LORD JAMES HARRINGTON AND
THE WHITSUN MYSTERY
by Lynn Florkiewicz

Welcome to the world of Lord James Harrington and the small village of Cavendish.

I hope you'll feel at home during your visit and that you'll enjoy getting involved in the Whitsun traditions and, of course, the mystery that James involves himself in.

Many thanks to those who have been with me since the first book and welcome to those who are new to the series. I hope that you enjoy these mysteries as much as I enjoy writing them.

LORD JAMES HARRINGTON AND THE WHITSUN MYSTERY

PROLOGUE

DAILY SKETCH 3rd APRIL 1950

STOP PRESS

The trial of Sean Kilty, who is charged with the murder of Mr Archibald Stanhope, 64, has been dismissed due to lack of evidence. It is rumoured that a key witness for the prosecution has declined to give evidence.

3

CHAPTER ONE

4th MAY 1959

Detective Chief Inspector George Lane held up a podgy index finger. 'Fact. Theodore Livingstone is living in Cavendish.' He held up a second finger. 'Fact: the man is living beyond his means yet can afford a mews house in Kensington and a huge lodge in Sussex.' A third finger appeared. 'Fact, on the surface, Theodore Livingstone is an upright pillar of the community. Fact–'

'All right, George,' Superintendent Higgins interrupted. 'I think you're sliding into the realm of assumption.'

George held his tongue.

James and Beth were seated with George and Higgins in the bar of a large hotel on the outskirts of Lewes. Looking through the door to the main function room, James could just make out the words on a banner that stretched the width of the stage at the far end. It read: *4th May 1959 Awards for Police Excellence and Gallantry*.

A voice behind Superintendent Higgins added: 'You'll never get anything on Livingstone.'

Higgins swung round. 'Ah, Inspector Fulton, you're away from your normal patch, aren't you?'

'Yes sir. My nephew's here. He recently joined up and is picking up an award. Always support family.'

Higgins made a brief introduction. Inspector Fulton was, James learned, based at Scotland Yard. In his late-forties with a big build and a squashed nose, he uttered a swift greeting then excused himself.

James picked up from where they'd left off by confirming that Theodore Livingstone was now in Cavendish. 'I thought the house was a second home. He seems to spend all of his time in London, which makes sense when Parliament's in session. He purchased Groom Lodge and the small property next door to it.'

'What do you make of him?' asked Higgins.

Theodore Livingstone, a Member of Parliament for the wealthy Kensington South constituency, was not a high-ranking MP but his name frequently appeared in the nationals as someone with the potential to rise through the political ranks. He was also described as being bullish and domineering. Ladies who continued to wave the equal rights banner were scathing of the man who was openly derogatory toward women, especially those who liked to carve out careers of their own. But, as James had never met the man, he said he couldn't comment on that side of his nature. 'All I can tell you is that he appears to have rubbed a few people up the wrong way in political circles and I only learned that from reading the papers. Why d'you ask?'

A gavel banging the lectern on the stage interrupted the conversation. George nudged him to their table where James straightened his tie. It was mid-afternoon and he had on a light grey suit, matching tie and a white shirt. The waiter topped up his glass of sparkling wine. Beth, who wore an elegant cream two-piece outfit with ivory shoes, sat to his right. James checked his tie again and took a sip of wine.

Beth sidled up. 'Are you nervous?'

'A little. It's not something I ever expected to happen.'

They sat down at one of ten large round tables, each accommodating twelve people, the majority of them in uniform. A handful of guests were civilians like James and Beth, along with the Mayor of Lewes who wore his mayoral gown and ceremonial chain of office. At the front were a reporter and photographer from the local press. Men and women from the Sussex constabulary were dressed in their finest; buttons gleaming, shoes polished and hair immaculate. Each table had been decorated with colourful ribbons and flowers. Attendees had enjoyed a light lunch of smoked mackerel and salad. A ripple of applause went around the room as a young police constable accepted a certificate for his efforts in preventing a local robbery.

George Lane, one of James' oldest friends, sat to his left. It had been a long time since James had seen him in anything other than an ill-fitting suit and fedora. James complimented his friend on his appearance.

George brushed some fluff from the pips on his epaulette and grunted. 'I'm all for recognising our people but I'd be far more comfortable in my normal get-up.' He was about to continue when he saw who was stepping on to the stage. 'Ah, I think this is us.'

James' stomach did a minor flip. He took another sip of wine and settled back in his chair.

Superintendent Higgins, looking every inch the professional with gold braid on his uniform and three medals on his chest, tapped the microphone and placed a sheet of paper on the wooden lectern. His thinning hair was swept back from his forehead. He cleared his throat.

'Ladies and gentleman, I'd like to thank everyone here for attending this award ceremony and commend our officers within the force for their continued service, loyalty, devotion and bravery in what can be a dangerous, yet fulfilling occupation. Being a police officer is a vocation. It is not a job that you simply step into. Every man and woman who wears this uniform does so knowing they will devote their energy to the job seven days a week and, for that, you have our undeniable gratitude. Not only from your peers and senior officers but from the public, who depend upon each and every one of you to do your job and help keep our streets safe from those who choose to break our laws.'

A round of applause broke out with the odd 'Here, here' thrown in. Higgins checked his notes.

'We have heard a good many stories today of the bravery, integrity and ingenuity of our people and I am proud to have you serve your county so well. To end this formal part of the afternoon, I have two awards to hand out. The first is one that I rarely have the pleasure of giving and one that fills me with a good deal of pride. The man receiving the Queen's Police Medal has served the Sussex Constabulary for over twenty-five years, rising from the rank of police constable to Detective Chief Inspector. It was my hope that he would continue through the ranks but his aversion to sitting behind a desk is well known.

'Whilst I'm disappointed not to see him rise to the position I believe he is more than qualified to fill, I am gratified to know that one of the best detectives in the country will continue to be heavily involved in solving some of our most difficult crimes.'

On his prompt, a young policewoman, who stood to the side of the stage, walked across to hand him a dark blue box. He opened it and addressed the audience.

'Ladies and gentleman, the man who will receive this award was responsible for solving the horrific canal murders in Chichester. His dogged determination when pursuing all leads meant that we were able to arrest our man sooner than anticipated and, no doubt, prevent further deaths. Not only was he active on this case, he also had a second, concurrent case to investigate, one that involved a skeleton found on the estate of Lord James Harrington. Again, an arrest was carried out; nine years after the crime was committed.' Higgins straightened up. 'It gives me enormous pleasure to invite the recipient of this award to the stage. Please join me in congratulating my friend and colleague, Detective Chief Inspector George Lane.'

The room erupted in cheers as George, looking embarrassed by the attention, picked up his cap and weaved his way through the crowd. James and Beth joined everyone else by standing to applaud. The local journalists eased forward to get the best photographs.

James looked on as his friend saluted Higgins while the medal was pinned to his uniform. Calls for a speech prevented George from leaving without saying something. He quietened the room down as Superintendent Higgins gestured to the microphone.

George leant in. 'Right, you know I don't go in for speeches.'

A chuckle and a shout of 'That's the most you've said all day,' gave rise to further guffaws.

'All right, all right. Look, most of you know me well enough. I come in, do the job to the best of my ability and if it takes a bit longer than normal, well, that happens and we have to get on with it. My motivation is getting justice. Always has been, always will be. When I see what happens to people affected by crime, whether it's a minor squabble or an act of violence, I see the consequences. I see the ripple of unrest and the upset it causes and that's my motivation. Getting justice for those people who are unfortunate enough to be the victims.'

He took a peek at his medal and held up the presentation box. 'It makes me proud to receive this but

I didn't do any of it on my own. We're a team. From the woman making us tea to the people in the thick of it. No one is any less important. Remember that. Never take any of your colleagues for granted, no matter what rank they are. All of you contribute and by doing that, it means justice gets served.' He shuffled his feet. 'Thank you everyone, and Superintendent Higgins, for your support and efforts.'

The applause continued well after he had taken his seat. Higgins asked that his audience remain seated for a couple more minutes.

'Before we finish, there is one more award that I am to present. Those of you who work alongside George will know of a certain gentleman who has assisted us with investigations in and around the Cavendish area. This particular person is a trusted and valued friend of DCI Lane's and I know he won't mind me saying that we were initially not happy for him to interfere with police business.'

James found himself the subject of friendly scrutiny from those at his table. He cleared his throat and took another sip of sparkling wine. Higgins continued.

'But, without the help of this man, who seems to possess the same dogged determination as George Lane, some of our cases would have been solved later than expected, or indeed, not at all. This man has the trust of his friends and neighbours and picks up on a number of things that would not necessarily reach the ears of the police. He's dipped into George's investigations on several occasions,' Higgins checked his paperwork, 'such as the deaths of Alec Grimes and Delphine Brooks-Hunter and you'll remember all that smuggling business that took place last summer.' This triggered plenty of nods. 'However, the man who initially was seen as a nuisance and considered a bungling amateur sleuth was a driving force behind identifying the skeleton found on his estate. DCI Lane assures me that, without his friend's help, the killer could still be at large. It gives me great pleasure, therefore, to present a certificate of commendation from the Chief Constable to Lord James Harrington.'

James squeezed George's shoulder as he passed him and made his way to the stage. The certificate was framed and presented with a pair of crystal whisky glasses in a satin-lined box. He smiled at the men and women in front of him who insisted that he, too, made a speech. He cleared his throat.

'Like George, I shan't keep you long. I'm sure you're all itching to descend on the bar. My interest in crime is simply that: an interest. I know I should stick to listening to Paul Temple or reading Maigret, but crime close to home fascinates me. I'm similar to George in that I see the damage that crime does to the victims and their families. I believe in righting a wrong and if someone has been robbed, attacked or simply feels aggrieved, I like to get to the bottom of it. I know I can be a nuisance, I know I step on toes that I shouldn't step on and George is the first to admonish me if I go too far. But I'm grateful for this recognition and would like to take this opportunity of thanking you, the men and women of our constabulary, for doing such a wonderful job in keeping us, the public, safe and secure. Thank you.'

The applause was warm and he received a pat on the back from the Superintendent who leant in and proposed they had a drink together in the bar. Knowing the formal presentations were now over, everyone began edging toward the drinks area. James thanked the many who passed by offering their congratulations. Beth held his hand and kissed him on the cheek.

'I'm so proud of you, sweetie.'

'They should be awarding you one of these. After all, you put up with me doing this and just lately you're as involved as me in these little mysteries.'

She held one of the crystal tumblers. 'Perhaps this is why you received two of these.'

He kissed the top of her head. 'Then it is well deserved and we'll be sure to christen these later.' He turned to George. 'Shall we adjourn to more comfortable seats?'

The three of them found a selection of armchairs in a lounge adjacent to the bar that overlooked the South Downs. No sooner had they made themselves comfortable than Superintendent Higgins asked if he could join them. He pulled a chair over and sat down with a sense of relief.

'I take it from your expression,' said James, 'that you're glad that's over.'

Higgins placed his uniform cap and gloves on the floor beside him. 'It's been a busy few weeks and if I'm being honest I could have happily snoozed in my favourite chair or had an afternoon fishing.'

'You fish?'

'I try to.'

'Well you should come over one afternoon. I have a stretch of river running through the estate that has some wonderful specimens for you to catch.'

The Superintendent's eyes lit up. 'I should like that very much.'

Beth opened her compact and checked her lipstick. 'You've been busy, you say? There doesn't seem to be much crime reported in the paper recently, or are you more involved in paperwork?'

Higgins explained that much of his role was shifting paper and ensuring the force was running as efficiently as possible. 'But every now and again I'm given notification about something that we may want to keep an eye on. That's when I keep people like George informed. Could be something that we've heard from an informant or, as an example, the jewel smuggling case you were caught up in, Lord Harrington. That began life as a rumour.'

'Does that mean,' said Beth, 'you have something to keep an eye on at the moment?'

James couldn't help but be surprised at the Superintendent's reaction as he shifted forward in his chair, careful not to be overheard.

'We were speaking of Theodore Livingstone earlier.'

'Yes,' James answered, turning to George. 'We were left with the impression that he wasn't high on your list of likeable people although I'm not entirely sure why. Although I don't like the reputation of the man, he is a renowned Member of Parliament, voted in by his constituents.'

George loosened his tie and undid his top button. 'I don't like the man.'

'You've met him?'

His friend was sour-faced. 'Not a nice individual and I can imagine him being involved in all sorts of underhand dealings.'

Higgins accepted a cigar from a passing waiter. 'You can't base your opinion on what you feel, George.'

'It's served me well so far, sir.'

'That's as may be but this is a man who covers his tracks.'

James met Beth's gaze. The Superintendent had captured their attention. George brought out his pipe and tobacco pouch. As he prepared it, he enlightened them.

'Theodore Livingstone is a well-respected MP in certain circles. He represents an area of London that has relatively few poor people, if any. Everyone who lives in Kensington South is rich. Incredibly rich. Anyone who isn't either commutes in to clean for these people or lives in to nanny for their kids.'

'Your point is?'

'We struggle to understand where he gets his money from. His lifestyle and spending exceed an MP's salary by some way.'

'Could it be a family inheritance?' asked Beth. She had, herself, received quite an inheritance when her parents, in Boston, had passed away.

George lit his pipe. 'No. His parents are from the north, Huddersfield, and worked in the factories. There's no money there.'

'If he's living beyond his means, what sort of evidence do you have for that?'

Superintendent Higgins took over. 'The house he has in Kensington is substantial. His neighbours are millionaires, private bankers, high court judges and suchlike. You can't afford that sort of property on a parliamentary wage. The property he's purchased near Cavendish is also substantial, especially when you consider that he bought the cottage next door too.'

'I say,' said James, 'isn't Maximillian Livingstone something to do with Theodore?'

'His son.'

James remembered reading about him a few months ago. The son had set up a grubby magazine that relied on gossip and tittle-tattle. A number of well-known faces had been victims of its rumours and found themselves sources of ridicule. In some cases, those within the entertainment business had been refused work as a result of the magazine's articles. He recalled a particularly beautiful girl who was lined up for a part alongside a leading actor. It was her break in show business and one that was snatched away because of an inappropriate relationship plastered across the pages of the magazine.

'*Guess What?* That's the name of the magazine, isn't it?'

Higgins drew on his cigar. 'Yes, rather an unsavoury publication.'

'How unpleasant,' said Beth. 'The pair of them sound completely undesirable.'

'And he's another who's living beyond his means,' said George. 'Sir, are you all right if I ask James and Beth?'

Higgins motioned for him to continue but to keep his voice down.

'The thing is, the rumour we have is that Theodore Livingstone is dealing in drugs. We believe that's where he gets his money from and we think he operates from that house in Cavendish. The problem we have is that, like all criminal masterminds, he doesn't get his own hands dirty.'

Beth huffed. 'How awful that a man with power should stoop so low. And I've read interviews with him. His views on working women are Dickensian. And, as for that awful magazine that his son runs, well…'

'Everything they do is above board, Beth. There are plenty of men who would prefer women to be tied to the kitchen sink. And it's not a crime to publish a magazine like that. They haven't broken the law.' He placed his pipe on the table. 'But if we do have information about someone that might know about Theodore, we're stifled.'

James met his gaze. 'How?'

'He's an MP, James, and a canny individual. He's friends with the Commissioner at Scotland Yard; he dines with the Prime Minister and lunches with influential men in business.'

'And, presumably, he uses these contacts of his when required. If there's any dealing going on, it's done by people beneath him. He has something on them or threatens them if they don't do as they're told.'

'How disgusting,' said Beth.

'The thing is,' said Superintendent Higgins, 'now he's got a bolthole in Cavendish, this may be the opportunity we've been looking for.'

James wanted to clarify things. 'Get him involved in village life and the community. Is that what you're speaking of?'

Higgins said that it was.

But James wasn't convinced. 'The man has been in that house for several months now and we don't see hide or hair of him – or his son for that matter.' He turned to Higgins. 'The thing is, Superintendent, we have a rather wonderful community and having these men turn up at our events is likely to cause some friction. I'm all for helping the police but not at the expense of ruining our community. Is there some other way?'

'Perhaps,' Beth suggested, 'we could just call in and tread gently.'

Higgins said that was exactly what he had in mind. 'I've no wish to spoil what you have in Cavendish. George has told me, on frequent occasions, that your village has a community to be proud of. You may be interested to know who has just moved to the cottage

15

next door to Groom Lodge.' After a pause he said, 'Dulcie Faye.'

Beth brought her hands to her mouth. '*The* Dulcie Faye?'

Both Higgins and George nodded.

'Goodness,' said James. Dulcie Faye was a young actress, who had come to everyone's notice in the last few months. She was predicted to be the next shining light in the British film industry. Many had described her as the British Doris Day. Her humble demeanour, looks and curvy figure had been the subject of a recent *Picturegoer* magazine feature. 'I take it she's the girlfriend of Maximillian.' The awkward silence was not lost on him. 'Are you saying she's with Theodore?'

'That's right, Lord Harrington,' said Higgins. 'How voluntary that is, we don't know.'

'That's our first port of call, James,' said Beth. 'Why would a beautiful young woman with the world at her feet be living in a cottage close to a man old enough to be her father? And a despicable-sounding man too.'

'Some women prefer older men,' James said. 'Perhaps those who lacked a father figure when they were children.'

'No! I read an interview with Dulcie Faye. She didn't come across like that at all. You read that, didn't you?'

'Oh yes, you're right. She was very complimentary about her parents and how they encouraged her to fulfil her dreams.' He shifted in his seat. 'I must admit that I'm surprised a girl like that would be attracted to a man like Theodore Livingstone. Or rather the other way around. She seems too independent for the likes of him. He must have some sort of hold over her.'

'It also seems odd that she's in that little property next door,' said Beth. 'Wouldn't she be better living in the city, close to the theatres and studios?'

'That's the ticket,' said Higgins, who reached down for his cap and gloves and rose from his seat. 'Keep George informed of anything you find out.' He made to go but stopped himself. 'What I will say is this. Theodore Livingstone has friends in high places and if you approach this in the wrong way, I'll know about it. The man will be on the phone to his contacts or he'll threaten you. Either option is not a good one. You must tread carefully, Lord and Lady Harrington. I am not asking you to solve a crime, simply to meet and observe the family to see what you can find out if anything. Perhaps see who comes and goes. Don't become friends with them. Your insights after one or two encounters could tell us quite a bit.'

'And report back to George,' James said, more to himself than anyone else.

'Either George or me. Livingstone has the police in his pocket. I'm not sure who we can trust at the moment.' Higgins bade them farewell.

George picked up his pipe. 'My instinct is normally right, James, and it tells me that Theodore and Maximillian are not nice people. If, once you've met them, you're not sure you want to continue, you stay away. Understood?'

'Message received, George.' He reached over and held Beth's hand. 'Are you all right with this?'

'I am. Like George said, if we're uncomfortable we simply stop. But I think our first port of call shouldn't be the Livingstone men. I think we should start with Dulcie Faye.'

'Good idea. We'll do that tomorrow morning, shall we? We have to be at the Half Moon later to discuss the steam festival and the Whitsun dance. Perhaps a few of our residents have met the Livingstone men. We could slip them into conversation and see what crops up.'

'Perhaps. Shall we make a move?'

They thanked George for what had turned out to be an interesting afternoon. James held his commendation tightly and had already decided where, in the study, it would hang. As they walked to the car, he wrapped an arm around Beth's shoulders.

'That was a curious discussion, wasn't it?'

'Yes, it was. I simply can't imagine why someone like Dulcie Faye should have anything to do with that dreadful man. Unless she's not as ordinary as she purports to be.'

'She is an actress. Perhaps she's putting on a performance for her public. She wouldn't be the first one. Hopefully we'll find out one way or another.' He opened the door to their gleaming red Jaguar. 'Sounds like we are at the beginning of a rather fascinating enquiry.'

CHAPTER TWO

It was early evening when James and Beth arrived at the Half Moon pub. Four newly-acquired bench seats had been placed on the cobbles outside and as they wandered across the village green, James could see they were the last to arrive. Ahead of them were the vicar and his wife, Stephen and Anne Merryweather, the village museum's curator, Professor Wilkins, the librarian Charlie Hawkins and the Cavendish Players director, Dorothy Forbes.

James tugged Beth back. 'Is that Mrs Withers sitting by the Professor?'

She mirrored his surprise. 'Yes, yes, it is. What's she doing here?'

Mrs Withers ran the sweet shop and made a point of becoming invisible during village events. She'd spent most of her life in the Women's Royal Naval Service, mainly in an operational capacity. Those years had left her with an incredibly organised and efficient manner that grated on most people who visited her shop. You were rarely welcomed into her establishment, more like capably moved on with little in the way of chit-chat. James knew she'd been married but that was long before she'd moved to Cavendish.

Their hope of an informal chat about the steam rally, James felt, would be anything but that with both the controlling Mrs Withers and the domineering Dorothy Forbes at the same table.

The landlord, Donovan Delaney, and his wife Kate had pushed the wooden benches together. James and Beth took the space opposite Stephen and Anne. Two other people came into view who didn't normally get involved in organising things — Mr Sharpe and Flora Armstrong.

Kate leaned out of the pub window and met James' expectant gaze. 'Let me know what you want and Donovan'll bring it out.'

'Ah splendid. I know you have some new ales on tap so bring me a half of whatever Donovan recommends. What about you, darling?'

'I think I'll have a Cinzano and lemonade.'

Kate shouted the orders to Donovan while James greeted everyone and commented on the new additions to the group. 'We don't often see you here,' he said, meeting the gazes of Mrs Withers, Mr Sharpe and Flora Armstrong.

'S-specialist knowledge,' Stephen responded.

Stephen and Anne, who had arrived in Cavendish just a couple of years previously, had become their close friends, so much so that they had recently holidayed together. They were in their early thirties, he tall and angular while she was short, almost pixie-like, with a mischievous glint in her eye. The villagers had welcomed them into the community and the congregation on a Sunday had tripled thanks to Stephen's humour and entertaining sermons. Their two boys, Luke and Mark, were playing ball on the green with Charlie's two children, Tommy and Susan.

Mr Sharpe was the first of the three newcomers to speak. Approaching fifty, he was old for his age. Indeed, James had often remarked to Beth that he couldn't imagine the man being anything but fifty. His attire didn't change from one day to the next; brown trousers, a green cable-knit cardigan and a shirt and tie. He was a confident man but one who attended events from a distance, preferring to observe rather than participate.

His presence at the table took James unawares although he was delighted to see him.

'My speciality is steam, Lord Harrington,' said Mr Sharpe. 'I've a passion for steamrollers and steam traction engines. You show me something run on steam and I'm there. I used to work on them years ago, when they were still in use but now the preservation societies are springing up, I'm very much involved again.'

Professor Wilkins patted him on the back. 'Mr Sharpe belongs to the Sussex Steam Guild. He's our point of contact.'

The steam rally was held over the course of a week and organised by the Sussex Steam Guild. They usually held it on a large showground near the Kent and Sussex border. Unfortunately, because those grounds were severely waterlogged, James had come to their rescue by loaning out two of his fields at Harrington's.

James welcomed Mr Sharpe warmly. 'How wonderful. It'll be good to have one of our residents here who knows what they're talking about. How are things going your end?'

'We're in the final stages. I'm helping with the guidebook. I've got interesting facts and historical references that I've put in, together with some wonderful photographs.'

Charlie added that the local council had offered to print the programme for visitors. 'They're doing that for free so we can charge a shilling per programme and we're splitting the profits with the Guild. That'll help pay for other events in the village.'

Donovan, his sleeves rolled up, brought out their drinks. 'Yer man, James,' he said in his melodic Dublin accent. 'Here you are. A half pint of King and Barnes Amber and a Cinzano and lemonade.'

21

'Wonderful,' said James holding the glass up. 'Cheers and have one yourself. I'll settle up with you later.'

'Don't you be leaving the country,' Donovan retorted. 'And count me and Kate in with whatever you're planning. You know we'll set a bar up somewhere. You just tell us where and when and we'll be there.'

Cavendish could always rely on the Delaneys to supply a bar at any event they staged. Kate appeared at the window again. 'And Graham Porter says he's sorry he couldn't make it but Sarah isn't feeling well and he's looking after the kids.'

'Yer man Graham is the same as me,' Donovan added. 'Supplying what'll be needed, just tell him when and where.'

The group thanked them. Graham, their local butcher, always supplied a hog roast or some other succulent offering. His smallholding was now a thriving business and he was becoming well known for his succulent home-cured gammon.

Dorothy Forbes jotted everything down on her clipboard. 'The WI, of course, are involved and Elsie is setting up a coffee bar — that seems to be a trend these days.'

James was pleased to know that Elsie Taylor, who ran his favourite café on the road between Cavendish and Charnley, would be taking part.

Beth caught Dorothy's attention. 'Shall we do a few of our Coffee Delight cakes? They'll complement what Elsie's doing.'

Anne's eyes lit up. 'Oh yes. I can help you with those. Shall we pop over to Elsie and ask if she'd mind?'

While Beth and Anne planned an hour out together, he turned his attention to Flora Armstrong and welcomed her to the group.

Flora Armstrong, a young woman of around eighteen or nineteen, seemed painfully aware that all eyes were upon her. She was not the most attractive girl and wore spectacles that did nothing to enhance the shape of her face. Her dark hair was cut just above the shoulder and Beth had remarked to him, some time ago, that a different style might make all the difference.

She spoke quietly and appeared a little in awe of the people around her. 'My parents said it would be a good idea to get more involved in things. I don't want to join the Women's Institute or anything but they thought I could perhaps help on a stall or something.'

Beth encouraged her. 'You're the sort of person we need at events like these. It's those little jobs like selling raffle tickets or taking entrance fees that people forget about.'

Flora was one of two women who worked in the telephone exchange at the back of the post office. She'd been there for around eighteen months now and was well thought of by the manager. James had spoken to her a few times when placing a call and she'd come across as professional in her manner.

'And how are things at work?' James said, more for small talk than anything else.

Unfortunately, whenever someone engaged with her, she reacted as if she'd been caught shoplifting. 'I'm enjoying it, thank you.' She finished the last of her drink and announced that she would go and buy another.

James couldn't help but feel sorry for her. Here was a girl who was so incredibly shy that her parents had forced her to get out and socialise. He wondered if she would ever be confident enough to do anything significant with her life.

The group began listing what had been done so far. The steam rally was still a couple of weeks away and most of the major arrangements were complete. Over forty participants would be arriving with their traction engines and taking their places in a large field at the far end of the Harrington estate. In addition to the traction engines, a specialist fair would be setting up to give children traditional rides, many of them run by steam. A number of food vendors were signed up to attend including, one of James' favourites, Paolo Rossi. His father ran an ice-cream parlour in Brighton and had just purchased a fleet of ice-cream vans, one of which would be standing on the main thoroughfare through the field.

Aside from the steam rally, the village would be holding its annual competition, Blooming Cavendish. This had been started several years ago by the villagers whose cottages surrounded the green. All took pride in their gardens and opened them up for visitors and judging. Stephen added that he was also getting his sermon together for the Pentecostal service.

Charlie reminded them not to forget the Whitsun dance, a tradition that had continued since the Great War. The men of the Morris dancing team were fighting in France and were missed in more ways than one. During a women's meeting, half a dozen ladies had decided that they would dance while the men were away. Every Whitsun Monday since, the ladies of Cavendish gathered outside the Half Moon to dance. The numbers now exceeded forty and the event had become quite a spectacle.

James rubbed his hands together. 'I say, this is going to be splendid, isn't it?'

'Turning back to the rally,' said Charlie, 'don't forget we've also got a few pre-war cars and motorbikes that'll be on show. We asked the Guild if they'd mind us doing that and they thought it was a good idea.'

'Yes, I'm going to put mine in for that.' Following his investigations over Easter, James was now a proud owner of a vintage Mercedes that he had every intention of showing off.

As the chatter continued, he realised that since he and Beth had arrived, Mrs Withers had not contributed a single word. He knew her to be standoffish and occasionally rude but the woman sitting at the end of the table appeared distant and drawn. Her drink, a glass of stout, was untouched and her shoulders slouched. The Professor was seated next to her; James caught his eye and they both moved to the entrance to the pub.

'How are you, your Lordship?' The Professor was a serious-minded individual and rarely smiled, much to the annoyance of Beth, who said the man had a grin that melted hearts and, whenever they were chatting, she made every effort to encourage that side of his personality. Nine times out of ten, she failed. No doubt, she would try again this evening.

'Very well, thanks,' James responded. 'Good to see you getting involved in our steam rally.'

'Like Mr Sharpe, I'm a traditionalist and there's no finer sight than a horde of traction engines and steam rollers trundling along together. I've managed to get hold of a man who has several miniature steam engines so I'll be keeping him company in that area.'

James steered him away from the group. 'I say, Wilkins, is Mrs Withers quite well? She seems out of sorts. And what's she doing here? She never gets involved in this sort of thing.'

25

The professor glanced over his shoulder. 'I don't know her very well, only to speak to in the newsagents, but she seems even more distant than normal. She doesn't look well either. I chivvied her into coming along because I thought it would do her good, you know, mix a bit. I know I'm not the most sociable person in the world but having people around is often the best thing. My suggestion doesn't appear to have had the desired effect, though.'

'I noticed she hasn't said a word and didn't acknowledge us when we arrived.'

'She was just as quiet before you arrived. As was Sharpe, although he's relaxed a little now.' He held out his glass. 'Do you want another?'

James said he was fine and, returning to the bench, took a pew by Mrs Withers. 'Mrs Withers, if you don't mind me saying, you look a little peaky. Can I get you a brandy or something to perk you up?'

He waited to be shot down in flames but was astonished to hear a forlorn sigh. 'I'm afraid a brandy won't solve the problem I have at the moment.'

'Anything I can help with?'

Her bottom lip trembled. 'No. No, you mustn't involve yourself. It has to remain with me.' She collected her things and left.

James turned to see everyone staring at him.

'Well,' said Stephen, 'what d-did you say to upset her?'

'She was upset well before you arrived,' Charlie pointed out.

'Oh dear,' said Beth. 'I'm not terribly enamoured with Mrs Withers but it's not like her to be so quiet. Doesn't anyone know?'

Anne fiddled with her glass and James sensed a reluctant desire to speak out. 'Anne? Any ideas?'

'Just something odd she said when she arrived. She was mumbling something about money and Maximillian Livingstone. I don't think she knew I was nearby. As soon as she saw me, she stopped speaking.'

James feigned ignorance. 'Maximillian Livingstone? Is he that young chap in Groom Lodge?'

Dorothy put her clipboard in her bag and gathered her coat. 'A very rude man, as is his father. I popped in with details about the steam rally and the Whitsun dance and they looked at me as if I was a piece of horse manure.' She shuddered. 'I've a list here of everything planned so far and what needs to be done. I hope you don't mind but my grandchildren are staying with me and I'd like to get back to them. I'll leave this with you, Anne. If you add anything to it, I'll type it up and have it distributed.' She collected her things and, after a cheery goodbye, left.

'Has anyone else had any dealings with the Livingstone men?' asked Beth.

Anne mentioned a chance meeting with the young actress, Dulcie Faye. 'She seems very nice. I've seen both her films and she came across as being like her characters, you know, the girl next door, although a little lost I thought.'

'Lost?' said James.

Anne reconsidered. 'No, not lost. Sad. I only met her the once but that's the impression she gave me. As if she regretted something and can't undo it.'

The Professor returned from the bar.

'Ah, Professor Wilkins?' said James. 'Have you had the pleasure of meeting the Livingstone men?'

'Never met them. I abhor Theodore Livingstone and what he stands for. Unless those Livingstone men are interested in history and traditions they won't be my cup of tea.'

'Doesn't Maximillian publish that awful magazine?' said Charlie. '*Guess What?*'

'Oh, how s-seedy,' Stephen said wincing in disgust. 'That's one of those awful magazines that spreads rumour and g-gossip and hang the consequences.'

'Mm, I bought a copy once,' said Anne. 'I thought it was a film magazine, you know, like *Picturegoer* or something like that. I read the first page and threw it in the bin. Full of gossip with no substance.'

'I w-wonder what she has to do with M-Maximillian Livingstone?'

A shout of 'Hello' from across the green caused them all to turn. Ken Scott, a lad of around seventeen was waving.

A sharp intake of breath caused them to turn the other way.

James leapt up to help Flora who had paled considerably — her legs buckled. 'I say, Flora, are you all right?' He helped her to the bench.

She put her drink down. 'Yes, yes, I'm sorry. I just felt a bit faint, that's all.'

Ken rushed to her side. 'Flora, what happened?'

She shrank back from all of the attention. 'I'm fine really. Please don't fuss.' She checked her watch. 'I promised to help my father with something.' Before James had even sat down, she was walking briskly across the green with Ken scrambling to keep up.

James, now back with Beth, leant in. 'That was all rather peculiar, wasn't it? And she left her drink.'

'I'll say. Both she and Mrs Withers are acting very strangely.'

'I wonder what Mrs Withers was talking to herself about that involves Maximillian.'

Charlie summoned Tommy and Susan over. 'Come on you two, it's getting late and you've got school tomorrow.'

Stephen did the same with his lads. As everyone prepared to go, the vicar caught James' eye. 'How did everything g-go this afternoon? We didn't get a chance to ask you.'

James described the award ceremony and, away from the main crowd, he and Beth went over their discussion with the Superintendent and George. Anne listened with increasing interest.

Stephen let out a whistle. 'P-perhaps Anne and I could call in to the Livingstone p-place and make our presence known in our official capacity. With the Pentecost service c-coming up, it would be a timely moment to ring the d-doorbell. We'll let you know how we get on.'

James thanked them but warned the pair of them not to be too intrusive. 'I get the impression that these men are ruthless. If you do go, just get a general feel for things. Your instincts are pretty good; first impressions and all that. Whatever you do, don't ask intrusive questions.'

He settled up with Donovan and then walked to the car with Beth. He liked a mystery but these Livingstones didn't sound like the sort of men he'd want to cross. He hoped they weren't biting off more than they could chew.

CHAPTER THREE

Valentine Plumb was sixty-four years old and dressed in coal-black trousers, a white shirt and an unbuttoned dark grey waistcoat. He wore round, black-framed spectacles and his bald head looked as if it had been polished. At this particular moment, he had returned to his study after enjoying a short tea break. The study faced a small garden where blue tits were feeding on some stale bread he'd thrown out that morning.

Surrounding Valentine Plumb were, from floor to ceiling, books. Anyone perusing the titles would soon discover that his chosen subject was psychology, with a particular focus on crime and body language. Only one shelf was dedicated to fiction: works that included Dickens, Austin, Twain, Conan Doyle and Christie.

His large, square desk dominated the centre of the room, with space to sit around it on all sides. Neat piles of foolscap paper were placed on it. He wandered around the table pointing to them, mumbling to himself as he went.

'Ongoing, research, editing, check facts, re-interview, new. Yes, yes, that'll do nicely.' He poured water from a jug into a glass and positioned himself at a part of the desk where a grey Olympia typewriter sat. He slotted a carbon sheet between two pieces of paper before carefully inserting them into the machine's roller.

He typed a heading: 'The Emotional Response to Victims of Crime. Sub-heading: Blackmail', then sat back.

After a few seconds, he got up from his chair and chewed on his pencil. 'Blackmail, yes,' he murmured as he stood by the open window. On a ledge in front of him was a reel-to-reel tape recorder. He rewound a section,

31

pressed the play button and listened to the recording he'd made earlier.

'For the affected victim of a violent crime, there are physical and emotional elements to consider. Physical injuries may take time to heal or the victim may need some help recuperating from a serious attack. Friends and relatives of the victim can see the impact and many will rally round to support the victim; most are aware that the emotional scars of such an attack will continue.' A pause. 'But for the victim of blackmail it is likely that their predicament will not be known to friends or relatives. People may comment on the behaviour of this person. It is likely they will become withdrawn, disengaged and argumentative should someone question their health or well-being.'

He stopped the recording and scanned the books to the side of him: Freud, Jung, Maslow... Various papers, from criminal court reports in London to the reports of investigative agents of the FBI in the United States, littered the surface. On the wall, a quote from Plato caught his eye: 'The measure of a man is what he does with power.'

He forwarded the tape to the end of the dictation and, speaking into the microphone, repeated the quote. 'This perhaps could be an opening paragraph. Those who blackmail assume power over another and gain enjoyment and satisfaction from that act. Would there be a difference between blackmailing someone you know and someone you don't know? For the victim, it could vary considerably. Knowing your blackmailer could lead you to commit a crime yourself — perhaps murder even. Not knowing your blackmailer, I would imagine, leaves you in fear of your safety — perhaps your life. Or

perhaps they would also resort to murder. Or suicide.'
He pressed the stop button.

'Yes, a nasty crime,' he muttered as he chose a pipe from several on a stand. 'Now to seek out the victims.'

He slid some papers around on the desk and frowned at the old copy of the *Daily Sketch*. Poor Jacqueline Simms.

CHAPTER FOUR

The comforting jingle of an ice-cream van broke the stillness. As if set loose from the traps, half a dozen children raced from all corners of the village to descend on the green, screaming: 'Ice cream! Ice cream!'

James, who was seated on a bench by the green, scanning the cricket coverage in the newspaper, watched as Luke and Mark dashed by him, brandishing handfuls of change. Tommy and Susan Hawkins caught up with them as they joined an orderly queue by the van.

Paolo Rossi slid the glass open and began taking orders. A van selling fresh fish pulled up just behind.

The theme to the radio show *Housewife's Choice* started up from inside one of the cottages nearby. James turned to discover that it came from the vicarage. Anne stood by the gate. She wandered across to him. She was wearing a floral apron and had her hair tied in a scarf.

'Housework day?' asked James.

He shifted along the seat to give her room. She sat down and her shoulders fell. 'The house always seems to need cleaning. Those two leave a trail of destruction behind them that I didn't think possible.'

James assured her that their twins had been the same. 'Don't worry,' he said with a cheeky grin. 'They grow out of it when they get to around eighteen.'

She groaned but brightened considerably when the boys returned. She smoothed back their shiny black hair. They had large brown eyes and long lashes. James remembered Beth saying she was quite jealous of the boys' eyelashes and wished hers were that length.

'I've got vanilla,' said Mark, the elder of the two, holding up a rectangular cone with a wedge of ice cream

34

in it. He winced as his teeth bit into the chill. 'Dad likes these but I think I like lollies better.'

'It's too cold,' said Luke, who had opted for a lolly. He thrust it up to within an inch of James' face. 'This is all sorts of flavours. See, it looks a bit like a rocket. Do you want some?'

Anne pulled his hand away. 'I'm sure Uncle James would prefer something a little more grown up, Luke. If it's too cold, Mark, just lick it, don't bite into it. Now run along into the house and when you've finished your ices, please tidy your bedrooms.'

Luke, who had decided to use the lolly as a rocket instead of as something to consume, ran after Mark to the vicarage.

Paolo Rossi was still serving a line of children but caught James' eye. He waved and tilted his head, indicating the advertisement of the treats on offer. James gestured that he would be across shortly.

'I say, Anne, do you fancy an ice cream before you get back to the hard toil of cleaning?'

'That would be wonderful. I'll have a vanilla cornet, like Mark had.'

He folded his paper and got up. 'Sit tight, I'll bring them over. Is Stephen here?'

'He's meeting a vicar who's standing in for us when we go away.'

'When's that?'

'Oh, not until next month. We're popping back to Oxfordshire to see our respective parents. We're picking Radley up too. My parents have been hiking in Wales and borrowed the dog We haven't seen them for a while and the children so love to visit their grandparents.'

James shouted back as he wandered toward Paolo. 'Nothing finer than the relationship between grandchildren and grandparents.'

He wondered when he and Beth would become grandparents and hoped it wouldn't be too late in life. His own grandfather had been an active man who had instilled a sense of adventure in him. Although Granddad had appeared to be as old as the hills that surrounded him, with white whiskers and a battered hat, he had been an agile man. He had walked with a cane that he didn't really need but it came in handy when hiking through the undergrowth. He and Grandma Harrington were unique for their time: titled individuals who took their own path through life and didn't always conform.

That was inevitably why he and his sister, Fiona, were now quite happy to mix with people of all walks of life. Their elder brother, Geoffrey, who had tragically died many years ago, had probably been the most formal of the family, feeling a need to be so when inheriting the title. But, although James now held the title, he didn't feel the need to change. If he ever thought about doing so, the image of his grandfather leaping around the grounds would spring to mind. Also, Beth would soon bring him to heel. Although from a prominent family in Boston, she had her feet on the ground and always alerted him to any shows of snobbery.

'Hello, Paolo,' he said as he reached the van. The blue and white paintwork gleamed and the chrome on the van sparkled in the sun. The framed menu of ices on sale added more colour. 'How's your father?'

'He's well, thank you, your Lordship. 'We've now got a fleet of vans as well as the parlour so business is good.'

'Splendid.'

The Rossi family were Italian immigrants who had arrived in England back in the 1920s. They'd established their first ice-cream parlour in Kent and the family moved to Brighton on the south coast during the 1930s. For a short while during World War II, Paolo's father had been rounded up, along with thousands of his countrymen, even though he had been resident in England for almost twenty years. James recalled the moment vividly. The Rossi family were well thought of by everyone but when the two countries found themselves on opposing sides, suspicion and accusations were rife. He remembered when the Rossi shop-front was boarded up after a particular nasty attack by people who had, just a few months previously, seen themselves as friends. It had taken the family time to heal emotional scars and James didn't think that Paolo's father had ever really forgiven anyone for that time. Paolo, of course, was a baby when this happened and, although well aware of his family's plight, had no time for looking back. The future, he said once to James, was what mattered and he intended to put Rossi's ice cream on the map.

Paolo had typically Italian looks — dark hair and eyes but could easily pass for an Englishman in the street with what was, effectively, a London accent. He was dressed in white trousers, white shirt, a white jacket and blue bow-tie. Perched on his head was a soda-jerk hat.

'What can I get for you?'

James put Anne's order in and requested a choc-ice for himself. 'Are we going to see you at the steam rally?'

'Oh yes. As soon as I saw your request come through I asked Dad if I could work on that one. It'll be a busy day but I'm looking forward to seeing those engines too.'

James sorted through some change as Paolo prepared the ices. The gentle hum of an expensive car distracted him. His rally driving days and love of cars meant James could tell the difference between an everyday vehicle and one of some quality. He leaned back to see a 1958 Bentley Continental cruise to a stop. It was a two-door maroon beauty and he didn't need to wonder who the owner was as the number plate identified him: TL 1.

Theodore Livingstone.

They'd not met but he recognised him from photographs in the newspapers. A large man who had over-indulged on rich food filled the driver's seat. He had a jowly face and the complexion of an individual who had drunk one too many glasses of claret. Theodore Livingstone, MP, was similar to a few of his ilk and their political parties: rich, arrogant and, once elected, there to make things better for himself rather than his constituents.

Paolo handed James his ice creams and groaned on seeing the car. 'Oh, for pity's sake, what does he want now?'

'You know him?'

The young man excused himself, took off his paper hat and slid the window shut. James wandered back across the green, taking occasional glimpses over his shoulder. Paolo and Theodore had got out of their respective vehicles but moved behind the van and out of view.

He gave Anne her ice cream. 'Do you know who owns the Bentley?'

'Haven't a clue. Someone rich presumably. I only got a glimpse but he seemed familiar.'

'Mmm, Theodore Livingstone, MP.'

Anne mouthed a silent 'oh' and licked her ice cream. 'Rose and Lilac Crumb were berating the Livingstones a few days ago.'

'Really?' Rose and Lilac Crumb, or the Snoop Sisters, as James referred to them, were the village gossips and spread rumours like wildfire. Stephen had managed to rein them in a little by including them more in village events but even so, James was wary of speaking if he knew they were in the vicinity. It was a pound to a penny they would make two and two equal thirteen.

'You'd best speak to Stephen,' said Anne. 'He mentioned it after our chat outside the pub last night but wouldn't go into detail.' She thanked James for the ice cream and got up. 'I'd best get on. The house won't clean itself.'

James waved a cheery goodbye with a promise that they would all get together soon. He turned his attention back to the road. Theodore reappeared and plodded to his car. The hum of the engine could barely be heard across the green as the Bentley drove past the van and into the distance. Paolo reappeared and opened the back door. He was wincing and massaging his wrist. James sat up. A couple more children ran toward the van and rapped on the window. He watched as Paolo gently slid the glass panel open but favouring his other hand.

Whatever had gone on between Theodore and Paolo was more than passing the time of day. He couldn't make a judgement on this alone but the rumour of Theodore being a bully seemed a reasonable one. And what was this business with Rose and Lilac? Had they also had a run-in with him?

The activities of a few residents caught his eye. They were in their gardens pruning and dead-heading in preparation for the Cavendish Blooms competition. He picked up his paper to focus again on the cricket news but found himself reading the same paragraph several times over. He slapped the paper in frustration.

Confound it! Theodore had got under his skin and he hadn't even met the man. He wondered if Beth had finished the shopping. The sooner they spoke to Dulcie Faye the better. And no doubt, George would be asking for an update in the next few days.

While James had been reading his paper, Beth had popped into the various shops in the village. The baker and milkman had made their respective home deliveries but she was keen to make use of the mobile fish stall that included Cavendish on its delivery route. Donald's fish stall was a small blue van with a colourful collage of various fish and shellfish painted on the side panels. The two back doors were opened and a wooden table folded out where customers could choose from a selection of fish. On the table today were cod, haddock, sole, plaice and kippers. Alongside were small portions of cockles, whelks, winkles and jellied eels.

Beth placed an order for two tail pieces of cod.

'A good choice, your Ladyship. No bones in the tail.' Donald wrapped the fish in several layers of paper before handing it over to her.

She heard footsteps approaching from behind.

'Oi, oi.'

She turned. 'Bert. How lovely to see you.'

Bert Briggs, a Cockney who had known James since they were children, put an order in for a portion of jellied eels.

She grimaced. 'Oh Bert, how do you eat those things?' In her native Boston, she'd been used to the fish she'd just purchased along with lobster and crab. Until she arrived in England to attend finishing school, she'd never heard of jellied eels.

James had introduced her to Bert early on in their relationship. It was, to outsiders, an odd friendship. A Lord with a family history dating back centuries and a poor East Ender who didn't have a penny to his name. They'd met on a school visit to the Natural History Museum. James was with a class from Ardingly, a private school in Sussex; Bert with Bethnal Green junior school. Both were seven years old. From that chance meeting, the pair had become firm friends.

Bert had insisted on showing Beth the real East End and had introduced her to pie and liquor, a dish only offered in that part of London. The pie had minced beef filling, a suet base and flaky pastry on top; the liquor was a green parsley sauce. She'd tried it and found she'd enjoyed it. But when Bert had asked her to try the jellied eels, she'd put her foot down.

'I'm sure they're lovely,' she'd said, almost heaving, 'but I'm afraid that is one step too far.'

Donald scooped the grey mass into a bag.

''ave you got a wooden fork,' Bert asked, 'I thought I'd 'ave 'em now.'

She shuddered. 'Don't eat them in front of me. Please!'

Bert's lined face creased as his suggestive laugh rang out. The ladies behind Beth couldn't help but join in. Donald handed Bert a fork and he began to dig into the delicacy. Beth said that her last stop was the butcher's so Bert accompanied her across the road.

The butcher's shop was owned and run by Graham Porter. He was a rotund, stocky man with a white apron that, more often than not, had bloodstains smeared down the front. Graham purchased all his joints from the local farms and butchered them himself in the room at the back. At the entrance to his shop was a model pig standing on its hind legs, wearing a red and white striped apron. The door was wedged open and a sprinkling of sawdust covered the tiled floor. To their left, there was a display of meats, hams and joints for roasting.

Graham held a huge hand up. 'Hello you two, how are you?'

Beth surveyed the meats as she answered him. 'We're very well, thank you, Graham. And thank you, as always, for putting yourself forward to help at the steam rally. Kate passed your message on.'

'My hog roast is a tradition and will continue to be so.'

Bert wandered to the end of the counter. 'Make sure you do the apple sauce as well. Sets the pork off nicely, that does. 'ere, that's a nice bi' of beef you've got there.'

'Comes up from Tilly's Farm over at Loxfield. He has his cattle grazing on some lush grass over there. Tender and tasty. D'you want some?'

'Nah mate, I'm off up to London.'

'Tea with the Queen?'

'Tea with *my* queen. Gladys has invited me up for a nosh with 'er and 'er family.'

'Oh,' said Beth, her eyes lighting up, 'how wonderful.'

He wagged a finger at her. 'Don't you go reading anything into it. It's a bi' of dinner and nothing else.'

42

Bert had recently become close to a lady he grew up with in the East End, Gladys. She ran a mission by Petticoat Lane market and, during one of James' investigations, they'd bumped into each other and rekindled that friendship. Gladys, who had a grown-up son, was now widowed and Beth was absolutely sure that romance was in the air. Bert was having none of it however and rapidly changed the subject.

'Where's Jimmy boy?'

Beth stood on tiptoe to scan the green. 'He's on the bench talking to Anne.'

Their friend scooped up another forkful of jellied eels, gave them a 'Cheerio' and made his way out.

A beautiful young woman passed him in the doorway, holding a wicker shopping basket. She had thick, glossy shoulder length hair that cascaded over her shoulders and wore jeans and a gingham blouse. Her full lips broke into a wide smile.

'Hello.'

Graham beamed. 'Miss Faye, lovely to see you again.'

Beth recognised her immediately. This was Dulcie Faye, the latest darling of the British cinema and pin-up for many young men around the country. Her face stared out from billboards and magazines and she'd become a role model for countless girls wanting to be just like her. She fluttered her eyelashes at Graham.

'You said, the last time I was in, that you cured your own ham, is that right?' She suddenly turned to Beth with a look of horror. 'Oh, I'm so sorry. You were here before me. Please, go ahead.'

Beth waved the offer away. 'I'm still wondering what to buy. I'm Beth Harrington by the way. We haven't met yet.'

Graham put in: '*Lady* Beth Harrington.'

'Oh heavens, how rude of me. I'm so sorry. Here am I barging in. You must think me terribly ill-mannered.'

'I think nothing of the sort,' said Beth. 'You're Dulcie Faye and we've enjoyed your recent films.'

Dulcie had a shyness about her and didn't appear to like the attention. Beth sensed a fragility and, knowing she was only about twenty, that was understandable.

'We heard that you'd moved into the village and I was just saying to James, my husband, that it's a shame we haven't seen much of you. We have so many events and clubs that you could come along to, although I guess you're busy much of the time with your commitments.'

'Oh, not really. In between films, it can be boring so it would be nice to get a little more involved. I'm not sure what with though.'

'Well we have the Women's Institute, of course, a tennis club, a choir, horticultural society and numerous events that we hold every year. Our next big thing is the steam rally, our Cavendish Blooms and the ladies' dancing on Whit Monday.'

Dulcie seemed positively enraptured by everything. 'It sounds wonderful.' She lowered her voice although only Beth and Graham were in the shop. 'I know that, because I'm an actress, people think I'm a socialite and brimming with confidence but, the truth is, I'm not. I'm terrible about meeting new people, especially in a crowd.'

Beth sympathised. 'We'll ease you in gently. Everyone is friendly and they'll make you most welcome.'

'Could I be a little forward and make a request?'

'Of course.'

'Just to begin with, could I just meet two or three people? That way, I'll know a few of the villagers when I do come along to something.'

'Why don't James and I visit you? We'll bring along Stephen and Anne Merryweather. That's the vicar and his wife who are dear friends. They only moved to the village a couple of years ago and can tell you how easy it was for them to be accepted.'

A look of relief swept over Dulcie. 'Oh, that would be perfect. Would you be able to make tomorrow afternoon, say two thirty? I have a script to read but it would be a lovely break in proceedings to meet you all.'

Beth accepted the invitation and hoped that the Merryweathers could make it. Either way, she was pleased that Dulcie had put the idea to her. It was a foot in the door to meeting Theodore Livingstone without appearing too forward.

CHAPTER FIVE

While Beth was chatting with Dulcie, James looked up to see Bert strolling toward him. He wore a scruffy jacket and a flat cap and was busy delving into a bag.

'Oi, oi, Jimmy boy,' he said as he plonked down next to him.

James peered into the bag and pulled a face. 'Disgusting. How on earth do you eat those?'

'You can talk. You posh toffs are always eating fish eggs and snails — this ain't no different.'

'For your information, I despise both but I take your point. Each to their own and all that. What brings you here?'

James was never entirely sure where Bert popped up from. More often than not he was in a bookmaker's shop, at a race meeting or in a pub. He had, on numerous occasions, asked to know exactly where his old friend lived but had never established it. He knew he had a small flat just down the road from Brighton racecourse but Bert had never invited James to visit or asked him to drive him there. The fact that he appeared to live from one day to the next caused James to assume that he might be embarrassed by his living quarters. Although they'd been friends since childhood, Bert kept much of his private life, private. All the same, James knew he could rely on Bert. He'd been at James' side during some of his escapades and had nothing but admiration for him.

Bert swallowed the last of his jellied eels and screwed the bag up. 'I'm on my way up to see Gladys.'

'Ah, Gladys, the light of your life at the moment.'

46

'Don't you start. You're as bad as the wimmin'.' He brought out a tin of tobacco and began preparing a roll-up. 'Mind you, between you and me, Jimmy boy, I think the world of her.' He slipped his cap back. 'But look at me, mate. I'm no catch, am I? She's up there and I'm down in Brighton. She won't leave 'er patch and I'm not sure I wanna leave mine.'

'I don't see why not. You were born and raised in the East End; you're part of the furniture up there. Beth said when you've taken her to Petticoat Lane, you seem to spend all of your time chatting to the stallholders. Do you have ties to Brighton?'

He shrugged and pulled a face. 'Not really. But I like being by the sea. It's nice to 'ave a gander up and down the prom. Clears your 'ead after a session in The King's Head.'

'Do I take it that you're considering a more serious relationship with Gladys?'

Bert stared across the green. Paolo was getting ready to drive to Charnley. He watched as the van disappeared. 'I'd like to, yeah. I'm getting older, I'd like to 'ave a companion, you know, a lady friend. It's all right drinking with the lads and going to the races but I want someone to come 'ome to.'

'Have you spoken to her about it?'

'Strewth no! I wouldn't know what to say. And she might turn me down!'

James turned. 'Bert, do you not see how much Gladys thinks of you? You're a fine catch as far as she's concerned. The pair of you would make a smashing couple. Don't let the lady slip through your hands because of where you want to live. You never know, she may like the idea of a move herself. You'll only know if you talk to her. Or you could compromise, find

47

somewhere you both like. Why don't you take her out for a meal and have a serious talk with her? I think you'll be surprised at what she may have to say.'

Bert scowled. ''ere, has she said something to you?'

'She doesn't need to, Bert. I know the ladies are more attuned to this than us but even I can see the way Gladys looks at you. She hangs on your every word.'

A sheepish look of pride crossed his face. 'We might go down the pie and liquor shop. They slop up some good nosh there.'

James grinned. 'That's the spirit.'

'And don't you be saying anything to Beth about this. I know she'll be on to Anne and then I get earache from the pair of 'em.'

James held his palms up. 'Your plan is safe with me.'

'Beth's in with Graham,' Bert continued. 'That actress passed me as I came out, that Dulcie Faye girl. Cor blimey, she's a stunner.'

Looking across the green, James could see the two chatting. 'I've not had the pleasure of meeting her yet. I understand that she's something to do with the Livingstone empire.'

Bert tilted his hand back and forth. 'I've seen her picture in the paper with that Theodore bloke. I ain't seen her get involved in politics and I'd be knocked sideways if she 'ad something to with tha' awful magazine.'

'Ah yes,' James mused, '*Guess What?* A rather salacious publication with little in the way of fact. It seems to delight in spreading rumours and causing the downfall of one celebrity or another.' He stretched his arm across the back of the bench. 'I say, do you know much about the Livingstone men?'

He went through what had happened a few minutes earlier between Theodore and Paolo.

'Poor ol' Paolo. Good lad, he is. Good family, the Rossis, shame about what happened to the dad during the war. Ol' Papa Rossi didn't deserve that. Never forgiven the British either. I think if he could, 'is dad would scarper back to Italy.'

'Does he really feel that bitter?'

His friend described a visit that he and Gladys had made to the ice-cream parlour just the previous year. Papa Rossi was always in the store but rarely served, leaving it instead to his son and daughter. 'I think he prefers making the stuff and staying in the background.'

'A great shame,' said James wondering if he would be able to coax Paolo's father out to visit the steam rally. He filed the thought away. As he had Bert there, he had a question to ask. Bert skated on the fine line of legalities during life and much of what he bought and sold could have been imagined as having fallen off the back of a lorry. James didn't get too involved with any of it, preferring Bert's friendship rather than to inquire too deeply into any activities he got up to. But Bert's contacts in London and the underworld had helped him solve a number of mysteries in the past and he was sure that he'd be able to assist with this one.

'Bert, what do you know about Theodore Livingstone?'

His friend groaned. 'Not someone you'd wanna cross. I could 'appily give him a bunch o' fives.'

'Why?'

'I've seen the papers. He thinks about 'imself and nothing else. I 'eard he's mixed up with the McCalls.'

James frowned. The McCalls were a gang of brothers who operated south of the river Thames. They were a hard bunch of criminals who thought nothing of putting anyone who crossed them in hospital. 'Is that a fact, or just a rumour?'

'It's always a rumour, Jimmy boy. Theodore Livingstone don't get his hands dirty. He lets others do that for him. He's detached, top o' the tree. No one can touch 'im; friends with the Prime Minister, lunches with Princess Margaret; has the Police Commissioner round for drinks. Everyone's scared to cross him. But Chatty Chatham, he's a mate o' mine — he lives up near Woolwich, he knows people in the McCalls' circle and they do 'is bidding now and again.'

'In exchange for what?'

'Money.' He flicked some ash from his cigarette. 'Chatty reckons Theodore Livingstone trades drugs and that, my friend, is big dosh. You don't get to live where he's living on an MP's salary. Drug money'll do it, though.'

'Is Maximillian of the same mould?'

Bert pulled a face. 'Max isn't into politics. Theodore set him up with that magazine. I fink it's about the fourth business he's set 'im up with. The others went bankrupt. Word is that Max thinks he's king of the jungle; pushing himself into parties he's not invited to, gate crashing private dinners, stalking celebrities. Looks like he's in his element running that magazine. Gets his kicks through humiliating people.'

'Would he help his father with the drugs business?'

'No idea. But, in the chain of humanity, I'd put 'em both down as cockroaches.'

'Have you met them?'

'Not me, mate. I don't move in those circles.' He stubbed his cigarette out. 'Why're you so interested anyway?'

50

James went through his conversation with George and Superintendent Higgins.

James started as Bert grabbed his lapel. 'Don't you get involved. Theodore Livingstone is not to be messed with. If he thinks you're sniffing around asking questions, he'll 'ave one of his cronies onto you with an iron bar.' He smoothed the lapel back. 'What the 'ell are the police thinking of? Just cos you got a commendation don't give them the right to put you in the firing line.'

James settled him down and assured him they were doing no such thing. 'I don't even have to talk to him. I was told to observe and if I see anything, I'm to pass it on.'

'Well, you've just seen him get under Rossi's skin. Pass that on and leave it.' The church bell chimed eleven o'clock. Bert got up. 'I'm serious, Jimmy boy. Don't you even think about treading on his toes or you'll 'ave me to answer to.'

Bert's expression emphasised his statement. It was one of concern as well as warning. Indeed, James felt a little unnerved as his friend walked toward the bus stop. It was unlike his friend to warn him off. This Theodore chap was clearly a nasty piece of work but, at the same time, held court with heads of state, police commissioners and royalty. Perhaps this would be a fruitless exercise. How on earth would his drug dealings be uncovered with friends in such high places?

Beth came toward him. It was a beautiful day and she wore a simple navy-blue dress with white piping around the collar. Her basket was full of shopping and she took out a KitKat as she settled beside him. She broke the chocolate bar in two and gave James half.

'I've been speaking with Dulcie Faye.'

'Yes, I saw. What's she like?'

'Surprisingly shy. She's so young and actually doesn't have much confidence at all.' Beth described Dulcie's hesitation at meeting new people in a group. 'She seems quite vulnerable in a way; but pleasant too.'

'What on earth is she doing with Theodore Livingstone then?' Before she could answer, he outlined his chat with Bert. 'We're going to have to tread carefully here, Beth. It's not like Bert to be so adamant and Theodore honestly sounds like a nasty piece of work.'

Beth sat for a while to consider what he'd said. 'Well, we'll do just that. And we have the perfect opening. Dulcie would much rather meet two or three people than a huge crowd so she's invited us to tea tomorrow afternoon. Two thirty. I said I'd bring Stephen and Anne — I hope they're free.'

James rolled up his newspaper. 'That's marvellous. It means we haven't put ourselves forward so there'll be no suspicion. Let's pop by the vicarage and break the news.'

Anne, excited at the prospect of meeting Dulcie Faye formally, eagerly said yes for the both of them. They arranged to meet at the cottage and he felt the familiar kick of adrenalin. He, too, was looking forward to meeting the famous Dulcie Faye but he was also keen to learn what sort of hold Theodore Livingstone had over her. Perhaps an afternoon with this new British starlet would yield some results.

CHAPTER SIX

The following morning, James breakfasted on a bowl of cornflakes. These last couple of months he'd felt less comfortable in his clothes and was appalled to see that he had put on five pounds in weight. He admonished himself.

'Do you know, Beth. I've never put on an ounce of fat in the past. It didn't matter what I ate or drank, my body seemed to burn it off.'

He received a sympathetic pout. 'I think it's a sign of age. A younger body works off more energy. I think. Didn't we read that somewhere? Anyway, summer's coming and you're always playing cricket or tennis so it'll soon come off.'

He checked his watch. 'Well, I'm making a start on shifting these excess pounds. I'm playing tennis with Charlie Hawkins this morning.'

'Isn't he working?'

'He's on holiday today.'

'Don't forget we have the Cavendish Blooms later; and we're seeing Dulcie Faye.'

Assuring her he'd be back in plenty of time James, dressed in long white trousers and plimsolls, arrived on court and played the first serve. He'd rolled the sleeves of his white shirt up and was grateful for the balmy breeze. Playing tennis with Charlie was competitive. He had an eye for a good stroke and thought nothing of slipping in the odd drop-volley which caused James to sprint forward on a number of occasions. The match went according to serve until the sixth game, where Charlie managed to break James and move on to take the first set.

With the sun heating up and the breeze dropping, Charlie suggested a break. 'We have the court for another hour but I wouldn't mind a drink.'

James was more than happy to stop. He'd regarded himself as a fit man but this last hour had proved how wrong he was. The doors to the large wooden pavilion were open and one of the long-serving members, Johnny Jones, who was now too old to play, was serving behind the counter.

'He's giving you a run for your money, your Lordship,' he said. 'Ready for a drink?'

James picked up his towel and wiped his face. 'He certainly is. Perhaps he'll get me fit for our tournament.'

Cavendish held an annual tennis tournament with the neighbouring village of Charnley. Last year's competition had been an enjoyable one except for the discovery of a smuggling network that had sent him and Beth on an intriguing yet thrilling adventure. He and Charlie ordered a glass of lemonade each. The telephone on the wall rang and Johnny went across to answer it. In two seconds, he indicated to Charlie that it was for him.

James looked on as the jovial Charlie became a little more serious.

'Right, no problem, I'll come straight over,' the librarian said, before hanging up. He gave an apologetic shrug. 'Tommy's fallen off something in the playground. They think he might've broken his arm so I'll have to pop to the hospital.'

'Oh Lord. D'you want a lift?'

'No thanks. I've got my bike here. They've taken him to the cottage hospital so I've not far to go.'

James leant back in his chair and sought out some company. He spotted Valentine Plumb seated on a deckchair outside. He picked up the two glasses of lemonade and wandered onto the veranda.

'Mr Plumb, I haven't seen you in a while.'

Valentine jumped to his feet. 'Thought I'd have some quiet time away from my writing. You play a good game, Lord Harrington.'

James rubbed his tummy. 'I would play a better game if I lost some of this. Too much good cooking and indulging in Elsie's lunches.'

Although only in her thirties, Elsie Taylor was adamant that marriage and children would not be a part of her life, preferring instead to bake and run her own café. So good was Elsie's cooking that he had entrusted her with some of Grandma Harrington's recipes and she'd done them justice.

He held up the spare lemonade. 'Charlie's had to attend to something. Would you care for his lemonade — he hasn't touched it.'

'Don't mind if I do.'

James dragged another deckchair alongside Plumb and they settled back. 'You say you're writing. You have another book in the offing?'

Plumb took off his spectacles and polished them with his tie. 'Yes, yes, I'm quite excited about this one. Something a little different to what I've done before and altogether much more interesting. It means getting out there and asking questions, meeting people affected by specific circumstances.'

'You have me fascinated,' said James, who had read a couple of Plumb's books. A qualified doctor and psychiatrist, he wrote without the aid of technical terms and medical jargon so the ordinary man on the street would understand it. 'What specific circumstances do you refer to?'

'This section I'm working on at the moment is blackmail.'

He had James' full attention. 'Blackmail. Just the psychology behind it or are you drawing on real cases?'

'Real cases. Something prompted me to study that area of crime. A case that was in the newspapers several years ago. It caught my eye again. I'd kept the clipping and it surfaced a few months ago when I was having a clear out.'

James sipped his drink. 'Is it a case I'd know about?'

'You may. It caught the attention of two or three nationals. A young nurse, Jacqueline Simms, was due to be a prosecution witness in the case of the murder of a patient in St Thomas' hospital. Do you recollect it?'

James repeated the name back and it suddenly sprang to mind. 'Yes, yes I do. If I remember correctly, she was the only witness. The prosecution was relying on her to put the killer in prison. She dropped out at the last minute.' His jaw dropped. 'Are you saying she was blackmailed?'

Valentine Plumb was almost gleeful. 'I visited her. Back in February and she had a story, I can tell you.' He shifted his chair to see James better. 'She'd contacted me, eager to meet; wanted me there as soon as I could. We arranged to meet the following day.'

James waited.

'She was dying. She had cancer, hadn't long to live and wanted me to know something. She'd apparently telephoned the police but they were not, how can I say, *open* to what she had to say. I can't say I blame them. When she told me, you could have knocked me down with a feather. I didn't believe her at first. I thought she just wanted some attention but when you know you're dying, you tend to want to confess and make things right.'

'And did she?'

'What?'

'Confess?'

'Ah,' said Plumb. 'Confession, where the confessor is generally asking for forgiveness for the sin of the crime. That is what you are thinking, yes?'

'That's generally the case but Jacqueline Simms did not kill the man in question. Your book is about blackmail so I presume she was forced into stepping down as the witness; that she was coerced, blackmailed or threatened in some way.'

'You've solved crimes, Lord Harrington. What do you observe about the people who commit those crimes?'

'I'm on the periphery of those investigations, Valentine. But what do I observe? In those cases that I've been involved in I have, in some respects, felt sorry for them. Not all of them, I hasten to add, but there are circumstances that motivate people to kill or steal.' He recounted his escapade in Cornwall. 'You know the chap responsible for that crime had the best of intentions. He just went about it the wrong way.'

Valentine loosened his tie. 'Have you ever come across pure evil?'

The words sent a chill through him. 'I'm pleased to say I haven't. I came across a young lady last Christmas who was mentally unstable, but I wouldn't say evil. This is to do with Jacqueline Simms?'

'Jacqueline Simms was a trained nurse. She'd been at St Thomas' for eight years without a blemish on her record. She received flowers and cards from grateful patients. She was an outstanding nurse who knew more than she needed to, medically. She was well thought of, a nice woman who had gone through some adversity. She'd given birth to a daughter. She named her Faith because Jacqueline had faith that everything would turn out for the best.'

'You speak as if you knew her.'

'I was a doctor at the hospital at that time. Nurse Simms often joined me as I did my rounds.'

'And what happened?'

'We had an admission one night. A Mr Archibald Stanhope. He'd had a fall. He was in his sixties and, to me, it appeared to be an unusual fall.'

'In what way?'

Valentine considered his words. 'Mr Stanhope was a fit man, medically sound and fully *compos mentis*. The fall he had, well...his explanation didn't seem quite right.' There was a brief pause. 'He said he'd tripped on the pavement but the injuries I treated him for gave me cause for suspicion. Oh, there were the normal grazes and bruises but he'd suffered a broken rib and I detected some pressure had been applied round the throat.'

'Good grief. Did you contact the police?'

'I had every intention of doing so but the look of fear in that man's eyes was one I will never forget. He gripped my arm and ordered me to say nothing. Nothing. He insisted he'd fallen over and that was an end to it.'

James puffed out his cheeks and felt for his cigarettes. He offered them to Plumb who gratefully accepted one. As James leant across to light the tip, he asked Valentine where Nurse Simms came into it.

'Nurse Simms worked on the ward that Stanhope was in. He was in a private room. He was to be with us for a while and at his age, it took some time for things to heal. Jacqueline tended to him, as she did all of the patients,

58

with no complaint and with tremendous care and empathy. I had no reason to think that anything untoward would happen. I was actually working my last week as a doctor the week before this all happened. My writing was leading to guest lectures and a possible position at a university. I wanted to delve into the mind, Lord Harrington, so I left St Thomas' hospital. The following week, Archibald Stanhope had been murdered and Jacqueline Simms had provided a statement.'

'But the court case was thrown out.'

'Not initially. But it collapsed. Once Jacqueline had withdrawn her statement, it all fell apart.'

'So, the next time you saw Jacqueline Simms was in February?'

'That's correct.'

Plumb took a long drag on his cigarette.

James smoothed his hair back. 'What did she tell you?'

'That the person on trial, a Sean Kilty, murdered Archibald Stanhope. She'd realised what had happened but was blackmailed, or rather threatened, into withdrawing her statement.'

'By whom?'

'Theodore Livingstone.'

CHAPTER SEVEN

'Theodore Livingstone!' James could hardly get the words out. He stared across to the courts where Helen Jackson and Sarah Porter, Graham's wife, were playing.

Theodore Livingstone.

He turned to Valentine. 'Did Jacqueline write this down?'

'In a sort of deathbed confession? No, she didn't. *Wouldn't*, is probably the better word for it. The mention of the Livingstone name made her hostile.'

'Hardly surprising. But what sort of hold did Theodore have over her?'

'Jacqueline Simms was a single woman. She became entangled with a young man, an upcoming politician who is now quite prominent. His career was mapped out for him. Ex-public school, family with money and position, that sort of thing. Well, he got the girl in trouble.'

'Resulting in Faith Simms.'

'Mmm. This chap wanted nothing to do with Jacqueline or his daughter. Gave them a lump sum and said he never wanted to see them again. Over the next few years, he'd ingratiated himself with Theodore Livingstone. Livingstone had become a sort of mentor.'

James could picture it. Egotistical MPs helping one another out on the ladder to success. Although he was part of the establishment himself, he abhorred people who took advantage of their position in such a way. A young man, buying people off and discarding his new-born daughter because of his own negligence? It was nothing short of disgraceful.

Valentine continued. 'Jacqueline told me that she was happy to cut ties with the father and didn't want him anywhere near her or her daughter. This chap started making a name for himself in the political world...'

'And Jacqueline, presumably after a few years, was beginning to struggle financially.'

'Yes, very much so. She followed him out of the Houses of Parliament one day and accosted him. Demanded money or she would go to the newspapers. I can't imagine Jacqueline doing that but she must have been desperate.'

James was struggling to keep up. 'I'm getting a little confused. I'm presuming that this young politician brushed her off and went begging to Theodore Livingstone. If that's the case, why wasn't Jacqueline the person who was killed?'

'Good question and the same question that I posed to Jacqueline. This is where it became most interesting. This Archibald Stanhope man had made an enemy of Theodore Livingstone. How or why I don't know but during some lucid moments while on painkillers he had spoken about his injuries. Said a little more than he should have done. Although Theodore was dining with the Duke of Kent when Stanhope was attacked, he knew the attack was down to Livingstone. I believe Theodore's son, Maximillian, paid Stanhope a visit while this was going on and Jacqueline was the duty nurse. Max recognised the name and must have fed this back to Theodore.'

Valentine dragged his chair closer and lowered his voice. 'After hearing the claims made by Stanhope, Jacqueline, being the conscientious nurse that she was, ensured that she remained close to Stanhope. She didn't like the way Maximillian behaved and there was something about him that made her wary. The next

61

evening, Sean Kilty came in, disguised as a doctor, and injected Stanhope with an overdose.'

'Conveniently witnessed by Jacqueline Simms.'

'Yes. He threatened her with the same if she opened her mouth. He told her to expect a visit from Theodore. But Jacqueline wanted the whole thing out in the open. To expose the people behind it.'

'An unwise decision.'

'They gave her an ultimatum. Refuse to testify or lose her daughter. And they told her to stay local. She did as she was told and the Livingstone men said they'd be watching her, making sure she never told anyone.'

James stroked his chin. 'Did she move away? I mean they couldn't follow her every move, could they?'

'You'd be surprised, Lord Harrington. The Livingstone men prefer to be in control. She had crossed the line with one of their own. The only options she had were the ones given to her.'

James felt his heart banging. Theodore and Maximillian, upper crust thugs who controlled people. No doubt charming and gracious in company but ruthless and manipulative underneath. 'Not only is this evil, Valentine, this shows how little empathy these men have.'

'Jacqueline reminded me of the proverb, kill two birds with one stone.'

'Yes, yes, of course. Stanhope had crossed the line, they wanted rid of him. Jacqueline had got herself acquainted with a now respectable MP, allegedly, and was causing problems. What better way than to kill Stanhope and put her in an impossible situation.' He held up a finger. 'But I still don't understand why they didn't kill Jacqueline? She was just as dangerous. A loose tongue and all that.'

'Because then the police would look further afield. Jacqueline got their man off by not testifying and was too terrified to cross them. If they'd have killed her, it would have instigated another investigation. It would have been too messy.'

'But couldn't the police use Jacqueline's statement in some way?'

'But how do you tie Theodore Livingstone to any crime? He's good friends with the Commissioner at Scotland Yard for heaven's sake. He stepped in and more or less stated that it was a ridiculous accusation. And he was dining with the Duke of Kent when the original attack took place, of course. No doubt the police thought her unstable.'

James thought this over. What an appalling situation for Jacqueline to have been in. To be held to ransom simply because, as a mother, she needed security for her child. What sort of man was this? To threaten an innocent, well-thought of nurse to serve his own agenda?

'I say, Valentine, what happened to the daughter?'

He shrugged. 'Jacqueline wouldn't say. She'd be around eighteen by now. Let's hope she's far away from here and doesn't come across the Livingstones.'

Helen Jackson jogged up to him. Her face was red from exertion. 'Hello James. Hello Valentine, don't often see you here. James, did you want another game? I've half an hour left on the court and Sarah has to get back?'

Valentine held his glass up. 'You go ahead. I'll sit and watch from the comfort of my deckchair.'

James eased himself out of his chair and picked up his racket. He turned to Valentine. 'I say, do you know Kushal Patel?'

Kushal Patel was a man whom James had befriended in a previous investigation. He helped debrief government agents after precarious and dangerous missions and was himself an esteemed and qualified psychologist.

'Yes, I do,' he replied with fondness. 'We bump into each other now and again. Charming man and a skilled psychologist.'

James trotted a few yards then turned again. 'One more thing, Valentine? You spoke about Theodore Livingstone as if you know him. Do you?'

James watched as Valentine struggled with his thoughts. 'We belong to the same club in London. The Wendover. I steer clear as much as I can. When I first set eyes on him, even back in the early days, I could see what sort of man he was.'

'The early days?'

'I was the Livingstone family GP when I first qualified.'

CHAPTER EIGHT

James splashed on aftershave and was grateful to feel more refreshed after the morning's exertions. He enjoyed a game of tennis as much as the next person but he hadn't reckoned on nearly two hours of play and with two good opponents. The day was still bright and warm and perusing the contents of his wardrobe, he chose a lemon cotton shirt and a pair of light linen trousers. Beth called up from the hall.

'Stephen's just telephoned. He seemed a little alarmed about something.'

'Oh?' James said as he came down the stairs. 'Did he say what?'

She shrugged. 'He wouldn't say. He has to judge the Cavendish Blooms so said he'll see you on the green.'

The Cavendish Blooms was something the residents who lived around the village green had started several years ago. Mr Bennett, James' childhood fishing tutor, had introduced the idea and a thoroughly good one it had turned out to be. The cottages around the village green were quaint and either whitewashed or built with some ornate brickwork around the windows and doors. Beth had always said images of the village deserved to be on the front of a biscuit tin and, when they pulled up alongside the vicarage, James had to agree.

It was early closing day and garden-gates were left open to allow people to wander in and out. It seemed fitting that the man who instigated the open garden tradition was also celebrating his birthday. Although he was a quiet and unassuming man, James and Beth were of the view that Bennett loved the attention of his fellow neighbours.

James reached into the car and brought out a bottle of whisky and a card. Their first port of call would be to Mr Bennett.

Bennett lived in one of the whitewashed cottages; a two-up, two-down residence with tiny rooms and lattice windows. Although nearing his 80th birthday, he was a fit man and painted his house every year to bring out the colour of the garden. He greeted them from his frayed deckchair by the garden gate.

'Oh Mr Bennett,' said Beth, 'your garden looks more spectacular every year.'

She helped him as he struggled to his feet and thanked her. 'Put more roses in this year and I've packed the place with colour.'

James followed close behind and repeated Beth's compliments. He handed over the bottle and card. 'Happy Birthday Mr Bennett.'

Blackie, Bennett's Border collie, came out of the open front door with his tail wagging. Beth reached into her bag. 'No, we haven't forgotten you.' She held up a bone. 'I've brought this from Graham's. Am I all right to give it to him?'

'Of course, your Ladyship. You'll have a friend for life now.'

She held the bone out for Blackie who gently took it from her and sought out some shade. Mr Bennett held up the bottle. 'Ooh, lovely, single malt. You shouldn't 'ave.'

James grinned. They went through the same routine every year and James didn't think that Bennett realised how much this man meant to him. He was a countryman, dressed in worn tweed trousers, a checked shirt and a waistcoat with various pockets. His hair peeped out from beneath a tatty bucket hat. His short beard was grey and a pipe was permanently lodged at the side of his mouth.

The fondness James had for him reached far beyond anything he could describe. When he was a child, the man was always up at the estate helping his father on the land and giving James and his late brother, Geoffrey, invaluable fishing lessons. Invaluable because not only did the man know how to fish, he knew where to fish depending on the flow of the river, the shallows, the shade, the weather and the seasons. On the land, his grasp of weather patterns, the animals and their behaviour, where and how to catch rabbits was endless. The man was a walking encyclopaedia on anything to do with country life.

He remembered a pony and trap that his father would allow Bennett to stable at the estate. Bennett would take James and Geoffrey deep into the forest and point out animals and teach them how to distinguish the various birds and their songs. Coming out of his reminiscing, he realised the Beth and Bennett were now at the back of the garden where the old man was pointing out new additions and old favourites.

'It's only the front gardens we show, as you know, your Ladyship, but you're welcome to go and have a look round the back.'

'Oh, I'd love to. You have so many vegetables planted. I wish I had the expertise to do this.'

'Takes a lot of time, your Ladyship, and I don't think that's something you have much of.'

Beth cast an eye over towards James, who agreed that life was rather hectic. 'Beth and I are popping over to meet Dulcie Faye this afternoon. Have you met her?'

Bennett's blue eyes twinkled. 'I have. Charming young girl. Quite shy and not as I'd imagine a film star to be. Took quite an interest in the garden, she did, and asked if I could give her some tips.'

'Mmm, I must admit I have the impression that those in the film world are all glamour and difficult to get near but, going by people I've spoken to, I'm sure I'll find her just as charming.'

After delighting in the mass of roses, ivory peonies, delicate sweet peas and sweet-smelling hyacinths, they thanked Bennett for the tour and popped next door to Mr Sharpe's house.

Unlike Bennett, Sharpe was not a country man but he had inherited his love of gardening from his mother whom he had lived with all his life. He'd not married and remained at home until her death two years ago. With the small inheritance she'd left him, he'd purchased a motor car and made some improvements to the rotting windows of his cottage.

Sharpe dressed formally as if always ready for Sunday service. Today, he wore dark trousers, the same green cable-knit cardigan he'd worn at the pub and a red tie. He had thinning brown hair swept back from his equine face. His cheeks were flushed. There was something a little jittery about the man and James couldn't put his finger on what troubled him. He didn't know Sharpe terribly well but he'd always come across as someone who was confident.

They chatted for a short while and admired the rows of hollyhocks and forsythia. As they turned to go, James spotted a bottle poking out of a brown paper bag hidden beneath his garden chair.

He steered Beth onto the pavement and bumped into Stephen. 'Ah, hello, you're doing the rounds as well I see.'

'Yes, I've just done the judging. Mr Bennett's come out top, as he did last year. He is the m-man to beat. Anne's o-over at Charlie's. It's a g-good turnout, isn't it?'

The number of villagers meandering in and out of the green was not a surprise. It was a lovely day and many women were examining the various blooms and getting ideas for their own gardens in between shopping and housework. Stephen tugged James across the road and onto the green. Beth followed with a quizzical expression.

'Everything all right?' asked James.

'I rang Beth e-earlier. Something that sounded a little q-queer.'

'Yes, she mentioned that you were somewhat alarmed.'

'It may b-be nothing. It may be me putting two and two together and making s-six.'

'Then again,' said James, 'it may be important. Spit it out.'

'Well. I came out early this morning. I th-thought I'd amble around the green and w-watch the last-minute preparations for the gardens. And I passed the telephone box.'

James and Beth exchanged sideways glances. James waited.

'Mr Sharpe was in there, making a call. Qu-quite agitated he was.'

James instinctively leaned in. 'About what?'

He received a helpless shrug. 'I-I don't know but it was m-more about what I overheard.' Stephen checked that no one was eavesdropping. 'He said "But I didn't kill her".'

The three of them stared at one another, not knowing what to say. James repeated the overheard phrase. 'And you've no idea who he was talking about?'

'No! I couldn't eavesdrop. I couldn't queue to make a call, could I? I-I have a telephone at the vicarage.'

'Did he mention who he was speaking with?'

'No. It may be n-nothing. He may have been talking about his pet r-rabbit. Oh. Does he have a pet rabbit?'

James said he didn't think he did and told him not to worry. 'Listen, we have to pop over and see Dulcie Faye. Are you coming?'

Stephen's eyes lit up and he adjusted his dog-collar. 'Oh yes. Let me get Anne. She's over at Charlie's house. We'll see you there.' He strode off..

Beth turned. 'That was a little odd, wasn't it?'

'I think we're making something out of nothing. Having said that, Sharpe doesn't seem to be his normal confident self. Did you notice the paper bag beneath his chair?'

'No.'

'Hiding a bottle of something and his cheeks were flushed. I know it's early afternoon but I believe he's already had a few swigs out of that bottle.'

'I thought he was teetotal.'

'I've seen him drink the odd glass of wine but this is secret drinking.' He stroked Beth's cheek. 'Something is playing on Sharpe's mind but I don't know if it's anything to do with the Livingstone men. Professor Wilkins mentioned him being quiet when we were at the pub.'

Beth checked her handbag was closed. 'Well, we can't very well go and demand to know what he was talking about. Let's visit Dulcie and see what we can find out.'

70

The bus to Brighton pulled in as they approached their car and James saw Bert step down on to the pavement. His friend had a brief chat with the driver then yelled across.

'Jimmy-boy, I'm not getting off, just wanted to check that you were in later.'

'We'll be at the pub. The folk club's on tonight.'

'Right, I'll see you there.' He went back to his seat.

Beth stood by the passenger door. 'Is Bert not stopping?'

'No, he's meeting us later at the folk club. He seemed keen to meet.' James held the car door open for her. 'Let's hope all of these discussions will be of some help to George and the Superintendent.'

CHAPTER NINE

Dulcie Faye's cottage was built around 1870 and, in its day, would have been a dwelling for a farmhand or estate worker. It reminded James of how children depict houses in their drawings: windows either side of a front door and a chimney in the middle of the roof. The gardens belonged to Groom Lodge about one hundred yards further up the lane, where Theodore's Bentley Continental was parked.

James took more of an interest in the car parked by Dulcie's residence. A sleek Rolls Royce Drophead coupé.

'My word, this is a beauty. Do you think it belongs to Miss Faye?'

'I haven't seen her drive and I've never seen this car in the village. It is a stunning vehicle, isn't it?'

He allowed his hand to pass along its flowing lines. This was certainly something he'd love to take out on to the open road. He leant in to look at the polished walnut dashboard with its array of dials and switches. What a beauty. Beth dragged him away and told him to stop torturing himself.

The cottage had a wooden porch which looked freshly painted in a gentle shade of grey and the front door beyond that was a glossy navy blue. Beth pressed the doorbell and they heard a distant chime inside, along with the sound of laughter. A few seconds later, Dulcie Faye answered the door.

'Lady Harrington, how lovely. I'm so pleased you could make it.' She cast a hesitant smile at James.

'Miss Faye, this is my husband, Lord James Harrington.'

'Lord Harrington, it's such a pleasure and I can't thank you enough for coming.'

James charmed her with a bow. 'I'm sure the pleasure is mine, Miss Faye.'

'Oh, call me Dulcie, please.' She gazed past him. 'Is the vicar coming?'

'We thought they'd be here by now.'

Stephen's rusty Austin 7 raced into view and slid to a halt on the gravel. He and Anne tumbled out of the car, uttering profuse apologies.

'Sorry, got caught up with the Crumb sisters,' Stephen said, reaching a hand out. 'Stephen Merryweather, vicar of Cavendish and this is my w-wife, Anne.'

With the formalities over, Dulcie invited them in, showing them through to a small lounge with a beamed ceiling and inglenook fireplace. James hardly had time to take it in when a handsome young man in tailored trousers and a white cotton shirt came in from the kitchen.

'Dulcie, the kettle's on.' He beamed at them. 'Hello all,' he said, 'I'm Tony Young.'

James didn't feel they needed confirmation. Tony Young was a famous British film star. Unlike Dulcie, who had admitted to being shy and timid, Tony was seen in all the newspapers and magazines as *the* man about town, in and out of nightclubs with a beautiful girl on his arm on most occasions. He oozed sex appeal with big brown eyes gazing mischievously out from under his floppy copper-brown fringe. Hollywood had already come calling for Tony Young and James thought that on looks alone he would be a success. Dulcie seemed a little hesitant and James wondered whether the confidence of her friend diminished her own.

73

'Shall I make tea?' Tony asked.

Dulcie jumped. 'Oh, yes, sorry.'

Tony gently pushed her into her seat. 'You sit down and entertain. I'll do the teas and then I must get going.' He addressed the group. 'We've been rehearsing.'

Anne's eyes lit up. 'Oh, how wonderful. What for?'

'A play. Tell them all about it, Dulce. It's going to be on at Drury Lane. Limited run because we both have films to do.'

Dulcie swallowed hard, overwhelmed by the sudden influx of people.

Beth moved to her side. 'Why don't we both sit on the sofa? Anne, come and join us. We can be all girls together and the men can take the armchairs.'

James caught Beth's eye. 'I'll pop in and help Tony bring the teas through.'

Knowing that Beth, Stephen and Anne would set Dulcie at ease by the time he returned, he entered the kitchen.

'Thought I'd help bring the tray through. Have you known Dulcie long?'

'Three years. We belonged to the same drama club and got our breaks more or less at the same time. Could you grab the tea caddy? It's just to your right there.'

James did so and, on Tony's instructions, scooped several spoons of tea into a large Brown Betty teapot. 'I understand she's quite shy?'

The young man leant on the counter. 'Yes, she's a funny thing really. Quite happy to act a part on camera or in front of an audience but, as herself, she can't seem to be comfortable. I've noticed it more just recently.'

'Oh? Why's that?'

Tony peered into the lounge and nudged the door to. 'Ever since she met up with that Theodore Livingstone, she seems like a nervous sparrow. I think he scares the living daylights out of her.'

'Are they actually a couple?'

He received a shrug. 'He likes to think so. Dulcie is a bit of glamour on his arm when he attends boring parliamentary functions. If he knows the press will be there, Dulcie is invited. He uses her. That's all he does. He hates women. Incredibly derogatory and ill-mannered. Thinks a woman's place is in the home and deserves to be put in her place if she steps out of line.'

Shocked, James asked: 'You mean he hits her?'

'No. But she has witnessed him hit another woman.' He turned the gas off on the stove and filled the pot. 'I think that's why Mrs Livingstone left.'

James lowered his voice. 'Why does she put up with it? She's a beautiful actress who could net a handsome young chap at any time. What on earth does she see in Theodore?'

'If you ask me,' Tony said, 'he has some sort of hold over her.'

'What_'

The door swung open and Anne offered to bring cups and saucers through. Tony raked a hand through his hair and signalled that he really should be making a move. Passing through to the lounge, he hugged Dulcie tight and kissed her on the cheek.

'We must, must, visit The Skyline. We'll get the whole company down from Drury Lane; let our hair down.'

The Skyline was the latest music club in the centre of London. It had become a hot spot for film stars, musicians and artists. Dulcie retreated into her chair. 'I'm not sure.'

'Nonsense,' he said picking up his car keys. 'I'll telephone you to arrange it. Don't let that dinosaur stop you from having some fun.'

Dulcie's gaze fell to the floor. The young man caught James' eye and gave him a knowing look, one that said Dulcie Faye was locked into an unpleasant relationship. He let himself out and they heard the roar of the engine as the Rolls Royce sped off into the distance.

After pouring tea, Dulcie expressed her devastation that she hadn't thought to buy cake or biscuits. 'I don't have them in the house otherwise I eat the lot and put on weight.'

'You have done me a favour, Miss Faye,' said James.

Stephen echoed him. 'Since I moved h-here, I seem to eat more and more. The vi-village has so many events that involve f-food.'

'Lady Harrington told me you have quite a few clubs and activities going on.'

Anne told her she should come and give the Cavendish players some acting lessons. 'Goodness knows, some of us could do with it.'

They laughed and spent a pleasant hour chatting about the village and what there was to do. Stephen and Anne described their arrival in Cavendish and how, even after just a couple of years, they felt as if they'd lived there all their lives.

'Y-you really must c-come along to something.'

Beth took Dulcie's hand. 'What are you interested in? Besides acting of course.'

Dulcie, now more relaxed and visibly happier, gazed at the ceiling in thought. 'That's a good question. I must admit, I do like tennis so I could get involved in that. I've never really been one for baking so I don't think I'd contribute in the food department. No, I'm definitely leaning more toward the arts. The studio that you mention at Harrington's sounds like my sort of thing. I've always fancied painting or drawing. Oh, and reading. I love to read. I quite like the idea of writing a book.'

James invited her to pop into the country hotel when she had a moment. 'GJ generally has something going on from April until December. We shut down after Christmas to decorate and make sure everything is shipshape in time for reopening. His wife, Catherine, also runs pottery classes.'

'That sounds wonderful. What a lovely community you've built here.' Her face sparkled in anticipation. It was the first time James had seen a genuine smile from her.

Beth delved into her handbag and brought out a postcard. The photograph on the front showed Harrington's in all its glory, mid-summer, with the tables and chairs out on the patio. On its reverse was printed its address, telephone number and rates. 'James, do you have a pen?'

James brought out his fountain pen and handed it to her. She scribbled on the card. 'This is our telephone number at home. When you want to go, let me know and we can come up with you. We'll introduce you to GJ and Catherine. They're not about much at the moment. I think Catherine's mother is unwell so they're back and forth quite a bit.'

'Oh, how kind. I really do appreciate it.'

Anne said that they, too, had some details for her. Stephen handed Dulcie a black and white leaflet. 'This tells you about the activities in the church hall. We have everything from the Cavendish players to the church choir.'

'The best place for everything else,' said Beth, 'is the library. If you like to read, you'll find a good selection of books there. Charlie Hawkins runs that from one of the cottages on the green. He's such a lovely man. A widower with two young children. You've no need to be shy with him. He'll make you most welcome.'

'Yes, he will,' said Anne. 'He was one of the first to come over and greet us when we moved here. I can introduce you to him if you'd like.'

'You really are all so kind. I do feel much more at home having met you.' She perched on the edge of her sofa. 'I will definitely contact you when I decide to come to one of these events.'

'Do you have an ear for music, Miss Faye?' James asked.

'Oh yes. My father loves all sorts, from classical through to the crooners. I think he even likes some of the new songs.'

'It's just that we have the folk club tonight at the Half Moon. It's a friendly little get-together and you'd be most welcome. We'll all be there.'

'I'll have to check with Theodore. I'm not sure if he has plans tonight.'

A pensive silence settled before James asked a question he already knew the answer to. But the answer would lead him to his preferred topic: 'I thought you and Tony were together, as a couple. You seem to get on well.'

Dulcie's eyes danced. 'No, although I don't know any woman who wouldn't want to be.'

'Me neither,' Anne said ignoring the astonished look from Stephen. 'He's as stunning in real life than on the screen. My mouth went dry as soon as I saw him.'

Stephen cleared his throat. 'You'll be wanting a ph-photo of him on the bedside cabinet next.'

'Anne's right,' said Beth. 'And now he has a starring role in a Hollywood film that *Picturegoer* was talking about. If that's a hit with the critics he'll be the next Robert Taylor.'

'Or Tony Curtis' added Anne and, after some thought, 'or David Niven.'

'A-Anne, I think we get the p-picture.'

Dulcie chuckled. 'Tony is a dear friend but any lady he courts tends to be more raucous than I will ever be. I think our relationship is more like brother and sister.'

'That's not a bad thing,' said James. 'He's clearly someone who thinks a good deal of you. I gather then that you are walking out with Maxi–'

'Oh no, no, not Max. Theodore.' Again, she fixed her eyes on the floor. The glimpse of the carefree and warm Dulcie they'd had had retreated.

Beth put her teacup down. 'You know I'm normally good at seeing how couples get together and when Tony was here I thought that you and he were well suited. Theodore Livingstone seems so different to you.'

The young lady rubbed her thumbs and fingers together, her gaze still on the floor. 'He's been very good to me. Introduced me to people and taken me to some lovely places.'

'A-and he's quite a prominent MP, isn't h-he? Have you been to the Houses of Parliament?' asked Stephen.

'No, no, he wouldn't take me there. It's all terribly highbrow and all they talk about is politics. He says it's not for women.'

James noted Beth baulk at the comment.

'Not for women?' she said. 'Hasn't he heard of the suffragette movement? We have the vote. He does know there are over twenty female Members of Parliament now?'

Dulcie gave a helpless shrug and Beth patted her hand. 'I'm sorry, Dulcie, it's not your fault. I do get irritable when a woman is not recognised for her knowledge and talents. I mean, look at you, an actress.'

'I don't think Theodore sees my acting as a serious thing.'

Anne insisted she should take it seriously. 'You're making a name for yourself, Miss Faye. Never let anyone take that opportunity away.'

'And when do you see Theodore?' asked James, keen to get back to the subject.

'Dinners and functions mainly. We had lunch with the Prime Minister just last week. I think that tomorrow we have to see Lord Huckleby and his wife.'

James was familiar with Lord Huckleby. He lived in Chelsea and was a rather boorish individual who wallowed in his own wealth and sense of superiority. This poor girl must go out of her mind with boredom, he thought. These people were the same age as Theodore with the same pompous old-fashioned attitude.

'That all must seem terribly mundane for you, Miss Faye,' he said. 'A bright young thing like you should be out having fun.'

'Oh, it's all right. It's only the odd evening here and there.'

'And does Theodore involve you in any of his business affairs?' He received a sharp look from Beth, implying he was being too direct.

'No. He's always going out at odd times in the evening. He doesn't let me know where though.'

James was beginning to get the measure of Theodore Livingstone. Young Miss Faye was simply a trophy, someone to show off when required. Someone who Theodore believed was unintelligent and posed no threat to him.

'W-when did you meet Theodore?' asked Stephen.

'Through a function of some sort. A man, who I later discovered was Maximillian, got chatting to me and introduced me to Theodore. Max was setting up that magazine of his and __ ' She brought out a handkerchief and wiped a tear away. 'Sorry, I suffer a little with hay fever.'

Beth's anxious eyes told him he had perhaps overstepped the mark.

He squatted down and handed Dulcie her tea. 'We'll have to introduce you to our GP, Philip Jackson. He may be able to help you with that.'

Anne, picking up on the diversion, asked Dulcie about the cottage and what she'd done to make it her own.

Beth joined him at the kitchen door. 'I don't think we can push any more, James. Those were tears, not hay fever.'

'Yes, you're right. Interesting that she broke down when we mentioned Max.'

'Do you think he featured her in *Guess What?*'

'Or perhaps threatened to feature her.'

Before she had a chance to answer, they heard a key in the lock. The front door swung open and Theodore and Maximillian Livingstone strode in. The two were similar in every sense of the word. Big, stocky men in ill-fitting suits; hair Brylcremed back from their faces, complexions that suggested they spent too much time drinking. They radiated entitlement.

Without a glance at the people gathered in the room, Theodore blustered: 'What was that blasted Tony Young doing here?'

Dulcie jumped up. 'Helping me with my lines, Theodore. You know he always helps me. It's not easy to learn them without another person playing the other parts. Theodore, I think you should meet my guests...'

'I must admit,' said Beth sitting back down, 'I find it difficult to learn lines. That's why I normally do the costumes.'

Theodore ignored her and stared at James. 'This woman with you?'

James felt his jaw tighten. 'This lady is my wife. And you are?'

'I've not seen you here before.' He walked further into the room and glared at Stephen. 'Local vicar? What the hell are you doing here?'

Anne bristled. 'I'm Anne Merryweather and this is Stephen, my husband. He's the vicar of Cavendish.'

Theodore spoke only to Stephen. 'Not a church man so if you've come here to preach or convert you're wasting your time. Dulcie, we have a dinner engagement tonight. Need to be ready at six o'clock sharp. Don't be late and wear something revealing. Max is driving us.'

James clenched his fists as he saw Max leering at Beth. She shifted uncomfortably in her seat.

'Theodore,' Dulcie said, 'I really think you should say hello to my guests.'

A thunderous expression crossed his face. 'Oh, you do, do you?'

Before he had a chance to continue, she motioned to James. 'This is Lord James Harrington. And this is his wife, Lady Beth Harrington. Stephen and Anne are their friends.'

James watched as Maximillian checked himself. He forced a smile.

Theodore glowered at Dulcie. 'You should have told me they would be visiting.'

James took the initiative. 'She didn't know we'd all be here. We popped in to welcome her to the village and see if she wanted to be included in a few activities.'

'And,' Beth added, 'I think you'll find that she was trying to introduce us when you arrived.'

Theodore had no choice but to accept their explanation. 'Lord and Lady Harrington. I must apologise for not meeting you sooner. I know you live locally. I've a few acquaintances who've stayed at Harrington's. I'm surprised you came here and not straight to us.'

Beth explained that she'd met Dulcie at the butcher's shop. 'We're a close-knit community and I said I'd call in. Had you made yourself known, I'm sure we would have come to you too.'

Theodore struggled to remain civil. James could tell simply by looking at him that he would have liked to challenge Beth and put her in her place. Had she been on her own with Dulcie, he was sure Theodore's reaction would have been very different.

Max diverted his attention from Beth to James. 'Perhaps we could all dine there together one evening.'

James suppressed the urge to refuse them entry. He hoped these men would never set foot on the drive let alone inside the restaurant. Instead, he remained silent.

Theodore reminded Dulcie of the dinner.

'What a shame you won't make it to the folk club tonight.' said Anne.

'Folk club,' Max said spluttering with laughter. 'Who goes to folk clubs?'

83

'Maximillian! Remember our guests.'

Max's subservient bowed head was not lost on James. Scowling, the young man inspected his shoes.

Dulcie fiddled with her earring. 'I can come to the folk club another time. I should really think about what to wear tonight.'

They took that as their cue to leave. James reluctantly shook hands with Theodore and Max and they left. The door was promptly slammed behind them. They made their way to their cars.

'How infuriatingly rude,' said Beth.

'I could have punched him,' added Anne.

'All God's ch-children and all that but I didn't l-like either of those men.'

Beth's eyes were full of anger. 'Did you see the way Max looked at me? I felt cheap.'

James opened the car door for her. 'I saw.' He gathered them close. 'This is not the place. We'll talk later at the Half Moon.'

Allowing Stephen and Anne to drive off first, James followed them to the end of the drive where he stopped. He reached an arm round Beth's shoulders. 'Are you all right, darling?'

'I'm absolutely livid. How can that man be so bullish and ill-mannered? Barging into that cottage without even knocking. He didn't even introduce himself. Did you notice that?'

'I did,' James said, edging the car forward so that he could see the road. He checked his rear-view mirror and did a double-take. He put the car in neutral, pulled the handbrake on and swung round. 'Oh Lord!'

Beth turned to see what he was looking at. 'What? What have you seen?'

James settled back. 'Not what. *Who.* Inspector Fulton. I've just seen him wander off with Theodore Livingstone.'

CHAPTER TEN

The room at the back of the Half Moon was normally reserved as a wooden skittles alley; but once a month Bob Tanner and the Taverners took over the area to open the Cavendish Folk Club. It had become a thriving venue for folk singers and a number of men and women with guitars, banjos, concertinas and fiddles crammed in. Tonight was scheduled as a Come-all-Ye which meant that all singers who wanted to perform could get up and do so.

Charlie Hawkins was on the door, asking people to make a donation to the club to help pay for their next guest artiste. To boost funds, the club sold raffle tickets, the winner receiving a bottle of sherry.

James and Beth were old hands at the club and made sure they arrived early to get a good seat. They'd found a couple of wooden chairs by the wall where Stephen and Anne promptly joined them. Each wooden table had a candle jammed into the neck an old beer bottle sitting on it. The room was thick with tobacco smoke but this only added to the atmosphere. There was an air of exclusivity about the club because it was so popular. Those arriving late were disappointed to find themselves standing at the back more or less in the main part of the pub.

Mr Bateson, artist, raconteur and Cavendish's sole solicitor, was introduced as the next performer. A cheer erupted as Bateson was someone who never took himself terribly seriously. He was a true entertainer. He'd said to James on numerous occasions that he had no singing voice to speak of but what he didn't lack was enthusiasm. He quietened the audience down.

'Now Pentecost is nearly upon us and I found this little ditty on a record. It's an enormously stirring hymn which will lend itself perfectly to some rousing harmonies.' He brought out a tuning fork and resonated it on the table. 'It's in E if anyone wants to add some accompaniment.'

The invitation caused several musicians to pick up their instruments and await the song.

Bateson, with his wild, overlong hair, launched into the chorus:

'Pentecostal fire is falling, Praise the Lord, it fell on me.

Pentecostal fire is falling, Brother, it will fall on thee.'

He repeated the chorus several times until everyone was singing. The harmonies gave James goose bumps as Bateson waved his arms to conduct the masses. Some knew the verses and joined in, others simply played an accompaniment. He gestured when to get loud and when to quieten down and, by the end of the hymn, received a tumultuous roar of approval.

Bob Tanner got up from his seat and applauded. 'I don't think we should wait until Pentecost to sing that again.' He checked his running order. 'Right, next up we have Aubrey Pipe who's come up from Brighton. It's his first time here, so give Aubrey a big hand.'

The young man took to the stage with a guitar. James felt a tap on his shoulder. He turned to see Bert who jerked his head towards the main bar.

'Keep my seat, darling,' James said to Beth. 'I'll be back in a while.'

He manoeuvred his way through to the bar, grateful to step away from the heat and smoke. Bert handed him a pint of beer.

'Let's go outside,' he said, steering his friend toward the door.

The sun remained high in the sky and there was still a balmy warmth that gave them a taste of what was to come. James breathed in the fresh air. A thunderous noise interrupted the quiet. At the end of the green, a huge steam traction engine came into view. Clouds of dark grey smoke billowed from the chimney and the driver pulled on a rope above him to sound the whistle.

'What a glorious spectacle, Bert.'

'Blimey, you're not wrong there. The rally ain't for a few days, is it?'

'No, but the Guild has several engines coming from all over the country so we told them they could pitch up when they arrived. The Guild is paying for Didier and his staff to sort out some sandwiches for the drivers until the day it starts. I understand the owners of these machines camp by their engines.'

'No wonder they're turning up early. Chance of a free lunch.'

'They'll get it back on entry fees. The weather forecast is good and I believe we're in for a spectacular show.'

The traction engine trundled into the distance. They sat on a bench and leaned against the wall of the pub, out of earshot of the regulars.

'So, Bert, you have news?'

'Jimmy-boy, the police 'ave no right asking you to get friendly with those Livingstone blokes. No right. You met 'em yet?'

James shifted on his chair and described their visit to Dulcie earlier in the day. 'I didn't take to them at all and they were rude beyond belief to Beth and Anne. When I look back on that conversation, those men didn't actually speak with them at all, just to me and Stephen. They didn't give any of us the time of day until Dulcie told them our title. Then he made an about turn. By that time, I loathed the man and couldn't wait to get out.'

'Well stay out. That's my advice to you.'

'You've yet to tell me why.'

'Chatty Chatham didn't want to tell me anything at first. Told me life was too precious to spill the beans on Theodore Livingstone. Everything I tell you is hearsay, you understand that don't you? No one knows anything for sure and no one wants to ask too many questions 'cos if it gets back to Livingstone then you may end up wearing concrete boots.'

A quiver shook James. He finally asked what the hearsay was.

'Livingstone is driven by money and he don't care how he gets it. But his dealings are in drugs.'

'George mentioned drugs. He rang earlier to say they believe a shipment is in motion. They don't know where though.'

'Livingstone seems to run a tidy racket and has half a dozen people in his pay. The McCalls mainly. Where the drugs are concerned, no one knows how he deals them or who deals them and no one is letting on either. It's a big business with just a handful of people. He makes a packet from that particular enterprise.

'And then there's Maximillian, who is charm personified when 'e wants to be. If any of those people have a weakness or a secret 'e whittles it out of 'em in some way. If they don't pay the money, Max gives them a few columns in that magazine of his.'

'I thought that was just celebrities.'

'Nah mate. He goes for anyone remotely famous who don't want their name dragged through the mud. Those are the circles he works in.'

'Going back to Theodore, surely he must slip up somewhere.'

Bert's head bobbed from side to side. 'People like Theodore don't slip up, they leave other people in the firing line. He's a powerful man. The McCalls love 'em because a lot of their crime is overlooked.'

'Good grief, how?'

'Don't forget Theodore's friends.'

James slumped back. 'Of course, the Commissioner of Scotland Yard, the Prime Minister and God knows how many others.'

'Yeah, and any dirty work that does go down happens when Theodore is cavorting about and it's splashed across the papers the next day. That way, he's always got an alibi.'

'But the police suspect him. They must do, otherwise they wouldn't be asking me to poke my nose in.'

'Of course they suspect. But they've nothing to pull 'em in on. The likelihood of you gleaning anything is pretty remote if you don't mind me saying. They're not gonna spill the beans to you, are they?'

'Does this Chatty man have any suggestions? Because if he doesn't then I shall, indeed, drop this.'

'There are a couple of ideas that came up. Theodore's a member of the Wendover. That's your club, ain't it?'

'It is. I have a good friend that I see there occasionally, 'Swiss' Cheeseman.'

Andrew 'Swiss' Cheeseman had helped him and Beth a while ago when trying to sort out the mystery of the death of a new resident. He'd earned the nickname 'Swiss' due to his love of cheese.

'Will 'e know Theodore?'

'Not intimately, no'

'Anyway,' Bert continued, 'Chatty reckoned that Livingstone has an office on the top floor of the Wendover. He uses it on a Monday and Tuesday afternoon. Why he doesn't use his office in Parliament, I don't know. Would he leave some papers locked there? Would your bloke know anything about that?'

James sipped his ale. 'He might do. I think the best thing I can do is arrange to have dinner with him at the club and see the lie of the land and all that.'

'Don't you do anything stupid.'

'Could you arrange to be in London on the same evening?'

His friend narrowed his eyes. 'What you planning?'

'If we know, for sure, that Theodore and Maximillian are at one of their 'must be seen' evenings, that means the office will be empty.'

'Oh no,' said Bert. 'It may be empty but it could also be watched or 'ave some sort of alarm. You're off your rocker and I ain't going to break in. I may not 'ave much of a life but I'd rather 'ave what I've got than be dead. Don't you even think about it, Jimmy boy or I'll cosh you over the head myself.'

'Well, what's the other suggestion?'

'Chatty 'eard a rumour. Word is that Theodore carries a notebook. Keeps a note about money coming in and out. Who owes them, who's in their pay, that sort of thing.' Bert gazed across the green. 'It makes sense that there would be something. He can't keep it all in his head. Theodore keeps it with him all the time. Chatty doesn't know how you'd get to look at it.'

'So, we need to find out how to get our hands on it.'

Bert swung round, his teeth gritted. 'You don't need to do any of that. Just tell George what I've told you. In fact, d'you know what? I'm gonna tell George. That way, you stay out of it.'

James abruptly turned to Bert. 'You say something normally happens when the Livingstones are at some sort of function?'

'That's what I said.'

'They're at something tonight. Theodore told Dulcie to wear something revealing.' He shuddered. 'That sounds like the press may be around.'

'Could be. But we don't know who's connected with Theodore. And anyway, even if something does 'appen, it won't get pinned on him.'

'Look, I know he has the ears of the Scotland Yard senior officers but surely there are some policemen who are trying to pin something on them.'

'That's the rub, Jimmy-boy. There are but none of 'em know who to trust. You've got George and that Superintendent who are worried about who to talk to. Theodore has a few of the senior ranks in his pocket.'

James snapped his finger and thumb. 'Yes, and one of those is Inspector Fulton.'

He received a sideways look from Bert. 'How d'you know that?'

'I saw him this afternoon with Theodore. I don't think he saw me although I'm sure Theodore updated him on our visit. But they behaved more like a couple of friends than a police Inspector and a suspect. And he overheard the Superintendent talking about Livingstone at the awards on Monday.' James took another swig of ale. 'I wonder what's going to happen tonight?'

Donovan appeared from the bar. 'Ah yer man, I've got Valentine Plumb on the phone for you.'

James checked his watch. 'I wondered where he was. He's normally here by now.' Pushing himself up from the bench he said: 'Perhaps he needs a lift.'

Donovan led him behind the bar to the small hallway where he picked up the receiver.

The singing from the folk club drifted down the hall. 'Hello, Plumb, car broken down? I can come and pick you up if you like.'

'Lord Harrington, I'm so sorry but I wondered if you could come here. I've had rather a shock.'

'Of course. Let me grab Beth and we'll be with you in a few minutes.'

'Oh no. No. Please don't bring your wife. I wouldn't want her to see this. It's not something for a lady to see. Please. I must ring off. I've telephoned the police. They may ring back.' The line went dead.

CHAPTER ELEVEN

Leaving Bert to notify Beth of his sudden absence, James jumped in the Austin Healey and hurried over to Plumb's house. He lived on the outskirts of the village in a substantial Victorian house surrounded by gardens. He'd never married and the house reflected the tastes of a confirmed bachelor and scholar. James had only ever seen the ground floor of the house but it was tastefully decorated with dark walnut cabinets and bookshelves.

The drive was a short one and took him out of the village and along a remote country lane. He was eager to know what had happened and Plumb's request that Beth remain at the pub had prompted more questions. He came to a halt on the narrow road to see Valentine waiting at the door.

James leapt from the car. 'Valentine, you had me worried, old man. Are you all right? What's happened?'

Valentine, who normally had quite a healthy glow about him, appeared fraught. 'I was coming to the folk club. I got out here and thought I'd adjust my little scarecrow over there. He was leaning quite a bit and no use to me like that so I went to straighten him up.'

James cast his eye across the vegetable plot to the scarecrow and then returned his attention to the man who seemed in some distress.

'The poor girl.'

The comment jolted James. 'Poor girl?' He moved toward Valentine. 'What d'you mean, poor girl? What's happened?'

Valentine's eyes sought out the scarecrow. 'Over there. That's why the blasted thing was leaning. She'd toppled it over.'

94

Unable to make sense of Valentine, James gave him a reassuring pat on the arm and made his way down a narrow strip of grass between vegetable patches. Getting closer, he slowed his pace. He'd felt quite brave a few seconds ago and now he was wary about what he was about to find. He heard Valentine behind him.

Reaching the raggedy scarecrow, James spotted the body of a young lady near it. She was lying on her front but the side of her face was visible. He squatted down and felt for a pulse. She was cold to the touch and he knew there was nothing he could do. Scrutinising the body, he put her in her late teens with short wavy dark brown hair, a little make-up and wearing a skirt and matching jacket. Her stockings were laddered but he couldn't see any sign of violence.

Valentine shuffled forward. 'Do you know who she is?'

James got up and brushed his trousers down. 'No, do you?'

The panic in his face suggested that Plumb did. 'It's Faith Simms.'

James tilted his head. 'Faith Simms?'

'You know! The girl I was talking about. Jacqueline Simms, the nurse. It's her daughter.'

'Oh Lord.' He grabbed Valentine's arm. 'I say, you haven't touched anything, have you?'

'No, no. Oh actually, yes, her handbag. I went through it to see if there was any identification. That's when I found out who she was.'

'Did you know she was coming here?'

His eyes opened in horror. 'No! I've never met her before.'

James spotted the handbag and, using his handkerchief, opened the clasp and peered in. He saw a

95

small purse, compact, comb and mirror along with a membership card to The Skyline, the music club frequented by Tony Young. Looking at the body again, he lifted the pocket on the jacket and peered inside. A scrap of paper. He slipped it out, careful not to touch it, read it and replaced it.

'She has your address in her pocket. You're sure she didn't contact you? Did you get any odd telephone calls or messages?'

Valentine denied receiving anything.

'Well the police should be here any minute now. Let's put the kettle on,' he said, steering Valentine back down the garden path and into the house. 'They'll be asking the same questions and you'd better tell them you've touched the handbag. They'll be wanting to check that for fingerprints.'

'Will they think I've put her there?'

'I wouldn't think so for one minute. But I would tell them everything you've told me. About Jacqueline Simms I mean.'

'Do you think that's relevant?'

'Oh yes,' said James, lighting the gas on the stove. 'I think it's extremely relevant.'

A few minutes later, James was relieved to see George pull up in a police car driven by a young constable.

Before he'd even stepped from the car, his friend hollered: 'What the devil are you doing here?'

James gave a brief outline of how he came to be at Plumb's house. 'I couldn't not come over, especially as he was so insistent I come. The chap is distraught.'

George brushed past and introduced himself to Valentine. Then he turned to the constable. 'Fulton, you wait for the ambulance and organise things out here.

Don't let them move the body until the photographer's been. I hope he gets here before it gets dark.' He turned to Plumb. 'Mr Plumb, shall we go inside?'

'Yes, yes.'

James tugged George back and lowered his voice. 'Fulton?'

'Yes, Constable Fulton, fresh from the academy. He's just joined us. He was at the awards ceremony on Monday. Picked up a commendation for preventing a robbery.'

'Is he any relation to Inspector Fulton?'

'Uncle, I think. Why?'

James pulled his friend closer. 'We need to talk.'

George lowered his voice. 'Is this about what we were discussing at the awards ceremony?'

'Yes.'

'I'll come to you. By the time we've finished up here, it'll be dark. I'm with Superintendent Higgins all day tomorrow. Will it wait a day?'

James said that it would have to. 'You'll probably find us at Harrington's.' He had a few things to do there, including going through menus with his chef, Didier, and ensuring that everything was place for the traction rally. 'We'll either be on the terrace with Didier or wandering around the far field.'

'Right, I'll catch up with you there.' He went to join Plumb in his study but as James followed him, he turned. 'James, this is police business.'

James stopped in his tracks and racked his brains for a reason to stay. Unfortunately, he didn't have one. Instead, he said: 'Make sure he tells you about Jacqueline Simms.'

Leaving George with a quizzical expression, James made his way to Constable Fulton.

97

'Constable Fulton? I understand you're new.'

The fresh-faced man couldn't have been more than twenty. He was a tall, slim man with sandy hair and a pleasing manner. 'Yes, sir. I came out of training and was posted to Lewes. I'm fortunate to be working for DCI Lane. He's one of the best detectives in the country.'

James agreed. 'And you are a relative of Inspector Fulton of Scotland Yard, is that correct?'

Wariness crept into the young man's voice. 'Ye...s. Do you know my uncle?'

'Not really, no. I was introduced to him a few days ago at an awards ceremony. He said he was with you.'

Constable Fulton frowned. 'He was there but I didn't invite him. I asked my dad but he couldn't get the time off work.'

Before James could ask anything else, the police photographer arrived, promptly followed by the ambulance. He moved towards the area where Faith Simms lay. What the devil was she doing in Valentine Plumb's vegetable patch? Why had she come here? It had to be something to do with her mother.

He fast came to the conclusion that this was the work of Theodore Livingstone. The link was there. From all angles. He hoped a post-mortem would find something odd. He was convinced Faith Simms had been murdered and that this was a result of her mother's witness statement.

He stepped to one side as the photographer brought his equipment over.

As he opened the car door, he spotted a black car pulling off in the distance. It could only have been waiting to see what had transpired. This country lane led only to the cottage and a bungalow about a hundred

98

yards further along. A shiver ran through him. Bert was right. He had to remain invisible where the Livingstones were concerned. He hoped he hadn't drawn attention to himself in any way. What was it that Bert had said? Concrete boots? He shuddered. Putting the car in gear, he drove toward the village. The fact that Theodore Livingstone was a loathsome man fuelled his determination to see justice done. At the same time, he wondered whether he should simply drop the requests of George and the Superintendent and let them get on with it. A chat with Beth would help sort his concerns out.

CHAPTER TWELVE

Knowing they had a busy day ahead, they arrived at Harrington's at eight o'clock on Friday morning and selected a table on the terrace. They spent some time chatting with their guests, many of whom were planning the day ahead. A few men were already wandering down to the river with their fishing rods; some couples had decided to ramble on the beautiful Sussex South Downs while others were finishing their breakfasts before going further afield in their cars. The wonderful location meant that many major towns and sightseeing spots were just a short drive away.

James and Beth waved to GJ who was entering the converted stables. GJ, a young man they had helped to get back on his feet after he'd spent several years as a homeless man was now using the block as an artist's gallery and tuition studio. The course he had scheduled this particular weekend was fully booked. He and his wife, Catherine, taught painting, drawing and pottery. It was proving to be a popular pastime with many of their guests, and both James and Beth were astonished at some of the work they'd produced.

Beth gazed across the fields. The two donkeys, Delphine and Sebastian, gifted to them by GJ, grazed under a tree. The sun was struggling to warm the slight chill in the air but the sky was promising a nice day ahead.

'Lord 'arrington, Lady 'arrington, forgive me please,' said Didier, their rotund French chef. He scurried to the table in his chef's whites, holding a few sheets of paper. Adam, a young waiter who had been with them for several years now, strode out after him with a look of expectation. Didier emitted an exasperated groan. 'Yes,

yes, come along.' He turned to James. 'Adam wishes to be more involved and wants to learn 'ow we do the menus.'

Beth beamed. 'Oh, how wonderful. Come and sit with us Adam. Are you wanting to train as a chef?'

James bit back a grin as Didier harrumphed at the young waiter.

Adam ignored Didier and pointed out that he didn't have the skills to be a chef but that he loved working at Harrington's and saw himself as someone who could perhaps rise through the ranks. 'I know that Paul will probably be here for years but I feel I'm ready to learn more and take on some responsibility. Paul said it was good to find out how all the areas worked so I'm listening in. Do you mind?'

'Not at all,' said Beth, who commended him for his attitude.

'Splendid idea,' said James. 'You're good at what you do, Adam, and professional with it. I'd be delighted to see you rise through the ranks. I'm sure Paul will be relieved to have someone he can rely on should he be on holiday or unwell.'

Paul, their maître d'hôtel, had been with them for ten years and, like Adam, thoroughly enjoyed working at Harrington's. But with the reputation of the hotel growing and its becoming ever more popular with the wealthy and elite, James thought it would be good to have two or three of their staff ready to step up if the need arose.

They seated themselves around the table and Paul popped his head out from the dining room. 'Your Lordship, Detective Chief Inspector Lane has just rung to ask your whereabouts. He asked that you remain here. He should be with you in about fifteen minutes.'

101

'Jolly good. Send him out here when he arrives.' He turned his attention to Didier. 'Now, my talented friend, what delights are you proposing for our guests?'

It never failed to amaze him how passionate Didier was about food. He'd discovered a good deal about the man during a particularly unpleasant episode over Christmas. But, without that affair, he would never have learned of the man's heroics during the Great War. As a teenager, he had risked his life by being a runner to and from the British lines, carrying not only messages and instructions, but bread and cakes that his family had baked in the local village. He fell in love with the process of baking and saw the pleasure it gave to the young soldiers on the battlefield.

That a love of cooking could blossom in such adversity was an eye-opener for James and he found he had so much respect for the man that he forgave him his temperament and impatience which, even he, as his employer, was on the receiving end of at times. He paid over the odds for Didier's services because he was the best and the thought of ever having to replace him was alarming to say the least.

Didier spread the papers out. 'I 'ave been speaking with the farmer on the coast. He has some beautiful braising steak so I think that *boeuf bourguignon* will be a lovely meal. It is more suited to winter, I know, but with spring vegetables and robust wine flavour, I believe our guests will enjoy it.'

'Sounds lovely,' said Beth.

'Now,' he continued, 'Mr Porter has offered me some of his 'ome cured gammon which I will serve with a poached egg and *pommes frites*.'

'I say, that sounds rather nice. Not the sort of thing you normally dish up.'

'*Oui, oui,* it is more suited to Elsie's café but I believe I can elevate it to something worthy of 'arringtons.'

'I'm sure you will,' James said knowing that this would look nothing like a café meal. He was interested to see what Didier would do with what was basically a thick slice of bacon. 'I think I shall have to put my name down to try that one.'

Beth agreed and asked if there would be a fish course.

'Of course,' Didier said, almost outraged that she would suggest there wouldn't be. 'I 'ave been in touch with your cousin, Lord 'arrington. Or, rather, he has been in touch with me.'

James perked up. 'You have some salmon?'

'*Oui, oui.* Served with mangetout and buttered new potatoes.'

James' cousin, Malcolm, lived in the Scottish Highlands and occasionally sent down a few bottles of cask-aged 12-year-old single malt. He had a salmon river running through his grounds so James had put Didier in touch with him recently and Scottish salmon was slowly becoming part of the menu. It didn't happen very often, only when Malcolm or one of his friends was visiting London or the south east. He wrapped it in ice and sent it down with whoever was travelling. They normally had enough for the week. After that, Didier changed his menu to the fresh fish caught along the coast at Brighton or Hastings.

James rubbed his hands together. 'So, we have beef, gammon and Scottish salmon. That's rather a lovely choice. What about entrées and desserts.'

Adam said he had those notes in front of him. 'Chef is making a pea and mint soup. He's also doing a selection of sautéed mushrooms with freshly baked bread and some smoked mackerel with onion and tomato.'

'Ooh, that sounds delicious,' said Beth. 'I won't have room for dessert.'

James watched as the young man blushed. He'd had a crush on Beth ever since he'd first started working here during the school holidays as a fourteen-year old. He hid it well but both James and Beth could read the signs. He was a pleasant-looking chap, now nineteen, and James had heard that he'd found himself a lady-friend, one of the waitresses.

A shuffle of paper brought him out of his musing as Didier revealed the dessert menu. 'I 'ave some fresh fruit with cream, your grandmother's lemon meringue pie.'

James groaned with a delight.

'And,' Didier continued, 'the cheeses from the farm are extremely varied at the moment so I will offer a cheese board with crackers and home-made chutney and pickles.'

'Splendid. Do you have any broad beans? They're in season now, aren't they?'

'*Oui, oui,* I will be serving them with the beef. That is a light, summer vegetable with the bright green colour to add to the dish.'

'Adam? Any thoughts?

Adam sat up straight, a little alarmed to be asked for some input. 'No, your Lordship, it all sounds lovely.'

'Well, do pitch in if you have thoughts in the future. Part of stepping up the ladder is to put your ideas and suggestions across, although I think you're wise to let Didier loose in the kitchen.'

Didier allowed himself a few seconds to bask in his glory then said he must get busy. He stood, collected his papers and, with a click of the heels and an *au revoir*, he left.

Adam thanked them for allowing him to sit in. 'I'll see if DCI Lane's arrived.'

A couple of minutes later George joined them at the table on the terrace. He loosened his tie and took in the view. 'Well this is better. Nice to get out from behind that desk and never-ending meetings.'

James scrutinised his friend. They were the same age with a shared interest in cricket and regular meetings for a pint in the Half Moon. He was a man who had passion for what he did and the medal he'd received at the awards ceremony was well deserved. The man sitting by him today, however, appeared tired and run-down. He sat forward. 'George, if you don't mind me saying, you look a little out of sorts.'

'I won't lie to you. I feel a bit worn out.'

Beth suggested he should take some time off. 'You never take a holiday and when you do you end up working.'

'It's not really to do with too much work. It's to do with the type of work.'

It didn't take long for James to understand. 'You're talking about this matter with Theodore Livingstone?'

George felt for his pipe. 'I'm not sure how to go about it, James. I've never come across a case where I'm not sure who to trust in my own force.'

'Perhaps it would be a good idea to divulge what you can here. You can trust us and that may be a good starting point.'

Beth asked how he had got on at Valentine Plumb's house.

'This is where I struggle to comprehend how to go about things. The victim was Faith Simms, daughter of Jacqueline Simms who withdrew her witness statement several years ago. James, did you update Beth on that?'

'I did.'

'I had quite a chat with Valentine Plumb. He knows that Jacqueline Simms has now died of her illness. He believes that she must have said something to her daughter to make her seek him out. He can think of no other reason for Faith to be in the area.'

'Can I ask,' said James, 'was Faith Simms murdered?'

'Difficult to say. There is a puncture mark on her arm and a syringe beneath her body which suggests suicide but…well, it looks to all of us as if it were staged. There are no other signs of drug use and why commit suicide at Plumb's, especially if she was trying to seek him out?'

'You believe she was murdered and placed at Plumb's cottage or do you think he's a suspect?'

'If it is murder, I'll have to treat him as a suspect for the time being. He has links to Livingstone through membership of the Wendover. That's your club, isn't it?'

'Mmm. He told you that he was also a doctor at the hospital Jacqueline worked in.'

'Yes, he did. From what he's said, this Jacqueline woman was set up and then blackmailed. I'll have to take a look at what happened back then. A lot of it's on file at Scotland Yard from the trial business. But I'd like to see where Faith Simms has been living and what prompted her to come to Cavendish. Would she have known Plumb?'

'Unlikely. And Plumb left the profession the week before that murder took place. Faith would have been very young.'

Beth held up a finger. 'You know what I think? I think that Jacqueline, knowing she was dying, decided to tell Faith the identity of her father and that she should speak to Valentine to find out more because she had confided in him. Jacqueline probably told Valentine everything.'

'I agree,' said George.

'Makes perfect sense,' said James. 'I wonder if she found out the identity of her father and confronted him, who then contacted Theodore or Maximillian who…'

'Sorted out a way to dispose of her,' said George, finishing James' sentence.

Beth wondered why they would put the body in Valentine Plumb's garden.

'He must have cropped up in the conversation,' he responded with a puff on his pipe. 'Theodore is perhaps trying to frame Plumb, I don't know.'

'Which confirms what Beth said,' added James, 'that Jacqueline felt comfortable with Plumb as her confidant. Told Faith to seek Valentine out, that she could trust him.'

Beth pursed her lips. 'What a foul man that Theodore is. Presumably he has an alibi.'

George said that both Theodore and Maximillian were at an opening night of a show in London on Wednesday and that last night Theodore and Dulcie had attended a première in Cambridge. 'They're plastered all over the papers today.'

James sat back. 'Bert has a contact, Chatty Chatham he calls him. He said that whenever something criminal was going to occur that involved Theodore, he made sure they were visible, as in plastered all over the papers.'

'Looks like this Chatty fella was right. Theodore wouldn't have got his hands dirty with this.'

'No, I know, but did you know that the McCalls are quite cosy with them?'

George said that he did. 'Those are the sort of people you don't want to mess with.' He clenched his jaw. 'I'm not happy about any of this. The only person I can speak to officially is Superintendent Higgins and I'm getting so paranoid that I'm wondering whether I can trust him!' He twisted in his chair. 'And why were you asking about Constable Fulton?'

'I would be careful with what you divulge to him too,' James said telling George about seeing Inspector Fulton with Theodore. 'I get the feeling that Constable Fulton is not his uncle's greatest fan but that could be some sort of cover.'

George flung a hand up. 'There, you see, who do we trust? This Chatty Chatham bloke, is he able to check anything out?'

'No, he won't touch it. And Bert told me to steer clear too.'

'Sweetie, don't forget to tell George about the notebook.'

'I'd forgotten about that. Thank you, darling. One thing this Chatty said was that he thinks Livingstone has a notebook that details all of his dealings; you know, what he's owed, meetings, payments etc.'

'Interesting.'

'Also, he uses an office at the top of the Wendover. I wondered if he kept any papers there, locked in a safe or a drawer.'

'Don't you even think about going in there.'

'I'm not, but I thought about having a word with a friend who's a fellow member. He may know more than me because he spends an awful lot of time there.'

George pushed his seat back and got up. 'That notebook may be the undoing of Theodore. If nothing else, perhaps we should all think about how to get hold of it. We can't just search him for no reason.' He gazed at the pair of them. 'And I mean *think* about it, not actually act on those thoughts. I've got to go. Promise me you'll not do anything stupid.'

A promise was good enough to appease him. James fondled Beth's hand. 'Shall we pop over to the field and see how everything's going? The rally starts tomorrow. I know the Steam Guild is organising it but as it's on our land, I feel somewhat responsible for its smooth running.'

As they sauntered across the grounds, Beth asked if he was going to take George's advice.

'I think so, yes. The fact that Bert doesn't want to lend a hand is ample enough warning for me. But it won't hurt to have a chat with a few people and Swiss is high on my list.'

'You may also want to speak with Rose and Lilac Crumb. Remember that Anne told you they had some sort of upset with the Livingstones.'

He held hands with her. 'Yes, along with Mrs Withers. She reacted oddly when the Livingstone name was mentioned.' Hopping over the stile to the event field, he spotted Mr Sharpe in the distance. 'Damn and blast, I forgot to tell George about Mr Sharpe and that odd comment that Stephen overheard.'

'Call him later.'

'And that encounter that Theodore had with Paolo Rossi.'

'Those Livingstone men are certainly forcing their way into people's lives.'

'And not in a good way. But let's have a chat with Sharpe while he's here.'

CHAPTER THIRTEEN

James had noticed, during his discussions with Didier and George, that a steady stream of traction engines was now congregating in the field and what a sight is was to behold. Steel clunked as drivers reversed the massive machines into their allocated spots. Puffs of steam billowed out of chimneys as pistons rattled back and forth. Their huge wheels carved paths through the field and many fellow engine owners buzzed to and fro, keen to see one another's machines. Some were pulling vibrantly-coloured Romany gypsy caravans which brightened the place up no end. The unique smell of coal and steam filled the air.

Steamrollers sat alongside threshing and ploughing machines, all of them in distinctive reds, blues and greens, with intricate gold calligraphy depicting their make or the name of the engineering works they'd been produced in.

Mr Sharpe was directing an ancient steamroller with a long black chimney and wooden roof. The driver was frantically turning the wheel to manoeuvre it into place.

Once he'd finished orchestrating this, Sharpe drifted back to what appeared to be his domain, an area filled with miniature steam engines that numerous men were studying.

Beth pulled a face. 'Why on earth do men want to stand around looking at an engine?'

'I think, darling, that is one of those many things that make us different. I'm equally perplexed as to why women are so curious about the colour of each other's lipstick.'

They grinned and Beth asked him how he would approach Mr Sharpe.

'I'm not entirely sure. He doesn't seem his normal confident self. Perhaps I should be firm with him. I don't mean I'm going to march him off and interrogate him but I do think we need to take him away from his muse. All the time he's standing there, people are going to want to chat to him and he, quite rightly, will want to speak about all things steam.'

'The refreshment stalls haven't set up yet.'

'No, but Paolo has just arrived with his ice-cream van.'

Her eyes lit up. 'Perfect timing. I'll make my way over.'

Mr Sharpe acknowledged him as he picked up a rag. 'Ah hello. Making sure everything is as it should be?'

'I am,' replied James, although he could see that there were no concerns from where he was standing. 'I say, Mr Sharpe, do you have a few moments? My wife is just buying some ice creams and one has your name on it.'

Sharpe wiped his hands before joining James. 'This is a perfectly splendid event to have locally. I'm quite pleased that the showground we normally use was too boggy. Having this on your doorstep for a week is a dream come true.'

They wandered toward the ice-cream van.

'I'm rather fond of these old things myself and, of course, I'm now the proud owner of a vintage car that will be taking its place for the classic car judging.'

'Yes, I heard about that. I'll look forward to seeing it.'

Beth stood by the side of the van with three ice creams and handed them out.

Mr Sharpe thanked her. He was still dressed in his green cardigan, shirt and tie and James wondered if he would ever vary what he wore. He only ever seemed to wear green or blue. He was clean and tidy but he could imagine his wardrobe holding several green and blue cardigans and nothing else. Still, that wasn't his concern and he was keen to find out what he could.

'If you don't mind me saying, Mr Sharpe, you seem a little under the weather just recently.'

Sharpe paused mid-lick of his ice-cream and his cheeks lost their colour. 'I…I don't know what you mean.'

James wasn't sure whether to push things or not. He didn't know Mr Sharpe terribly well and, at this precise moment, he looked like a man on the run. Instinct told him to come straight to the point. 'I think you possibly do.'

His eyes darted from pillar to post as he took a step back. 'How could you possibly know anything about it? I haven't… he wouldn't…' He stopped abruptly with an expression that divulged his feeling that he'd said too much.

In truth, James hadn't a clue as to whether he had given him any leads except one. The man was clearly hiding something.

Beth put on her most sympathetic expression. 'This is obviously worrying you, Mr Sharpe, is there anything we can do to help?'

'No! No, nothing. You can't do anything.'

'Strange,' said James, 'that a couple of other villagers have reacted like that just recently.'

'Oh?' Sharpe's hands trembled as he licked his ice cream.

'Yes, it was the night we were outside the Half Moon. We were talking about the Livingstone men.'

The mention of the name caused Sharpe to catch his breath. Fear flashed in his eyes and again he scanned the fields as if a sniper would be picking him off at any moment. James drew him close. 'Mr Sharpe, if the Livingstone men are threatening you in any way, you must speak to my friend, DCI Lane. He can protect you.'

He almost dropped his ice cream. 'Oh no. No, you must leave this be.' He handed his cornet back to Beth. 'Thank you, I really must be on my way.'

James turned. 'Mr Sharpe?' Getting his attention, he asked: 'What did you mean, you didn't kill her?'

With a strangled cry Sharpe insisted he had to go. He rushed back to his engines, picked up his belongings and headed for his car. Beth deposited the man's unfinished ice cream in the bin and linked arms with James. 'That poor man is terrified.'

'I wonder what it is that Theodore has over him. He's clearly been accused of killing someone.'

'Faith Simms?'

'I wondered that although, according to Mr Bennett, he's been jittery for some time. And that comment was surely made before Faith Simms was killed, don't you think? Does he have any other family?'

'I don't think so. He lived with his mother until her death a couple of years ago.'

'Do you think he's being accused of killing her?'

'Now that would be a frightening accusation. I think that might be something to give to George. If we have proof, of course. But what has any of this to do with drugs?'

Not knowing the answer to that particular question, they made their way across the field and watched as engines continued arriving. A few traders were also filing in and setting up in time for the following morning. The rally would be here for a week and the weather was set fair. As much as he was looking forward to it, the fact that several residents in the village appeared to be under some threat disturbed him.

He patted Beth's hand as they made their way toward the entrance. 'Stephen's here, let's see what we can glean about the Snoop Sisters.'

'I'd r-recommend you speak with them direct,' said Stephen admiring a huge steamroller in front of him. 'Luke and Mark are going to love it here.' He gave them his full attention. 'I c-can tell you that it is to do with the Livingstones and they may have m-met their match.'

Beth tilted her head. 'In what way?'

'It is not my s-secret to tell, Beth.'

'Oh Stephen, I wouldn't put you in that position, you know that, but telling us they've met their match is a bold statement, especially knowing how ruthless those men are.'

Stephen grimaced. 'Yes, I know w-what you mean. Let me say this. M-Maximillian had something on Rose and Lilac.'

'Maximillian!'

'Yes.'

'I don't believe it.'

'L-let me finish. He had something on the sisters but the sisters c-came to me and I gave them advice which will mean he has no hold.'

James frowned. 'Are you saying that they're being blackmailed?'

Stephen scanned the area, leaned in and whispered. 'Yes.' He stood straight. 'I can't tell you anymore but please visit them. After my ch-chat with them, I'm sure they'll be happy to spill the b-beans.'

James checked his watch. A visit to the Snoop Sisters wouldn't be any hardship. 'Are they at home, do you know?'

Stephen told them they were helping Anne with the flowers in the church. 'They only arrived as I left so they'll be there for a while.' His face brightened. 'Oh look, there's Dulcie Faye.'

They turned to see the beautiful Dulcie signing an autograph for one of the engine-drivers. On seeing them, she waved and made her way over.

'Hello, how lovely to see you! I wasn't sure whether we were allowed in yet.'

James said that the field was open for exhibitors to come in and set up but that residents were invited to see this as a quiet day to visit. 'Tomorrow is the official opening day. We'll have a couple of people on the gate selling programmes and the vendors will all be up and running.'

Stephen asked if she'd had a good time during her evening out with Theodore.

Dulcie shrugged. 'Oh, it was all right. A bit boring really but it's one of those functions that Theodore likes me to attend with him so attend I must.'

'Y-you were in the paper these last two mornings.'

James detected a hint of sadness. No doubt, she had tolerated a couple of tedious evenings with the pompous Theodore.

'I say,' he said, 'I hope you're going to join us at the rally. Why don't you come along with us? Beth and Anne will both be here and we can introduce you to a few of our villagers who get involved with everything.'

Her face lit up. 'I'd like that very much. Providing, of course, there are no last-minute functions to attend.'

Beth asked if there were many 'last-minute' functions.

'It feels as if they're all last minute but that's probably my imagination and the fact that I don't particularly want to go.'

'D-do you *have* to g-go?'

She started. 'Oh yes. Yes, I have to go. Theodore wouldn't forgive me if I let him down.'

'You know,' said Beth, 'if someone had said to me that you and Theodore were a couple, well, I don't think I'd have believed them.'

Dulcie let out a hesitant laugh. 'Well, you know what they say, opposites attract. What time will you be here tomorrow?'

Beth said that they would all be there around nine in the morning. 'The Guild is taking on the main bit of organising but we each have our different jobs to do so we have to be in place for when the show opens at ten.'

'Is there anything I can do?'

James guaranteed her that her presence would be enough. 'Having a film star at our little shindig will brighten up many of our visitors' days.'

Her smile was genuine as she wandered away.

'Come along,' he said to Beth, 'let's you and I see if we can ingratiate ourselves with the Snoop Sisters.'

CHAPTER FOURTEEN

As the car wound through the country lanes toward Cavendish, Beth commented that it was much safer speaking to people they felt were affected by the Livingstone men. 'I mean people like the Crumbs and Mrs Withers. That way we don't have to do anything that forces us into meeting with those awful men.'

James parked the car alongside the vicarage. 'I think you're right,' he said, distracted by the image in his rear-view mirror. The black car that he'd seen at the end of the lane at Valentine Plumb's cottage had kept its distance, but he was sure that the same vehicle had now followed them from Harrington's. He waited for it to go by but whoever was driving was hidden by a wide-brimmed hat, their face obscured from his view.

'Are you all right, sweetie?'

He dismissed his concern. 'Of course. In a bit of a dream, that's all,' he said as he got out of the car. He opened the passenger door for Beth, all the while wondering if Theodore was onto him. But how? He thought he'd been very discreet. They'd dropped by on Dulcie at her invitation; Bert, he knew, would not have spoken to anyone he didn't trust. Inspector Fulton! He would have seen him when they'd visited Dulcie; Theodore no doubt told him they were there. Blast. Fulton knew James had been speaking about the Livingstone men at the police awards. Perhaps his nephew had alerted him to the fact that he was at Valentine Plumb's when Faith's body was found. Confound it!

Beth had stopped to observe him. 'James, what's going on?'

'Mmm?'

'You're acting terribly strange. You have something on your mind. What is it?'

He improvised. 'I'm just trying to fathom out a way to get hold of that notebook of Livingstone's.'

She appeared unconvinced of the answer but didn't push the subject. 'If you do find out, you must get on to George. I don't want us taking any risks with these people.'

He slipped his hand into hers. 'No, I don't either.'

They entered the church to see Anne and several members of the WI replacing wilting flowers with fresh blooms, polishing floors and preparing the building for Stephen's Pentecost service. James loved the Pentecost service, especially since Stephen had taken over as vicar of Cavendish. It was a time for celebration, when the villagers remembered the gift of the Holy Spirit. Stephen made a point of wearing robes ornamented with a deep red design depicting the flames in which the Holy Spirit came to earth.

Anne was placing hymn sheets on the pews as she welcomed them. 'Oh hello, I thought you were spending the morning at Harrington's.'

'We finished what we needed to do,' said Beth. 'Do you need a hand here? I don't have anything on at the moment.'

Anne put her hand to her forehead and scanned the scene. 'I think we're about finished. I do have some paper doves to hang up that Luke and Mark made, bless them. They've been busy the past few days with papier mâché and having a marvellous time. I'm putting the hymns out for people. We're singing three specific hymns and Stephen thought it would be good to have a song-sheet rather than flick through the books. And the print is so small in the hymn books, we're certain that a

119

lot of people don't sing because they can't read the words. That's what Stephen likes to think. Personally, I know a lot of people hate singing in public.'

James asked for a copy of the hymn sheet. '"Come Down O Love Divine". That's a lovely hymn. D'you remember, darling, we heard the King's College Choir sing that?'

'It's beautiful. What else do you have?'

'"Breathe on me Breath of God".'

'I chose that one,' said Anne.

'And you've included "Pentecostal Fire is Falling".'

'Oh, how wonderful,' said Beth, 'that is such an exhilarating hymn.'

Anne agreed. 'We're leaving that one for last and Bob Tanner is going to lead the congregation.'

Everyone agreed this was going to be a most enjoyable service. James took a note of who was helping in the nave but could see neither Rose or Lilac Crumb. He asked Anne.

'They're in our garden picking some flowers to display in the entrance.'

Beth turned to him. 'I'll stay here while you go and speak with them. They are cantankerous beyond reason but they do like it when you take an interest in them.'

'Mmm, I'm not sure that what I'm going to ask could be termed taking an interest, more being blatantly nosy.' He pecked her on the cheek and made his way across to the vicarage.

Rose and Lilac Crumb were two elderly sisters who had lived together their whole lives, neither having married or shown any inclination to want to leave the other. They had moved into the Cavendish area several years ago and the rumour was that they had been driven out from their last residence. The gossip being that they had stolen money from their WI kitty and spent a night in the West End of London at a theatre. They vehemently denied any criminal activity and swore that they were upstanding citizens and would never stoop to such inexcusable behaviour. The rumours died down and, although they were nosy and occasionally rude, the sisters had integrated themselves into the Cavendish community.

The last few events held in the village had seen them become more involved and it appeared that this fed the sisters' need to be included. In some ways, they were egotistical, enjoying the attention they received. But, James thought, if that made them happier and more accepted, why should anyone mind?

Each carrying a trug, Rose and Lilac Crumb were bending over studying the various cottage flowers and ferns in the vicarage garden and cutting stems of those they felt suitable for their display. So far, they had several examples of roses, pansies, marigolds and foxgloves. He leaned on the wooden gate.

'Hello there,' said James. 'Looks like you're doing a splendid job.'

The Snoop Sisters bustled across to him.

'You found a body,' said Lilac.

'That seems to be your hobby now,' added Rose.

'Anyone we know?'

'Was Mr Plumb arrested?'

'Always the quiet ones, that's what they say.'

James insisted that the police hadn't established whether it was foul play but the sisters would not be moved.

'How did she get there?'

'Suffocated, was she?'

After several more irritating and irrational questions, he held his hands up to stop them. 'I think making assumptions is the last thing any of us should be doing. This is a young woman whose life was cut short, for whatever reason, and it's not our place to lay blame or surmise what happened in her life.' He felt a little sheepish for stating something that he knew he was clearly guilty of but, if he didn't stop these sisters in their stride, rumours would be rife in the village. And if Livingstone got to hear about it…well, that didn't bear thinking about.

Suitably chastised, the sisters remained quiet. He took a breath.

'I wondered if I might ask you a personal question, one that may help unlock a little mystery that I'm working on.'

Their eyes gleamed and they moved closer.

He sent up a silent prayer and hoped they would be forthcoming. 'Ladies, the Reverend Merryweather has not, I promise, divulged anything to me. However, I understand that you may have had an unpleasant encounter with that man Livingstone. Is that correct?'

He braced himself, ready for the pair of them to puff out their cheeks and tell him to mind his own business. What he didn't expect was for Lilac Crumb to dissolve into tears and for Rose to look despairing.

'I say, I didn't mean to upset you.' He dashed through the gate, delved in his pocket and brought out a clean handkerchief. 'Ladies, will you please allow me to help? I rather think that I may be in a position to do so.'

Rose guided her sister over to the wooden garden bench by the front door where Lilac gradually composed herself. He dragged over a wrought-iron chair. He wasn't quite sure what to say next and wondered if Beth should have come with him. She was much better at this sort of thing than he was. But Rose saved him the worry.

'Lord Harrington, we shall tell you what happened. In fact, we're happy to tell you everything because we want it out in the open. If it's out in the open, then no one can say anything.'

Lilac sniffed. 'Or do anything.'

James clasped his hands together. 'Ladies, you're making it sound as if you've committed some heinous crime.'

'To us, it was. It wasn't awful in the context of many crimes but, to us, it was awful. Bringing shame on our family.'

'You must remember, Lilac dear, that mother and father were dead when this happened.'

'It doesn't matter,' Lilac replied, her eyes brimming again with tears. 'Our brother isn't dead and it would have brought shame on him. We were not brought up to behave the way we did. Whatever were we thinking?'

James watched as the two sisters consoled each other. He didn't always have much time for these two women but, at the moment, he was happy to stay with them for several hours if he knew he could make a difference.

Rose patted her sister's hand. 'There, there. We've already told the vicar. He gave us good advice. He told us to bring it out in the open. So, sister dear, we may as well start with Lord Harrington. He says he's in a position to help so perhaps he can help smooth the waters.'

James reached out and held their hands. 'Anything I can do, I will. Now why don't you unload this burden that you carry.'

Rose rested the trug of flowers on her lap and gently stroked the velvety marigold flowers she'd picked.

'Many years ago, Lord Harrington, we did a wicked thing.'

'A wicked, wicked thing.'

'We deceived a good many people, people that trusted us, depended on our goodwill.'

'This was in your previous residence?' asked James.

Rose nodded. 'We're not silly, we know that rumours surrounded us a few weeks after we arrived but we denied everything.'

Lilac's shoulders sank. 'What were we thinking.'

James was keen to move this along and already knew what this was all about. He shifted forward on his seat. 'The rumour being the theft of money from the Women's Institute?'

Lilac took a sharp intake of breath and the tears began to fall again.

He moved beside her. 'Please, Miss Crumb, don't upset yourself. Tell me what has happened. I take it that someone is using this against you in some way?'

Rose was seated the other side of her sister and, between them, they comforted and soothed her. She continued the story. 'We were treasurers and banked the membership funds and any monies that came into the Institute at our local branch.'

'But we didn't bank all of it,' Lilac brought her hands to her mouth. 'We kept some back in a piggy bank.'

'It became second nature. If we had an amount to bank, we would put some by.'

'And then we said that when the piggy bank was full, we would break it and treat ourselves to a night at the theatre, in London.'

'We became carried away with the whole idea of it. We didn't think about accounts or anything like that.'

'No, we didn't. The pig filled up and we went to see a show in London. We'd never seen a West End show before and we sat in the stalls. Oh, it was wonderful. We didn't think anyone would know.'

James was beginning to see what had happened. 'Someone else did the accounts?'

'Yes,' said Rose. 'When they handed the money to us to bank, they kept a record of things. It was to ensure that what we did didn't happen.'

'Oh, the shame of it,' Lilac said grabbing James' forearm. 'We were banished from the WI and the village turned against us.'

'So much so that we decided to move from the area – from the county and start afresh.'

'And,' James said, 'you found yourself in Cavendish and here you've been ever since.'

Between them, the sisters insisted that they had remained law-abiding citizens and vowed never to do anything like that again. Their mother and father, they said, would have been devastated to learn that their daughters had committed such an act. They fretted together and comforted each other as James tried to move them on to where Livingstone came into things.

'Do I take it, ladies, that Maximillian found out about this?'

Rose answered. 'It's been such a worry,' she continued, explaining that Maximillian had paid them a visit. 'We thought he was being neighbourly, introducing himself but no, he'd found out. He wanted money from us, he said, or he would make sure it was in the paper.'

James frowned. 'But, you're not famous so you wouldn't be in *Guess What?*'

'Oh yes we would,' the sisters said more or less in unison.

Rose clarified. 'That paper does little snippets of information. Fillers we think they're called. We would take up a paragraph but that's all it would take.'

'Our brother is an eminent scientist, Lord Harrington. We would have been named as Felix Crumb's sisters. His reputation would be ruined.'

'But how did Maximillian find out?'

'We don't know,' Lilac replied.

James smoothed his hair back. 'Well someone must know, mustn't they? You're absolutely sure you haven't told anyone in the village?'

'Only Felix.'

Rose said that he lived in Kent. 'Near Rochester, he is. We confided in him many years ago and asked for his forgiveness. He was such a dear. He wrote a cheque for us to repay what we had taken.'

'And that didn't stop Maximillian?'

'Oh no. He seemed positively delighted to hear about our indiscretion and he wouldn't have printed anything about us paying the money back.'

'How much did he ask for?'

'Fifty pounds?'

Well, well, well, James thought, that's an awful lot of money. What foul and malicious men these Livingstones seemed to be. To blackmail two elderly ladies because of one lapse. How low could one stoop? And why? Why would he want to do that? It's not as if he didn't have money? What would another fifty pounds be to a family that clearly had thousands? But this was becoming frustrating. He was searching for a link with Theodore and drugs but, at the moment, all untoward behaviour

126

was being exhibited by Maximillian. Could this be linked to Theodore's drug empire? He didn't think so.

'I still don't understand how Maximillian could have known,' James said. 'Were you overheard?'

Rose shrugged. 'Felix visits us regularly. We've spoken about it, of course, but not in company.' She turned to Lilac. 'I can't even remember where we would have been for people to hear.'

Lilac couldn't fathom it either.

'You say that Stephen gave you some advice,' prompted James.

Rose disclosed that the Reverend had suggested they confess to the theft and admit that it was all an awful mistake, that they paid the money back and assure people they would never betray a trust again. 'You are our first,' she said with a glimmer of expectation. 'Felix is not hard up and he said that if Maximillian does print anything, he will sue him.'

'Well I forgive you and I am more than happy to accompany you to any function or meeting where you want to own up to this. The more people you tell, the less hold Maximillian will have over you. Indeed, I'd be surprised if he darkened your doorstep again.'

A look of relief washed over the sisters' faces and they began planning a list of people to confess to. James told them to let him know when he was wanted and suggested that Stephen and Anne would also be happy to support them. He went to go but, before leaving, he had one last question.

'Ladies, would you be willing to speak to DCI Lane about this and make an official statement?'

Horror returned to their faces.

'I couldn't,' said Rose.

'What if Mr Livingstone found out?'

He sat back down again. 'No one will know. This is between us, the three of us. I can take you to Lewes and the only other person to see you would be George. Or, we could meet at Elsie's and …'

'Yes,' said Rose, 'I don't want anyone seeing us go into a police station. A tea shop is much more civilised.'

'Yes,' said Lilac. 'But it must remain between us.'

'What about Lady Harrington?' Rose asked her sister.

'She must swear not to speak to anyone.'

James convinced her that they would swear on the lives of their sons that they would not speak to anyone about this except for George. 'I'll get him to contact you.' He made to go. 'Now, ladies, are you settled with those arrangements?'

Lilac shrank back. 'But what if Inspector Lane charges us with theft?'

James was certain that his friend would not interfere with a petty crime that happened years ago, especially as the money was returned and it occurred in another county.

Satisfied with his assurances, the sisters agreed that they were comfortable with the suggestion and would wait to hear from George. He left them discussing their list of people to tell. The inspiration was a simple one and one that did not involve liaising with those awful Livingstone men. If he could gather enough statements from people affected by Maximillian, this might lead to an arrest. It wouldn't help with finding information out about Theodore but arresting Maximillian might put a chink in his armour.

He wondered how open Mrs Withers and Mr Sharpe would be if he approached them as he had the Snoop Sisters. He felt certain that their worries stemmed from

Maximillian's threats. But then his heart skipped a beat at the thought – what if word got back to Theodore or Maximillian about his interfering? He'd already been followed and now he instinctively scanned the area for the dark car. He couldn't see anything suspicious. Was he getting paranoid?

Beth was at the church door waving. She met him on the gravel outside. 'How did you get on?'

'Enlightening. I've been sworn to secrecy. Just us, George and the sisters. Let's pop home. I have a severe fear of being overheard or being seen to act suspiciously.'

Beth's look was incredulous as she followed him to the car. 'You look a little pale, James, are you coming down with something?'

James said that he wasn't. Nothing medical anyway. But on the way home, he kept one eye on his rear-view mirror.

At home, they made lunch – Grandma Harrington's Welsh Rarebit.

'What I don't understand,' said James as he stirred the grated cheese into the sauce, 'is why Maximillian Livingstone should bother with people like Rose and Lilac. That *Guess What?* publication is all about celebrities and famous people. Those sorts of magazines don't normally bother with tittle-tattle like that. I know the brother is a scientist but he's not what I would think of as a celebrity.'

Beth checked the bread under the grill. 'I must admit, I always thought the magazine was about film stars and television personalities, although I've never read it so I'm not an expert.'

129

There was a knock on the front door. James turned the gas down and went through to the hall where he opened the door to Charlie Hawkins.

'Charlie, how's Tommy? Does he need a plaster cast signing?'

'No, thank the lord. Turned out to be just a bad knock with some impressive bruising.'

'Come on through – we're just doing a spot of lunch.'

'Oh, sorry, I can come back it you like.'

James nudged him through to the kitchen. 'Do you want some? I've prepared far too much cheese sauce and we can put another slice of bread under the grill.'

Charlie breathed in the smell of Grandma Harrington's cheese sauce and said that he didn't need asking twice. In ten minutes, the three of them were sitting on the small terrace in the back garden where Charlie told them he'd simply popped in to confirm arrangements for the first day of the steam rally. He held up a programme.

'Hot off the press from the Sussex Steam Guild. We're opening up at ten o'clock and Flora Armstrong and Anne are going to be selling programmes and raffle tickets. I think Dulcie Faye is helping with the entrance money too.'

James asked if there was a raffle every day, at which point Beth reminded him that it was a grand raffle. 'People buying tickets are putting their names and addresses on the back and the Guild are doing a grand draw on the final day.'

'Of course,' James said, forgetting that the prize was a weekend for two at The Grand Hotel on Brighton's seafront.

Charlie went over who would be manning the stalls set up by the local residents. He handed them a roster. 'It's a long day so we're all taking it in turns to be at specific places. I've got you two down to help with the hog roast at midday tomorrow. That'll give Graham a few extra pairs of hands. Is that all right with you?'

'Absolutely.'

'Oh, but you're showing your old car, aren't you?' He flipped through his notebook. 'Oh no, that's not until the final day.'

'Midday is fine,' said James.

Beth asked if the WI marquee had been set up.

Charlie said that it was. 'I've just come from there and all the marquees are up for the WI, Donovan's mobile bar and Elsie's little café. The Steam Guild have a few marquees with engine parts for sale and steam-themed gifts, you know, tea towels and beer mats, that sort of thing.'

'Splendid,' James said, finishing off the last of his cheese on toast. He turned to Beth. 'Did you and Anne bake some of Grandma's Coffee Delights?'

'Time was running short, so Dorothy and Kate are cooking them this evening and taking them over first thing tomorrow. We'll replenish as we go through the week.'

Over the next ten minutes they discussed the rally and future events being put on until the subject turned to Dulcie Faye.

Charlie's eyes twinkled. 'Dulcie Faye came into the library this morning. You'd told her that I was very welcoming apparently.'

Beth said that the Merryweathers had mentioned it to the actress. 'She's incredibly shy.'

'Yes, I found that out. You don't expect an actress to be withdrawn, do you? Anyway, we had quite a chat about her career and her likes and dislikes. She's a bit of a bookworm, so I gave her a tour of the library and she's now a member. The kids met her too. They came home for lunch from school and sat there staring at her until Susan finally plucked up courage to open her mouth. Of course, once she started, Tommy joined in and I couldn't stop the pair of 'em. I was glad to get them back to school. She's lovely with children, they really liked her.'

James stole a glance at Beth who raised an eyebrow. Charlie with smitten with Dulcie Faye. As if reading their minds, Charlie asked if Dulcie and Theodore were really a couple.

Beth almost jumped from her seat. 'Oh Charlie, don't even think about asking her out. Theodore Livingstone is a horrible, detestable man who would stop at nothing to dissuade you from even talking to her.'

Charlie sought confirmation from James.

'She's absolutely right, Charlie. Lovely as Dulcie is, Theodore Livingstone is not a man to be messed with on even the slightest of matters. The lady is out of bounds.'

'But what does she see in him? She doesn't appear terribly happy there and that man, Theodore, well, he's not the sort of bloke I'd expect her to be with.'

James repeated he should steer clear. 'Anyway, she's a career girl, destined for stardom and all that.'

He watched as his friend shrugged. 'I s'pose you're right. It doesn't seem like a happy house over there though. Apparently, Theodore and his son had a right big argument this morning.'

James sat up. 'Really? Do you know what about?'

'Something about having to bail the son out again.' He got up. 'I'd best get back to the library. I wasn't planning to stop for lunch but that was really nice, thanks.'

At the front door, as he waved Charlie goodbye he saw Bert strolling up the drive. James went down to meet him. 'What on earth are you doing here?'

'I got the bus to drop me off. There's another one about ten minutes behind this one so I'll flag that down. Listen,' he said, motioning for James to walk back down the drive with him. 'I've heard news about that magazine that Maximillian runs. Turns out that it's in a bit of trouble, financially.'

'That confirms what Charlie's just told me,' James went over the librarian's visit. 'I say, Bert, do you know if that magazine has always covered celebrity gossip? Does Maximillian go in for local gossip, you know, about people who aren't famous.'

'Funny you should ask that, Jimmy boy, he's recently been adding a column called And Another Thing. Little paragraphs about everyday people who 'ave perhaps done something they shouldn't 'ave. They normally have loose links to someone well-known or mildly famous. That's a sure sign that he's desperate for gossip.' They arrived at the end of the drive. 'Chatty Chatham's keeping his ear to the ground and has it on good authority that Theodore does have a notebook but probably keeps it with him at all times. I suppose he must put it somewhere safe when he goes to bed, though.' The sound of an approaching bus caused him to turn and flag it down. 'Perhaps you should get George to think of an excuse to search his offices or the Wendover.'

The bus slowed down and Bert hopped on board. 'I'll see you tomorrow at the steam rally. Gladys is coming.'

James waved goodbye. Gladys was beginning to be a permanent fixture in his friend's life. He wondered if they would tie the knot. He hoped so. Gladys was a bundle of kindness and would be a perfect match for Bert.

Back in the hall, he skimmed through a number of business cards in his address book and pulled one out. Picking up the receiver, he dialled and waited a few seconds.

'NTN Insurance.'

'Ah, hello, could you put me through to Andrew Cheeseman please?'

After a minute, he heard the familiar 'Putting you through' announcement. 'Swiss?'

'Yes. Who's this?

'James Harrington.'

'James, how the devil are you? Haven't seen you for a few months. How's Beth?'

'We're fine, both fine. Swiss, I wondered whether I could possibly meet you?'

'At the Wendover?'

'Yes. I'll explain more when I see you.'

'All sounds a bit cloak and dagger. Do we need to be somewhere undisturbed and free from eavesdropping?'

James said that was exactly what he would like.

'Well, the Wendover is perfect for that as you know. There are a few rooms secreted here and there that we could make use of. Will Beth be coming? Shall I book a table for supper?'

'Yes, I'm sure she would love that. Listen, speaking of rooms, am I correct that Theodore Livingstone has a room at the top of the club?'

He received a groan down the line. 'Yes, he has. Put a few people's backs up, that has. These rooms are supposed to be for everyone but he's commandeered that one for a lot of the time. At least two days a week. Why he can't use the offices at Parliament, I don't know. The members' committee doesn't do anything about it.'

'Why not?'

'That man has people in his pocket, James. I got on to him about that room and told him he wasn't playing by the rules. I said to him, why don't you work from Parliament? Damn near hoisted me off my feet by the lapels and told me to sue him. Nasty piece of work. Anyway, enough about that...oh, that's probably what you want to talk about isn't it?'

'This is between you and me, Swiss. No one else is to know that I'm asking.'

'Mum's the word. Anything I can do to discredit his membership and all that...so, when do you want to meet? Evening?'

'How about Monday, seven o'clock?'

'I'll book a table and make sure we're not disturbed.'

James jotted the arrangements down. 'Splendid, we'll see you then.'

Beth skipped down the stairs and James updated her about the arrangements. 'Oh, that'll be perfect,' she said. 'We haven't seen him since all that business in the autumn. Is this about Theodore?'

'Mmmm.'

'Well, darling, we're well ahead of schedule and we have the afternoon free. How about we go visit Mrs Withers?'

'Her shop doesn't open until two.' He checked the clock. 'That gives us quarter of an hour. Appleton's out the front trimming some of the shrubs. I'm going to ask him about some flowers along that drive. It looks a little bare.'

'I'll wash up the dishes. I'll be out in ten minutes.'

Ernest Appleton, their gardener, was at the far corner of the house tidying a few things. But before James had a chance to go over to him, a dark blue car came up the drive and he was aware of a lump in his throat. Was this the same car that had been following him? He couldn't be sure. He thought that had been black. The grille seemed different too. He wished he'd paid attention when he'd first spotted it. Through the windscreen, he identified the driver and that didn't make him feel any better. Inspector Fulton. What on earth was he doing here?

Fulton got out of the car and put his hat on.

'You're a bit off the beaten track, aren't you?' said James, hoping to sound relaxed. 'Aren't you Scotland Yard?'

The man shambled over. 'Just popped in to see a couple of people.'

James waited. That was a lie, he was sure of it.

The Inspector cast an eye over the Jaguar. 'Nice car.'

'Yes, a comfortable ride.'

'Get it serviced regularly do you?'

'It's all legal and above board if that's what you mean.' James could feel the tension in his shoulders. 'Did you call by for a reason?'

'You're friends with DCI Lane, is that right? And you've got on friendly terms with Superintendent Higgins. Offered him some fishing.'

Frustrated with the man skirting around the issue, James felt his tension turn to annoyance. 'Inspector, you've clearly come here for a reason and I'd much rather you say what you want instead of side-stepping the matter.'

Fulton's eyes were dark and an expression of pure dislike crossed his face. 'You need to know who you can trust, Lord Harrington.' He pointed to the Jaguar with his hat. 'And check those brakes. They're the things people always forget about.'

Back at his car, he threw his hat onto the passenger seat and, seeing Beth emerge, waved a greeting before driving off.

'What did he want?'

James strode over to the Jaguar and checked under the engine. The brake cable was sound. He lifted the bonnet and checked the mechanics, the oil and brake fluid. Everything was in order. 'Most peculiar, Beth. I think the man was warning me off or threatening me, I'm not sure which. Told me that I need to know who to trust.'

'I wouldn't trust him!' She got into the Jaguar.

Leaving his chat with Appleton until later, he settled himself in the driver's seat. Certain that Fulton was in the Livingstone camp, he knew he had to tread carefully. He was clearly skirting danger. One question too many could be disastrous.

CHAPTER FIFTEEN

Mrs Withers was in her late fifties. Her hair was dyed jet black. Unfortunately, the colour clashed with her pasty complexion and James recalled that Beth had said ages ago that she thought a subtler shade would suit her better. She wore a floral dress that had seen better days and a mauve cardigan was draped over her shoulders. At her feet was Winnie, the British bulldog.

She had just turned the sign to 'Open' when James and Beth arrived. The bell above the door jangled.

She uttered a weary greeting but, as James turned the sign to 'Closed', her expression became fierce. 'You can't do that. I'm always open at two o'clock prompt. People will be wondering what I'm doing.'

James selected a pen from the counter and wrote 'Opening at 2:30 today.' To one side of the till was a roll of Sellotape which he used to stick the notice to the door. 'Mrs Withers, we have something important to discuss. It's a personal matter but it may help resolve some rather nasty criminal activity that's going on.'

Beth gave Mrs Withers a smile that indicated she hoped she would help. She added that her efficient naval background would mean they received factual information instead of tittle-tattle.

The reference caused her straighten up and she softened slightly. James could imagine her in her WRNS uniform standing to attention and dishing out orders.

She ushered them through to the back room. 'Come along, Winnie, we'll put the kettle on.'

The room at the back housed stock: tins of fruit, bags of flour and sugar, boxes of sweets and cereals. The only furnishings were a small desk and a couple of wooden chairs. Beth took one of the chairs. After a few minutes, Mrs Withers appeared from a side room with a tray, which she placed on the table. The wooden chair creaked as she installed her large frame on it. James perched on the corner of the desk and stirred the tea in the pot.

Mrs Withers focussed on placing cups on saucers and pouring milk.

'Mrs Withers, have you heard about the girl that was found on Valentine Plumb's land?'

'I heard about it. Nothing to do with me. Do you think I should know her?'

'Not at all. It's just that the police believe she may have been threatened or blackmailed by someone.'

Mrs Wither's hand stopped for a second before continuing with the tea ceremony. 'Why are you telling me this?'

Beth filled the silence. 'Mrs Withers, you were awfully quiet at the pub the other night and you've been looking tired. Something is worrying you. Some*one* is worrying you.'

'You have concerns about Maximillian Livingstone, is that right?' James asked.

Her eyes blazed. 'Who told you? No one knows about it. What do you know?'

James, uncomfortable on the table, pulled over a sturdy wooden crate to sit on. 'It was simply something someone overheard. The thing is, you're not alone. Maximillian Livingstone has his sights on a few people here in Cavendish to help his grotty little magazine and I believe he may have latched onto something that you've been involved with. If we're wide of the mark, please tell us to go on our way.'

139

Beth slid her chair closer. 'We're not prying. It's just that people are beginning to get hurt and we want to help. The police___'

She swung round. 'You haven't told the police!'

Beth stared at James who was quick to reassure her. 'Absolutely not. We'll be led by you. Having said that, are you going to confide in us or bottle this up and make yourself ill?'

The woman composed herself and a sign of the Mrs Withers they were more familiar with showed itself. 'You can't do anything.'

'You'd be surprised what we can do,' said Beth.

They waited. James watched as she wrestled with her thoughts. Even Winnie picked up on the anxiety and began to paw at her. She reached down to stroke him and assured him that everything was fine. Finally, she sat up straight.

'Maximillian Livingstone has discovered something from my past that I would prefer to have kept there.'

'And he's using this against you?'

She met his gaze. 'Yes,' she said, seeming almost relieved that the statement was out in the open. 'It was something that occurred during the war, an indiscretion. The person involved was high ranking within the Navy. It would be more than an embarrassment to him and his family to have this incident publicised: it would be damaging for them. And the Navy,' She shrugged. 'I'll have to pay him.'

'No,' Beth said in horror. 'That's the last thing you should do.'

'I have no choice, Lady Harrington. He's given me a deadline.'

'But what if he asks for more?'

James asked how much Maximillian had asked for.

'One hundred pounds.'

'My word, that's an awful lot of money. And who's to say that he won't ask for more in a few months' time?'

She shrugged again. 'What else can I do?'

He saw Beth's livid face as she said: 'You can go to the police. Tell them what's happened.'

Mrs Withers' reaction was one that suggested Beth was naïve. 'I can't face the consequences of going to the police.' She bent down and hugged Winnie. 'This adorable creature is my companion and I could never hurt him.'

James frowned. 'You mean he's threatened your dog?'

'Threatened to kill the dog and ruin the business.'

Good grief, how low would this man stoop?

'Mrs Withers, people like you are the backbone of this country. You're a strong, determined woman who has served your country. You cannot let a snake like Maximillian control how you live your life. Is this indiscretion so awful that you can't speak about it? By speaking about it, you'll take control back. He'll have no power over you.'

Her eyes took on a haunted look. 'I have few friends, Lord Harrington, but I could not cut ties with my oldest school-friend. She would be devastated by this and that is why I will pay.'

They finished their tea. She checked the clock. 'I should go and open the shop.'

'Before you do,' said James, 'let me put a proposal to you. By all means pay the man, if that's what you've decided, but please speak with DCI Lane. Put a statement together. The more people who provide statements, the more evidence the police have to act on.'

141

She contemplated what he'd said, before getting up. With an earnest look, she promised she would consider it. 'If DCI Lane can promise this would not get back to my friend, I will seriously look into speaking to him.' They went through to the shop, where Mrs Withers saw them out.

On the street, James felt for his keys. 'What d'you think?' he asked as they walked toward the car.

'She had an affair.'

'Yes, that's what I thought. She was married during the war. Her husband was killed in an accident a few months after VE day.'

'It sounds to me like the husband of this school-friend is the high-ranking naval officer.'

'What the devil is Maximillian playing at? He's messing up people's lives for the sake of the odd fifty or hundred pounds. That's pocket money to him. Is this to try to save his magazine? It seems an awfully stupid way to go about it.'

'Do you think she'll go to see George?'

'She is at least thinking about it. I hope that common sense will prevail and that she'll do the right thing.'

In the car, Beth turned to him. 'All we have so far is the awful blackmailing by Maximillian. What do we have or Theodore? He's the one running the drug business a. ve have no gossip on that whatsoever.'

'Do you think it's worth chatting with Dulcie?'

'No! We don't know her well enough. She may tell Theodore.'

The ignition fired. 'You're right. We need to speak to a few more people. Shall we try Mr Sharpe again. I feel he may be on the edge of talking.'

'He is a nervous sparrow, isn't he?'

James turned the ignition off. 'And nervous people tend to chat. Come on.'

CHAPTER SIXTEEN

Mr Sharpe was in his front garden, polishing a tiny engine. It was clearly some sort of steam contraption with a thin funnel and miniature pistons. The steel shone and the bright yellow and blue paintwork gleamed.

'Goodness,' said James, leaning on the garden fence, 'that's a rather natty little thing.'

He noted the anxiety in Sharpe's eyes. 'Yes, yes, it's something that I've had for some time. I'm taking it up to the rally to show alongside the others. Have you taken your car up yet?'

'I'm giving it a last-minute polish when I get back and then I'll take her over.'

Sharpe stretched his back and wiped his hands on an old rag. Although working on what could be a dirty job, he still had his trademark cable-knit cardigan on, along with a shirt and tie. 'I won't keep you chatting,' he said, 'I've things to do anyway.' He made to scurry inside.

'We rather wondered if we could have a word.'

Sharpe looked at Beth, who suggested they go inside and sit down. 'It'll only take a few minutes and we promise not to be a nuisance.'

His eyes darted between the two of them and then across the green before beckoning them in as if on a secret liaison. Inside, the living room was cluttered with armchairs, a huge old wireless and magazines on agricultural machinery. He cleared the papers and motioned for them to sit down. No offer of refreshments was made but, James thought, the poor chap was so on edge the thought had probably not entered his mind.

His Adam's apple bobbed. 'Lord Harrington. Lady Harrington. I do not wish to be rude. There's no doubt that you are kind people and when mother died you were

144

so caring and sympathetic but I fear you are planning to interrogate me again and I simply can't cope with it.'

Beth's expression softened. 'Oh Mr Sharpe, we're not here to interrogate you. We're worried about you. Something is making you ill and you can't simply bottle it up.'

James offered a cigarette to Mr Sharpe, who received it with shaky hands.

'Mr Sharpe, you don't have to tell us anything. I'm simply going to ask a couple of questions and all you need to do is answer yes or no. Are you happier with that?'

Sharpe watched as James lit the cigarettes and blew the match out. He took a drag and appeared to be close to tears. Finally, he bobbed his head.

'Is the subject of your distress something to do with Maximillian Livingstone?'

He stared into the distance for a while, then gave a curt nod.

'Does he have some sort of story on you that, if made public, would cause you embarrassment or something worse?'

'Something worse,' Sharpe stated, 'something much worse.'

'Mr Sharpe,' Beth said. 'We promise you the utmost discretion. You're not the only person to have this cloud hovering over you. If you're strong enough to divulge what information you can, James may be able to help.'

'How?' Mr Sharpe exclaimed. 'That man is ruthless. He's already shown me what he's capable of.'

James straightened up.

'I was to pay him one hundred pounds. One hundred pounds. That's about all I have in the bank.'

'You refused?'

'Of course I refused. I didn't know Maximillian Livingstone at all. He knocked on the door one day and introduced himself. I just knew him as one of those people who had moved in down the road. He was charming at first, until he sat down. Said he had some business that I was a part of.' Sharpe harrumphed. 'I asked him, what sort of business could he have with me? Then it all came out.' Sharpe jumped up and paced the room.

James spotted a bottle of brandy. He grabbed a glass and poured a measure. 'Here, I think you should drink this. I know this is difficult for you but remember, this stays with us and you may actually feel better for sharing the burden.'

'We're on your side, Mr Sharpe,' Beth added. 'Please let us help you.'

Sharpe swigged the brandy down in one and held the glass out for a top up; James duly obliged.

'When I refused, he behaved abominably. His attitude was menacing. He sent shivers through me, I can tell you. Then, he got up and went to that wall.' A picture had recently been hanging there; James could make out the outline. 'Started talking to me about mother. I had an oil painting of her up there. I had it done when she was sixty years old. She'd always wanted it and I managed to get someone in Brighton to do it. Lovely it was. She'd put her best frock on and a few bits of jewellery. Really pleased with it she was.'

James didn't like where this was going and warily asked where the painting was now.

Mr Sharpe stifled a cry. 'Behind the sideboard.'

James, who had not taken one puff of his cigarette, stubbed it out and went over to the sideboard. Reaching down the back, he pulled on a large wooden frame about four feet square. Freeing it from its confines, he saw the canvas had been ripped. When he turned it around, Mr Sharpe struggled to hold his tears back. Beth brought her hands to her mouth.

James studied the canvas. Whoever had painted Mrs Sharpe had done a marvellous job. He placed the painting on the dining table and folded the strip back in place. She was a lovely lady, with hazel eyes, greying hair and a warmth about her He'd always seen her as a grandmother although he knew she had no grandchildren. But she had that air about her; that warmth and love in her eyes that a typical grandmother had. Mr Sharpe's stifled weeping interrupted his thoughts.

'Maximillian did this?'

'He accused me of killing my mother. Told me that if I didn't give him the money, he'd put his accusations in his magazine. I'd never heard of it and told him that. But he had a couple of back issues and left them with me. They're over there. Dreadful, dreadful publication. I couldn't bear the thought of my name being dragged through the mud, and mother's too. I said to him, how dare you come into my house and make false accusations?'

Beth motioned for him to sit down. 'And what did he do?'

He continued pacing the floor. 'He said, but they're not false are they. I've proof. I said, that's rubbish, you know nothing and I'm not paying you a penny. Then he gave me a look that made my blood run cold. He stood up and brought out a knife. I thought he was going to kill me. But then he yanked that painting from the wall and plunged that knife in. Not only that, he brought the knife

147

to my chin. Here. He actually pierced the skin. Told me he'd do the same to me if I didn't pay up.'

Beth's urgent stare told James one thing and one thing only: *we must do something*.

'Mr Sharpe, can I ask a very personal question? If we're to help you, you must be completely honest with me.'

'Ask me anything.' He swigged his brandy and wiped his tears. 'I've told you everything, I have no secrets anymore.'

'Maximillian accused you of killing your mother. Why would he think that? What proof was he speaking of?'

Revealing this information appeared to have instilled some composure. 'You know that my mother had cancer, don't you? Well, toward the end, the pain was unbearable for her. She wanted to stay at home, she wouldn't let any hospital staff near her because she thought they'd take her away. So, I cared for her. Dr Jackson was the only person she'd let in. He was very good and prescribed morphine to ease her pain. He showed me how to administer it.' He stared out of the window. 'I stuck religiously to the prescription, every day.'

James closed his eyes. He had an inkling what the man would say next.

'The day she died, the morphine was having no effect.' He turned and grabbed James by the arm. 'I gave her more. I thought, what harm could it do? Whatever I did, she was going to die so why not let her go peacefully?'

'And did she go peacefully?'

148

For the first time since they'd arrived, Sharpe appeared relaxed and his shoulders less tense. 'Yes,' he said with relief. 'She went peacefully.'

'This is what you meant when you were overheard saying "*I didn't kill her*".'

'Yes, yes, I was telephoning that awful man, trying to plead my case. He was having none of it though. Pay up and stop moaning. Those were his words.'

After thinking for a few seconds, Beth said: 'How on earth did Maximillian find out about this? And what sort of proof could he have? He wasn't here. This happened before he arrived in the village. And giving an extra dose of morphine could simply be down to error. You were tired, you didn't realise you had administered too much. I can't imagine any judge in the land would class this as murder. That is what Maximillian would accuse you of in the magazine.'

'I couldn't put up with the stress of it. I've been living on my nerves.'

James allowed all this information to sink in. He still couldn't fathom why someone would behave in such a way toward a perfect stranger. And where did Theodore Livingstone come into this? He was the man George and Superintendent Higgins wanted them to watch. Instead, they'd stumbled upon his son's unpleasant activities. Perhaps this would lead to something though and, now he knew about it, he wanted to put a stop to it. Ordinary, wonderful villagers were being put through the mill by this grotty individual. He wanted the man brought to justice and the sooner the better.

Beth brought him out of his thoughts. 'James, what are we going to do?'

'Mr Sharpe, you've taken the biggest step by divulging this information. Anything you do from now on will be much easier than you think. Now you've confided in us, it's little steps from there on. Do you understand?'

'Yes, yes I do. But I still don't know how you can help.'

'Other people have been affected by this chap. The only way we're going to throw the book at him is to provide evidence. To provide evidence, people must make statements.'

'Oh no!'

'Yes! Yes, Mr Sharpe. Others are coming forward. They are visiting DCI Lane and putting this all in official statements. The more statements there are, the more evidence there is and the greater chance of a conviction. It would be confidential, Mr Sharpe. That statement will be between you and the police. Do not speak to anyone except George Lane, is that clear? He's tasked with collating this information.'

Beth sat up. 'I've an idea. For evidence.'

James and Mr Sharpe waited.

'If Maximillian has visited here, he's also visited the others. His fingerprints will be everywhere.'

James beamed. 'I didn't even think of that.'

Even Mr Sharpe appeared buoyed by that news. 'Oh, excellent, do you think they will? I don't clean much, as you can see, and he sat in that chair over there. No one else has sat in it.'

'Keep it that way,' said James. 'Are you happy for me to call George and get him to come over?'

'Could he come at night, when it's dark, and not in a police car?'

'Of course he can. Let me arrange it.'

They went to go but Beth moved to study the painting first. 'What a shame. This is a lovely portrait and something to remember her by.'

'That's more upsetting than parting with money. I'd happily part with one hundred pounds to have that fixed.'

James smiled. 'You know, you may be able to salvage it.'

'But how?' said Beth. 'It's ruined.'

'No, it's not. That knife was a sharp one. See here, one perfect cut, no fraying of the canvas. I'm sure if we have a word with GJ, he could repair it.'

'Oh James, that would be wonderful.'

'D'you think he could?' said Sharpe.

'Did Maximillian touch this?'

'Yes, yes, he did.'

'Let George come over and get fingerprints. We'll have a word with GJ and get him to take a look after that's done. He's a splendid artist and I'm certain he's done some restoration work. If he can't do it, I'll get onto my cousin, Herbie; he'll have some contacts.'

Herbie Harrington was, in James's view, a snob and a boor but he couldn't deny that the man knew his art and would have the contacts to help.

Sharpe began to weep again. 'I don't know how to thank you.'

'Chin up, old man. And not a word to anyone about this. This stays with the three of us and DCI Lane, is that clear? Don't speak to any other policeman about it, even one in authority.'

Sharpe drew back. 'Are you saying we can't trust the police?'

'I'm saying that Theodore and his son have friends in high places and I know for a fact that George Lane is not part of their circle. And don't let Maximillian see you looking anything other than frightened. Can you manage that?'

'Yes, the man scares me. I don't need to pretend in that regard.'

'Mr Sharpe,' said Beth, 'you didn't answer James' question earlier. How could Maximillian have known?'

He opened the front door. 'I don't know. I've been trying to rack my brains. I spoke to Dr Jackson but I know he wouldn't have said anything.'

'I say,' said James, 'was your mother famous for anything?'

His face lit up. 'I don't know about famous but she was the recipient of an OBE for services to charity.'

'Of course! I remember that.' He couldn't believe he'd forgotten. She'd been presented the medal by King George VI. Her photograph had been in the county papers and her name mentioned in *The Times*. It was a proud day for her and one she'd said she'd treasured. Having the accusation of murdering such a lovely lady published in *Guess What?* would destroy Mr Sharpe and tarnish his mother's memory.

With a few reassuring words, they left Mr Sharpe to continue shining his engine. James and Beth made their way back to the car. He switched the ignition on and pressed the starter button. The motor roared to life.

'Do you fancy an excursion to Elsie's?'

Beth opened her handbag and brought out her purse. 'I'll go to the call box and telephone George. I think we need to speak with him about this. Perhaps he could meet us there.'

'Good idea.'

When Beth returned, he happened to look across the green. Seated on a bench with his legs crossed at the

152

ankles was Maximillian Livingstone. He was too far away to be sure but James was pretty certain that the man was smirking at him.

CHAPTER SEVENTEEN

Elsie Taylor's café was on the road between Cavendish and Charnley. It was an old run-down cottage when Elsie had inherited it from her grandmother, a stalwart of the Charnley community. Elsie, who was born a few miles down the road in Burgess Hill, had discussed her plans for the house with her mum and dad and they had given their blessing for their only child to embark on a business to turn the premises into a café.

James was astounded at the sheer energy and work that Elsie had put into the property. She'd had a builder in to knock one wall out between the two small front rooms and, once that was completed, she'd spent months decorating the whole house. Upstairs, he learned, were her own bedroom, a small bathroom and a lounge. Downstairs, the converted rooms housed several wooden tables and chairs, with beautiful flower displays, chequered tablecloths and napkins. She'd also instructed the builder to install bow windows which provided a lovely view of the country road and the trees beyond. Behind her counter, a huge dresser dominated the area, housing a number of Victorian teapots and crockery. To the side of the kitchen, she'd added a room to serve as an area for stock.

He couldn't remember a time when Elsie wasn't here because she'd made such a mark on the area with her home-made scones, cakes and light lunches. But, it must have been around fifteen years since: Elsie would have been in her early twenties. What a brave girl to launch a business on her own. Over the years, he'd discovered how driven she was, forsaking marriage and children to pursue her two loves, baking and running the café. He even trusted her with his grandmother's recipes and she made sure she advertised them as 'Grandma Harrington's' and explained to anyone who asked who Grandma Harrington was.

Today's menu, chalked up on the board, included one of Grandma's dishes: German pancakes. It was a recipe that his grandmother had been given at the turn of the century although he wasn't sure that it came from that country or whether someone had simply given it that name. Whatever the story, he was delighted to see it on the menu as it was a particularly lovely snack. He closed the door behind Beth and they scanned the room for a table.

He couldn't help but be impressed. True to form, Elsie had embraced whatever was happening in the villages and had laid her hands on several toy traction engines. She'd dotted them around the café and slotted leaflets about the rally into the menu-folders.

A couple was leaving at the far end and they made their way to the vacated table. Elsie grabbed a cloth and reached them as they sat down.

'Sorry your favourite table by the window isn't free,' she said. 'Seems to be busy today, lots of new people coming and going. I expect it's that steam rally up at your place.'

'I think so,' said James, 'there seem to be a few followers of steam spending the whole week here. Harrington's is full and I know a few people are putting up friends and family for the few days that it's on. Good business for you, Else.'

'And,' Beth said, noting the chalkboard, 'you have German pancakes on the menu.'

'Oh yes. Well old farmer Park down the road dropped off so many eggs I didn't know what to do with 'em so I thought this would be the best use.'

James agreed, remembering that the last time he and Beth had made the dish, they had to get a good supply of eggs.

Elsie collected the used crockery onto a tray and brushed the crumbs from the table. 'Now, what is it you'll be having?'

'We're waiting for DCI Lane,' said James, 'but shall we order tea to be going on with?'

'Here's George now,' said Beth.

George took off his felt hat as he entered the café. Spotting James and Beth, he threaded his way through the tables and, after greeting Elsie, he unbuttoned his jacket and took a seat.

Beth asked if they wanted to share a portion of German pancakes. She turned to James. 'I know you're trying to cut down but if we have a portion between us that shouldn't cause too much harm.'

With their order made and tea delivered, George looked over his shoulder. James watched as he did so and was certain his friend was ensuring that no one linked to their forthcoming discussion was in the room. He'd never seen George quite so unnerved as by this current investigation and instinct caused him to bring his chair forward. As if reading his mind, Beth did the same.

'Thank you for coming, George,' said James. 'I know it's short notice.'

George appeared strained. 'I wish Superintendent Higgins hadn't asked you to spy on these men. I haven't told him what I'm asking you to do but I know he'll stand by the decision.'

Beth frowned. 'What decision?'

'That you forget you were asked and go back to normal. Don't call on Dulcie Faye or try to engage with the Livingstones. Don't make enquiries and don't ask questions. Leave it up to the police.'

'Can't do, old chap,' replied James.

'And,' Beth said as she stirred the pot, 'we've really taken quite a shine to Dulcie. She's delightful and seems to be living under a cloud at that house. We can't leave her floundering.'

'George, the reason we've asked you here is that we seem to have stumbled across a few things that are more to do with Maximillian than Theodore.'

'Oh?'

Beth outlined the visit to Dulcie Faye. 'She was charming, as we knew she'd be, and she had Tony Young with her and he told James that Theodore has some sort of hold over Dulcie but he didn't know what. The problem was he had to go because he had a rehearsal or something.'

'But then Theodore and Maximillian came in.'

'Blundered in more like,' said Beth, bristling. 'What rude and ill-mannered men they are, George. I think Steve and Anne's little dog has more decorum than those two put together.'

George pulled a face. 'This isn't evidence, Beth. All you have here is gossip.'

'There's more,' said James. 'That was just the start. We began chatting to a few people who physically shrank when these men were mentioned. In particular, when Maximillian's name came up. Did you know that he doesn't just target well-known people?'

Elsie arrived with the German pancakes and placed them in the middle of the table. 'There's golden syrup in this bowl and lemon and sugar here.'

Beth asked for strawberry jam. 'I do love these with a smear of strawberries.'

With all the toppings to hand, Elsie left them to it. James tore off a section of the fluffy pancake and put it on his plate. He trickled some golden syrup over the dish.

George did the same and then updated them on what he knew. '*Guess What?* is struggling. Has been for quite a while. I'm not sure that it's because the British public don't like that sort of thing or whether Maximillian isn't cut out for business. The information I have suggests it's the latter. Theodore has set Max up with a number of businesses and none of them last very long. He doesn't keep employees long, he doesn't pay them well and those who complain about it have met with an accident after crossing him. This magazine is the latest in a long line of defunct businesses. Theodore seems to bail him out now and again but then brings the whole thing to a close. So, yes, he writes about all sorts of people in the public eye, private sector and the general public too; those with a passing acquaintance with being in the public eye. Beginning to scrape the barrel. I mean, who's going to be interested in the life of an obscure villager?'

'How despicable,' said Beth.

'That explains Theodore's behaviour toward his son.' James said as he turned to Beth. 'Did you notice that Maximillian seems a little subservient in his father's presence?'

'I did. And he's getting rid of his frustration by threatening our villagers. Trying to prove he's a man. What he's doing is unforgivable.'

George sat up. 'What exactly is he doing?'

'Wait a minute,' said James, 'are you saying that the police have never received complaints against Maximillian?'

158

'Complaints about what?'

'Blackmail.'

'There are always rumours about both men, of course, but like we said before, people are too scared to say anything. We did have intelligence on one person. You remember that actor, David Simpson, he came forward.'

Beth covered her mouth. 'David Simpson! He was being blackmailed?'

'Maximillian had something on him and Simpson caved in.'

'He paid up?' said James.

'Yes.' George took a bite of his pancake. 'But never mind him, what's all this about the villagers?'

James and Beth described the events so far; the behaviour of Mrs Withers and the way Maximillian had approached her; the shame felt by the Snoop Sisters over their theft of WI funds and the pain that Mr Sharpe was going through with the accusation being directed at him.

George listened quietly. 'But, if thcy're as scared as you say they are, they won't come forward. I haven't heard anything from them yet.'

'Ah ha,' said James, holding up a finger, 'we think we have convinced them to speak with you.'

'We guessed,' Beth continued, 'that if they knew that others in the same predicament were going to make statements, then they would feel safety in numbers. Especially if the others are fellow residents.'

George couldn't hide his delight. 'And you've convinced them?'

James grinned. 'We think so. They're petrified of Maximillian but I think they realise that something must be done. But,' James said meeting George's gaze, 'they will only deal with you. In fact, I told them to deal only with you, what with this trust issue at the moment.'

He went on to outline that the Snoop Sisters were coming clean about their indiscretion and would supply a statement. 'They want you to meet them here or somewhere that Maximillian and his like don't go to. They refuse to go to the police station. I could put a room aside at Harrington's if you'd like.'

'The same with Mrs Withers,' said Beth. 'I think she'd come around if you went to her.'

'And Mr Sharpe?' said George.

'You may have something more there,' said James. 'Maximillian visited him at home a couple of times and Sharpe is not house-proud.'

George grinned. 'Fingerprints.'

'And plenty of them. Again, he wants discretion. His house looks out onto the green and he's petrified that Maximillian will see you enter.'

'The poor man has turned to drink,' said Beth.

'And you say that the Snoop Sisters indiscretion is now out in the open. Can you tell me what the respective secrets are for Mrs Withers and Mr Sharpe?'

'I'm afraid not,' said James. 'They are not our secrets to tell but each of them has been threatened and Sharpe had some property damaged.'

George jotted everything down in his notebook. 'We'll do everything as discreetly as possible.'

'Not we, George. *You.* I promised these people that you would deal with it and, quite honestly, I'm not sure who to trust in your department.'

His friend's face darkened. 'What d'you mean?'

James reminded him of the sighting of Inspector Fulton after they had met with Dulcie Faye. 'That young constable of yours is his nephew. My impression was that the nephew didn't have much to do with his uncle but that could just be a cover.'

George mulled everything over and finished his tea. 'Right. I'll see them personally. I'll keep an eye on Constable Fulton.' He straightened his tie. 'How did Maximillian find out about the indiscretions of your villagers?'

Both James and Beth shrugged.

'I suppose,' said Beth, 'if you find that out, you may be able to add more statements to the pile.'

George got ready to leave but James stopped him. 'What about Theodore? He never uses his office at Parliament. You know he has an office at the Wendover and Bert's source seems sure there's a written record of transactions that could be linked to his drug ring.'

'You stop this now. What you've told me will hopefully give me enough to arrest Maximillian. Let me and the Superintendent deal with Theodore.'

James sighed. 'Have you nothing at all on Theodore?'

His friend rolled his hat around his fingers. 'Nothing to link him directly, no. But I had a check on all that business a few years ago, you know, the trial where Jacqueline Simms was going to testify. Seems that the man who was murdered, Archie Stanhope, worked for Livingstone at his constituency. Posting leaflets, that sort of thing. He'd been arrested a few times for minor things but the last offence was to do with drugs.'

'Do you think he was trying to get a cut of the action?'

'I'm sure of it. Theodore finds out and takes the necessary steps.'

James couldn't find the words.

Beth mirrored his disbelief.

George left them to their thoughts and, for a minute, they didn't speak. James absentmindedly split the last piece of pancake. 'I forgot to ask him about Faith Simms,' he said before a thought sprang to mind. 'You know that Valentine Plumb is doing a book about blackmail.'

'Who belongs to the same club as Theodore,' added Beth. 'I know you said Valentine doesn't like Theodore but could that be a ruse?' She closed her eyes in frustration. 'Oh, James, I really don't know who to trust.'

'We trust the people we truly know. In the police, it's George and he is the only one I will deal with.' He dabbed his lips with a napkin.' I know someone who may be able to shed light on Plumb. Kushal Patel.'

Kushal Patel had assisted James during his investigation into the death of an elderly lady the previous year. Although born in India, he had spent the majority of his seventy years in and around London as a psychiatrist and psychologist. He worked from his home in a glorious Georgian mansion in Richmond but was also in the pay of the British government. His role there was to counsel and debrief agents and spies on their return from particularly dangerous missions.

James had remained in contact with him. First, he was an informative man and second, because he loved spending time in his company. The man was exceptionally well-read, knowledgeable and gracious. He had an air about him that made one feel relaxed and calm simply by being in his presence. He wondered if Kushal ever practised things like meditation or quiet reflection. He'd read quite a bit about it in various books about India. Maybe, though, that inner calm was simply part of his natural persona.

Returning home, he dialled Kushal's number and sat on the bottom stair in their hall to chat. Once the usual pleasantries were out of the way, Kushal allowed a few seconds of silence to pass before answering James' questions. He spoke with a slight accent.

'Valentine Plumb is renowned in his field, James. I am most sure that he would not involve himself in criminal activity. He has no reason to. He is not a poor man, he is in demand by many of his peers to give talks and I know of several universities that would like him to dedicate his efforts to the service of their particular institution.'

'My problem is something that you probably can't answer. Do you know if he has a secret that he would prefer to keep quiet?'

'Ah,' came the response and James could almost see the man smiling at the other end of the phone. 'I know Valentine Plumb as much as he knows me. Valentine does not know my secrets so I am unlikely to know his. But, a question for you, James. The criminal activity that you speak of involves personal secrets, I assume. Valentine is writing a book on the subject of blackmail, that much I know from talking with his peers in the circles we move in. I presume you are wondering if he has been blackmailed.'

James didn't interrupt. He knew Kushal was thinking aloud.

'Is this to do with Jacqueline Simms?' Kushal continued.

'You know about that?'

'Yes. He and I were speaking at a conference a few weeks after she had pulled out of the trial.'

'What did he tell you?'

'That the nurse had been scared. It is clear, from his description, that those responsible for the crime had threatened her. Blackmailed her.'

'Did Valentine Plumb continue to see Jacqueline Simms?'

'Only for a few weeks after she pulled out of the trial. I believe he felt responsible for her. He was, effectively, her superior on the ward. She was good at her job and he tried to develop her skills.'

'Do you know anything about the daughter?'

'No, nothing. I would hope that she and her mother are far away from the people who cast such a shadow over them.'

'Oh Lord, you haven't heard, have you?'

Kushal listened as James described the devastating disease that took Jacqueline Simms' life and the fact that her daughter, Faith, was found dead in Plumb's garden.

'That is most curious,' said Kushal. 'Faith Simms has opened up old wounds and spoken to the wrong people.'

'My thoughts exactly. Valentine belongs to the same club as me, the Wendover. Theodore Livingstone is a member too. You know Valentine used to be his GP. Has he ever mentioned being friends with him at all?'

'I cannot imagine a less likely friendship.'

'Oh?'

'My understanding is that he cut ties with the family after Theodore's wife died. She was committed to an institution for a while because of mental illness.'

'Had he discovered something?'

'Discover? No. But sometimes it is more a matter of instinct. From the little he said to me, I got the impression that he came to dislike Theodore and decided to resign from being the family GP.' After a pause, he added: 'Perhaps this is Theodore's way of getting back

164

at him; placing the dead body of Faith Simms in his garden.'

James wasn't surprised. It was just the sort of thing the Livingstons would stoop to. He heard a distant chime down the line.

'Ah, James, my next appointment is here. Perhaps we should meet one day when we are less busy.'

'Yes. Come down to stay. Beth would be delighted to see you. Take care of yourself.'

He wandered through to the lounge to see the French doors open and Beth sitting on a wrought iron chair, doing some needlework. He took a chair opposite and updated her on the call.

In the distance, he could see steam puffing from a few traction engines' chimneys. It was coming up to five o'clock and he pondered on what an exceptionally long day it had been; but there were still things to do before the rally started the next day. And, no doubt, a few of the villagers returning from work would be popping in to see the engines this evening before tomorrow's opening. He leapt up. 'I'm going to give the Mercedes an inspection before I take her down to the show.'

Wearing his overalls, he manoeuvred the huge veteran car on to the drive and rummaged around in the garage for some polish and a clean rag. Rolling up his sleeves, he walked round the car to touch up any areas that had dulled over the last couple of weeks. Even being this close to such a spectacular car sent his heart racing. Cream paintwork covered the bonnet and the massive wheel fenders. The oak running-boards gleamed and the black leather seats had been brought to life with Beth's leather restoring kit that she'd spotted in the local ironmongery shop. Between them, they had brought the car up to showroom condition and he was itching to display it at the steam rally.

So engrossed was he in polishing the fog lights and banishing any mote of dust, he failed to see Bert Briggs waving at him. It wasn't until his friend shouted his familiar 'Oi oi' that he looked up. Rubbing his hands on his overalls, he went over to greet him.

'Are we supposed to be meeting?'

'Nah, nah, nothing like that. I'm on my way down to the steam rally. Said I'd help set a few things up. You coming down?'

'Yes, I'm taking this beauty along with us. Give me a few minutes and we'll all toddle off down. I'll drive this down and Beth's following on with the Jaguar. Pick which vehicle you'd prefer.'

Half an hour later and the three of them arrived at the far field of Harrington's. Still getting to grips with the odd function of gears, brakes and levers, James edged the Mercedes forward into its allocated space. Its presence drew a number of villagers who began taking photographs.

Professor Wilkins' expression said everything. 'What a beauty, Lord Harrington. You should enter that into the London to Brighton rally.'

'I'm considering doing that. Indeed, I've already contacted the RAC to see how to go about it.'

Leaving half a dozen people to admire his car, he felt Bert pull him away and beckon Beth across.

'Right, Jimmy boy, you know that I've been telling you to keep your nose out of Theodore Livingstone's affairs.'

James waited.

'Well, I think I've found a way to at least glimpse inside that office without being noticed.'

'How?'

'Chatty Chatham asked around and 'as managed to get hold of the bloke who cleans the windows at The Wendover. He does the whole street. If you want him to, he could ask him to take a look.'

James swallowed his nerves. The mere mention of Theodore made him anxious and the man wasn't even targeting them.

Beth edged closer. 'Oh Bert, I don't think we should ask anyone to risk anything. George has already told us to stop.'

Their friend visibly brightened. 'Good. It's not often we agree on something but that's exactly what you should do.' He turned to go. 'Right, I'm off to help the Delaneys.'

'No, wait a minute,' said James. 'I think it's a good idea.' He caught Beth's horrified look and asked her to hear him out. 'This window-cleaner is a regular. No one's going to take any notice of him, are they? All he'll be doing is looking in. Perhaps he could spot a particularly awkward mark that takes him a while to clean and give him a couple of extra minutes to scan the room. He can at least see if there's a safe or something.'

'And then report back to George,' Beth ordered.

'Of course. I'll keep our dinner date with Swiss and we could meet this window-cleaner somewhere to find out if he's seen anything.'

'You're like a bloody dog with a bone, you are. I'll get Chatty to sort it out.' Bert stomped off.

Behind them, a raised voice caused them to turn.

'Why didn't you tell me before?'

The question came from Flora Armstrong's beau, Ken Scott. His dark hair flopped over his forehead as he shouted at the girl in front of him.

'It wasn't anything to do with you and it's nothing to do with you now,' she replied.

'Yes it is. You're my girl. It's up to me to look after you. I can't believe it. How could you fall for someone like that? Couldn't you tell he was trying it on?'

The girl wrestled her arm free and stormed off.

James turned to Beth. 'Was that Flora Armstrong?'

'Yes. I wonder what that was about.'

Beth spotted Anne over at the WI tent. 'Darling, I think I should spend at least half an hour helping the ladies out.'

He watched her disappear and strolled past some of the traction engines. One in particular caught his eye, a forlorn rusty old thing that had seen better days and was so dilapidated it had to be brought in on a lorry. But there was something rather lovely about it and, on the placard at the front, he was delighted to read that the owners had found it at the back of an old barn and were going to restore it.

Wandering around the back, he squatted down to look underneath the metalwork and became aware of someone behind him. He went to get up but a hand kept him squashed uncomfortably. The man, smelling of tobacco, leaned into him.

'You ought to be careful, Lord Harrington,' the voice whispered. 'If you start asking too many questions, the wrong people might hear about it.'

James felt something at his ribs and his mouth went dry.

'If you look around now, you'll regret it. You close your eyes and count to fifty. You open them before that, you'll be sorry.'

James closed his eyes and listened as the footfall on the long grass faded. He waited a while and eased himself up before tentatively stepping to the front of the engine. Ahead of him, enjoying the spectacle in the brilliant sunshine, were about forty villagers. Dulcie Faye was laughing with Beth and Anne at the entrance to the WI marquee.

Standing by Paolo Rossi's ice-cream van was Theodore who stared fixedly across the field. James followed his gaze and swallowed a wave of nausea. Inspector Fulton. Feeling a sudden need to sit down, he headed to the beer tent.

CHAPTER EIGHTEEN

The brandy provided the warmth he sought and the unease that had crept into his bones slowly dissipated. Donovan stopped work on setting the bar up and approached him, flinging a tea towel over his shoulder.

'You look a little shaky there, if you don't mind me saying. Are you feeling all right?'

James assured him he was quite well but wondered if he had a slight cold coming. 'Just felt a bit chilled, but this brandy is doing the trick.'

'Don't be telling everyone I'm pouring drinks. I'm only supposed to be setting up.'

James gave him his empty glass. 'Mum's the word old chap. Appreciate your kindness. Ah, here's Beth.'

He strode toward her and she pressed him for his thoughts. 'What's happened? You look dreadful.'

'Nothing for you to worry about.'

She slapped him on the arm. 'Don't patronise me, James, you look as if someone has walked over your grave.'

He steered her to the corner of the WI tent, sat her down in a chair and pulled his own chair closer. After he'd described the unnerving event she became increasingly shocked and couldn't find the words to react.

Finally, she grabbed his hands. 'You must tell George about this. If that was Inspector Fulton, they'll need to start following him or whatever they do. The man is clearly in the Livingstones' pay, stooping so low as to threaten people. Did you think it was a weapon he had?'

170

'I don't know. Now I'm sitting here thinking about it, I'd say it was unlikely. Whatever he was threatening to do would draw attention to him. He stank of tobacco.'

'Well, he does smoke like a chimney. If he stank of tobacco, he's your likely suspect.' She peered round the opening of the marquee. 'Theodore is speaking with Paolo.'

James pulled his chair along to see Theodore wag a finger at the young man and walk off. Maximillian joined his father and appeared to be downcast, as if he was in his father's bad books. Inspector Fulton stood staring at the ice-cream vendor for a short while, then followed.

James reached for Beth's hand. 'Come on.'

Although the rally wasn't starting until the next day, Paolo had taken that opportunity to open up and also spend some time looking at the engines.

James knocked on the frame of the van's back door. 'Open for visitors?'

The young man beamed. 'Lord Harrington, Lady Harrington. I can't thank you enough for inviting us to be here. I've already taken a good look at the engines. Amazing vehicles, aren't they?'

'They are indeed,' said James. 'You know that we're opening up the next field so that some of the working farm engines can do some ploughing?'

Paolo couldn't have been happier. 'How fantastic. I'll see if I can bring dad along. I think he'd love to see those old engines doing what they were made for.'

Beth added that it would be lovely to see Papa Rossi at the event. 'Even if it's just for a couple of hours. You know that James could arrange for him to be picked up and taken home if he didn't want to stay for too long.'

'I must admit, it's difficult to get the old man out of the house.' He gave a helpless shrug. 'I have very vague memories of my dad actually in the shop, serving customers. Everyone tells me he was the happiest man they ever knew.' He cast his gaze down at his teacup. 'It's difficult enough to get him to show his face in the shop so the likelihood of him coming here is pretty remote.'

'Paolo,' said James, 'does your father ever speak about what happened during the war?'

'He says little things now and again. Over the years, I've gathered lots of snippets and pieced together what I think happened.' He closed the shutters on the van. 'Shall we sit outside for a bit?'

They moved to the grass at the back of the van where there were half a dozen wooden folding chairs. He unfolded three and they sat down.

'I'm sorry, did you want an ice cream?' he asked.

They declined. James was eager to hear what the young man had to say and didn't want to interrupt his flow.

Paolo cradled his cup of tea. 'I was born in 1938 and, when the war began, my father was proud to be supporting the Allies. He was ashamed of how his fellow countrymen in Italy could support a man like Hitler. But all of that changed a couple of years later. You know the story, I don't need to tell you.'

James and Beth knew. It had been a horrendous time for a number of Italians and, indeed, all the immigrants who had made their homes in England, hoping to make a better life for themselves and their families. When Mussolini came out in support of Germany, normally reasonable people began to attack foreigners. Papa Rossi, a stalwart within the community, was branded a

172

spy, his shop attacked, windows smashed and graffiti painted on the walls. Both James and Beth had felt an anger they didn't know they were capable of but could do nothing. Papa Rossi had been a Category C alien, supposedly posing no risk. His wife was English and Paolo and his siblings were born in England. But that didn't stop the suspicion of people who had once spoken of Papa Rossi as a friend and good neighbour.

'But when the war ended,' said Beth, 'didn't things change? I mean, Italy switched allegiance. Didn't these people who had targeted your father try to make amends?'

'A few did. Some brought gifts and said they couldn't believe they'd behaved so badly toward him. Some stayed indifferent and never spoke to him again.'

'But that's terrible. Heavens, it's not your father's fault that Mussolini should make such a decision, thousands of miles away.'

'Not everyone thinks like that.'

'That war created divisions like no other,' James said. 'It pitted neighbour against neighbour and it really amounts to the fact that people were scared. Men, in particular, do not like to admit to being scared. They didn't know who to trust and they didn't know your father intimately. When you don't know someone, you make guesses and assumptions. You listen to people goading you and telling you stories that you come to believe are true. Then suddenly, the man you considered your friend is now your enemy. And peer pressure also causes such behaviour. No one man wants to go against a crowd on the warpath.'

The three sat in silence for a while. Paolo swigged the last of his tea. 'Well, the war was years ago. A new generation have grown up and they come into the shop.

They know about the war, of course they do, but they come in for ice cream. If they see dad out the back they wave hello. He waves back but he puts no effort into chatting with them.'

'If I were to have a word with your father, do you think he would visit the rally if I promised to take him home straight after?'

'You can try. I don't want to give you a false promise.'

A young boy shouted in the distance. 'Mummy, look at that car.'

Paolo turned to see what had attracted the lad's attention. He scowled. Theodore drove slowly past in his Bentley, with Max alongside him and Fulton in the rear. Fulton lifted a hand and tipped his head. James gritted his teeth. Paolo witnessed his reaction.

'You don't like him either?'

The subject of his anger, at that time, was Fulton but he couldn't let on to Paolo. 'I can't comment. I don't know them. I've only met them once but first impressions stay with me.'

'I've got a few names for 'em, none of which I can repeat here.'

Beth told him he needn't stand on ceremony. 'I received the same impression as my husband.'

'And being a woman, I would think it's probably a worse impression. They like women to know their place. I think they like everyone to know their place.'

'Where do you stand?' asked James.

Paolo shifted. 'What d'you mean?'

'You had quite an altercation with Theodore in the village a few days ago. What was that all about?'

'Just a misunderstanding.' Paolo turned the cup around in his hand. 'I'd best get on.'

James asked him to wait. 'The Livingstones are not people you want to cross, Paolo. Are you involved with them in some way? I mean in a way that makes you or your family uncomfortable? Has Maximillian intimidated you at all? Because if he has, you won't be the first. He's proving to be a nasty piece of work.'

Confusion crossed the young man's face. 'Maximillian? I've nothing to do with Maximillian.'

James stole a look at Beth and returned his attention to Paolo. 'Are you saying that you're being threatened by Theodore?'

A bead of sweat appeared on Paolo's top lip. 'No, I've no problem with either of them. I told you, that business with Theodore was a misunderstanding, that's all. I'd best get on.' He slammed the door shut and James could hear him slide the panels open to begin serving again.

They folded the chairs and leaned them up against the van. James went to the front and gave Paolo a card. 'If you ever need to talk, you know where we are.'

Paolo slipped the card in his pocket and beckoned the children across. The colour had drained from his normally healthy-looking face and he struggled to keep cheerful for the kiddies.

James guided Beth away. 'Well, that was interesting, wasn't it?'

'Darling, I hope he's not in cahoots with Theodore.'

'Yes, I do too. That'll be another thing for his father to worry about. I say, shall we pop down to the ice-cream shop, see if we can talk Papa Rossi into coming up?'

Beth checked her watch. 'They'll still be open. I really fancy putting my feet up but it would be nice to convince Mr Rossi to come.'

'We'll be back by nine at the latest. What do you think?'

'I think that's a wonderful idea. Let me tell Anne what we're doing. I'll have to make sure I help the WI and everyone tomorrow. I feel a fraud just wandering around here as if I own the place.'

James laughed. 'But darling, you do own the place.'

Twenty minutes later the Jaguar was parked on the seafront between Brighton and Hove, two towns which blended into each other, each lined with impressive cream-coloured Georgian townhouses overlooking the English Channel.

Rossi's Ice Cream Parlour was situated at the end of a small parade of shops and, alongside it was the forecourt of a garage that Rossi had taken over. It now housed a small fleet of new ice-cream vans that served the area. Advertising hoardings provided a colourful backdrop to the cobbled area, promoting Rossi's home-made Italian ice cream in a variety of delicious flavours. A van was up on a jack, being repaired by a mechanic and a young lady was polishing one of the ice-cream bicycles displaying the invitation to 'Stop Me and Buy One'.

Inside, a lady in her mid-twenties greeted them from behind the counter. 'Hello, welcome to Rossi's. What can I get you?'

The family resemblance confirmed to James that this was Paolo's sister. It had been a while since he'd seen her. After giving their first names he asked if his presumption was correct.

'Oh yes, Paolo's my younger brother,' she said. 'I'm Sophia.' Her uniform was the same as Paolo's although she had made alterations to flatter her figure.

She had inherited her father's Italian features: dark brown eyes, thick chestnut hair and full lips. The soda jerk hat was perched just off centre. To the side of her was a glass case full of various flavoured ice-creams and stacked to the rear were columns of wafers and cones. Alongside those were sculpted sundae glasses for those wanting to eat at the tables.

The walls were white and the family had updated the tables and chairs since James and Beth had last been in. Now, they had square tables and cushioned chairs. Above the menu board was a blue and white striped awning to give the impression that you were still outside. All in all, it was pristine and uplifting.

'The last time we were here,' said Beth, 'it was just the shop and a few bicycles. We see you now have the yard.'

'Oh yes. We've had that about two years now. We've twenty bicycles and six vans. Most of them are out and about at the moment.' She tilted her head. 'James and Beth… you're Lord and Lady Harrington. I thought I recognised you. How lovely that you should call in. Paolo is up at Harrington's at the moment.'

'Yes, we spoke to him earlier,' said James. 'I understand he volunteered to work that particular shift.'

'Oh yes, anything to do with cars and engines. Put a steam engine in front of him and you keep him entertained for hours.' She caught Beth's eye. 'That's men for you.'

Beth agreed.

'I say, Sophia, we popped by to have a chat with your father. Is he about?'

'Yes, yes, he is. He's always mixing up various concoctions to add to the flavours we have. Some of them are quite scrummy and others end up being

177

discarded. But we've twelve flavours now and, of course, we're famous for our ice-cream sundaes here in the shop.' Without waiting for a response, she disappeared through candy-pink fly curtains. 'Dad. Lord and Lady Harrington are here asking for you.'

Papa Rossi flung his arms up and rushed out. '*Mamma mia, che sorpresa.*' He held the curtain open and invited them through. 'Come, come.'

As they entered, he dragged two stools over from his preparation area. Surrounding them were a number of containers, fridges and contraptions for making ice cream. Papa Rossi wiped his hands and sat on a third stool.

'You want ice cream. It's complimentary.' His accent was still strong.

They declined, admitting that they would be having plenty over the next few days up at the steam rally.

'You are good people,' the old man said. He'd kept his olive complexion but the years during the war had taken their toll. His face was lined and there was a wariness about the man that James knew hadn't been there before the troubles. 'You always ask the Rossis to provide the ice cream and Paolo was as excited as a boy with the sweets. But you come here. Is there a problem?' His brow knitted together. 'Has Paolo done something? I don't know why he is being so angry.'

'He's doing a magnificent job,' said Beth. 'You should be very proud of him.'

'Mr Rossi, we were rather hoping that we could persuade you to come over for a couple of hours. We'd pick you up and bring you home. It's just that Paolo said that you'd love to see the rally so here we are.'

The old man considered the offer. His hands showed signs of arthritis and his hair that had been so black and shiny years ago was now greying and wiry. 'I don't know. I am not a social man, not since my wife… she died… I don't like to go out much. Of course, it is kind of you to ask but I am no company.'

'We didn't ask that you come to entertain us, Mr Rossi. We'd simply take you up and you can have a look around, spend some time with your son and enjoy the rally.'

'Do say you'll come,' said Beth.

Sophia stood in the doorway. 'It'll be a grand day out for you, Dad; you never go anywhere and you'd love to see those engines as much as Paolo. Why don't you? I can hold the fort here. I'm sure the shop can go a couple of hours without you toiling away back here.'

All eyes were upon Papa Rossi as he suddenly sat up. '*Si.* I will come.' He visibly brightened. 'Tomorrow. I will come tomorrow.'

James confirmed that either he or the Reverend Merryweather would collect him at eleven o'clock and, whenever he was ready to return home, they would deliver him to his doorstep. Papa Rossi was more than happy with the arrangements and began to mutter to himself about what he should wear. Beth made to leave but James had a question to ask. Something he'd said earlier had piqued his curiosity.

'What did you mean about Paolo being so angry?'

The energy that had rushed through the old man disappeared. 'The last few weeks, the boy is different. He's normally such a happy boy but, recently, he has a look. What do you call it… haunted, that is the word, haunted, as if he has problems.' He shrugged. 'What problems can he have? He has a job, a business, a family. We are a family. We talk to each other, talk out our problems and worries, but Paolo, he is not doing that.' He met their gaze. 'He used to do that. He used to tell us if something worried him but not these last few weeks. Something has happened. It worries me. He is my boy. I worry about him. I tell Sophia I worry but even she cannot get him to speak.'

James offered to talk with him. 'Perhaps I can glean some information.' He held out little hope after their discussion earlier.

Papa Rossi followed them through to the shop door. 'It is not your worry. You are not to concern yourself with Paolo. You have more important things than this.'

Beth took his hand. 'People are important. Families are important, we know that as well as anyone. If we can help, we will.'

Tears welled. 'You are good people.'

'We'll give you a day to remember.'

CHAPTER NINETEEN

The following day was the official opening day of the Sussex Steam Guild Rally and the crowds descended. It was a warm, breezy day; fluffy white clouds scudded high in the sky as residents and visitors made their way in through the gate.

It was taking some time for people to get through as Dulcie Faye was helping Anne at the entrance. Not only were people paying their admittance, they also wanted to have their photograph taken with the young actress while youngsters clamoured for an autograph. Fortunately, everyone was in good spirits and didn't mind a few minutes' wait. Those who had come by car were parked in a field further down the road and streams of people were walking up from their vehicles. Charlie Hawkins, who had plenty of acquaintances in the council, had managed to secure an ad-hoc bus stop outside the showground so that people from the outlying villages could be dropped there.

Stephen had volunteered to pick up Paolo's father and had safely delivered him to the ice-cream van where he seemed rather buoyant serving the customers. The Reverend had commented to James that perhaps chatting to the public might bring the old man out of himself.

Beth, in a beautiful swing skirt, pumps and a short-sleeved jumper stood a few yards from the entrance with Flora Armstrong, selling raffle tickets. Flora, in her first attempt at being involved in the traditions and festivities in Cavendish, took her lead from Beth. James looked on from a distance. Beth was making an easy job of enticing people across while Flora tore out the appropriate number of tickets. But, in between times, he could see Beth had to coax the young telephonist out of her shell. He couldn't help but feel the girl was not herself. She seemed frightened, as if seeking out an assassin.

Her boyfriend, Ken Scott, joined them and handed them both glasses of lemonade. James studied their body language. The disagreement from the previous day had clearly continued. Flora appeared distant and cool toward her boyfriend who, himself, seemed worried.

The young man excused himself and made his way toward the steam engines. James came into step with him.

'Ken, isn't it?'

'Yes, yes, it is. Lord Harrington.' He put out a hand.

'You work on one of the outlying farms, don't you?'

'Not any more, no, I'm helping Mr Mitchell up at the orchard.'

Pete Mitchell and his young wife had taken the orchard over after Mitchell's father had died and they were turning it into a profitable business. Unfortunately, a couple of years previously, when his wife was away, Pete had had a brief fling with a lady who had remained anonymous. It had only come to light during James' investigation into the death of a local farmer. Pete was completely embarrassed by the whole thing and swore to James that he had mended his ways. It would appear that he had certainly done so. The couple were often seen together and Mrs Mitchell was now expecting.

Ken continued, 'It's a fairly big orchard and you know that Mr Mitchell gets people in during the harvest to get the apples in. But there's lots of other stuff to do during the year so I'm a sort of odd job man, fixing fences, weeding, checking the leaves for disease, that sort of thing.'

'You sound as if you enjoy it.'

'I do, yes.'

'And how long have you been courting Flora?'

'About six months now.'

'Going well?'

The fondness turned to a shrug. The young man put his hands in his pockets. 'I think so.'

'You don't sound so sure.'

'It's just that she's been so secretive lately, as if she's got something happening but she won't tell me. Well, I get bits but not the whole story. I wondered if she was seeing someone else. But if that's the case, why doesn't she tell me? I don't want to be made a fool of.'

They stopped to study the miniature engines presided over by Mr Sharpe. Sharpe acknowledged James with a beaming smile and seemed back to his normal confident self.

James turned to Ken. 'Flora doesn't seem the type to be disloyal. She strikes me as a very shy woman lacking in confidence. I'm not sure that it would be in her nature to upset someone close to her.'

Ken raked a hand through his hair. 'Perhaps. Whenever I ask what's wrong, she just shrugs it off and says it's none of my business and that I'm not to worry. But I do worry. She's my girl and I don't want her to be unhappy.'

'I couldn't help but overhear the disagreement that you had late yesterday. You asked why she hadn't told you before.'

His jaw tensed. 'She mentioned something about that bloke Mr Livingstone and that he'd been pestering her.'

'Theodore?'

'No, the son, Maximillian. I couldn't believe it when she told me.'

'Told you what?'

'It just didn't make sense. You're right, she is shy and lacking confidence, that's why I couldn't understand it but it only lasted a short while.'

'What only lasted a short while?'

James sensed an undercurrent of frustration within the young man.

'It was pretty clear what with him being such a b_, sorry, pompous oaf.'

James pulled a face. 'Are you telling me they had some sort of relationship?'

'Yes. Probably swayed by his charm and money.'

'Are you sure?'

'She told me herself. Yesterday. It was before they moved here. Maximillian was down here looking at properties and got friendly with her, put the charm on and wined and dined her. Then he just ditched her. It made her really ill. I think she'd fallen for him hook, line and sinker. I don't know why he did it. He's the sort of person that has a model on his arm, not someone like Flora. Sorry, that sounds really awful but people like Maximillian don't court girls like Flora. I think it was her first love. She was off work for a week, just kept crying.'

A group of three young men caught Ken's attention and waved him over to the bar area. Ken went to join them but not before James gave him his card and an invitation to chat if he needed to.

Well, that's a turn up for the books, James thought, as he made his way toward Beth.

She linked arms with him. 'Come on, darling, let's enjoy the day. Flora and Dulcie have teamed up with Dorothy Forbes, so everything is in safe hands.'

They strode toward the main arena where the threshing machines were being put through their paces.

The smell of steam, oil and smoke drifted across the field and Beth remarked on how unique the mixture was and that if they could bottle it, she'd buy some. Men, young and old, were working the engines and inviting youngsters up to the footplate to pull the whistle cord. The vision was a colourful one and it was easy to imagine that you had been transported back to the turn of the century, especially as many owners were dressed in old-style clothing.

Professor Wilkins stood by the entrance to the arena, holding a clipboard. He waited for them to get closer and produced a rare smile. 'Ah, hello, this is marvellous, isn't it? They don't make machines like this anymore.'

'Sadly not,' said James, 'but as long as we keep these traditions alive, we can at least preserve their history. I wonder if we could convince the Steam Guild to hold the event here every year.'

'And,' added Beth, 'the children love it. These engines are so enormous and to children they must seem like giants.'

'What's next in the arena?'

Wilkins checked his notes. 'Vintage motorbikes. We've about twenty-five entries, all in good condition and we have Mr Bateson judging them. You know that he's a big motorbike enthusiast and a member of the Steam Guild.'

'Yes indeed,' James said recalling that he often saw the village's solicitor on a summer's day, wearing a leather helmet and gauntlets as he took his Brough Superior along the country lanes.

Beth said that they had nicknamed him Lawrence of Arabia, knowing that the famous officer who did some intelligence work in the Middle East had ridden the same type of bike.

'I do exactly the same. Are you popping to the next field to see the ploughing? That's going on this afternoon at around two o'clock.'

'We most certainly are,' said James. Before they moved on, he took a few photographs of those engines closest to them. Beth accepted an invitation to climb on board one and pull the whistle, which she did with childish glee.

Along from the arena, the WI had set up their tent and Elsie Taylor had positioned a mini version of her café at the far end. She seemed to work in conjunction with the Women's Institute and was always quite happy for people to purchase their cake from the stalls and come over to her for tea, although she had ensured that a few dozen Grandma Harrington's Coffee Delights were displayed on her table.

As normal, the WI had done themselves proud and a number of sponges, buns, fairy cakes and pastries were on offer. Further along, sales of home-made jam and pickles were proving to be popular.

Anne already carried a basket full of goodies. They spotted her and she made her way over. 'I've just bought some of the lemon curd and Rose and Lilac told me it was your grandmother's recipe. Is that true?'

'Ah yes, Grandma was very fond of all things lemon: lemon drizzle, lemon meringue, lemon curd. If it had lemon in it then Grandma would make it. Stephen about?'

'We've just finished having some tea. He's chatting to Elsie with the boys.' She turned to Beth. 'I have a lovely dress-pattern that my mother-in-law sent me. I think the style would suit you better than me.'

James left them talking and went over to catch Stephen, whose two boys, Luke and Mark, were itching

186

to get back outside to see the engines. Although two years separated them, they were similar in height with the same dark hair and eyes with freckles across their cheeks.

'Have you seen the threshing machines, Uncle James?' asked Mark.

'I have indeed.'

'They're like huge dragons waiting to eat you up,' said Luke. 'I stood up by the steering wheel and tooted the whistle. It was really loud.' He giggled.

'I'd like to be a train driver when I grow up,' said Mark. 'Do you think I'll be able to do that?'

'I don't see why not. My father always told me that if you worked hard and did your best, you could be anything you wanted to be.'

'I could be a pilot and zoom up into space,' said Luke. 'I could take people to Mars.'

'You can't do that, stupid,' Mark said. 'Planes can't go to Mars, only rockets.'

'Dan Dare does, he goes across the galaxy and everything.'

James ruffled his hair. 'Dan Dare is a very brave man,' he said with a sly wink to Stephen. 'But being a spaceman is the same as being a train driver. You have to work hard.'

Mark gave his young brother an old-fashioned look. 'Can we go and sit by the arena, Dad?'

Stephen handed them a couple of sausage rolls and told them to sit close to Professor Wilkins. 'Then I know exactly where you are. Stay out of trouble and don't g-get run over.'

The boys raced out of the tent. Stephen bit into his sausage roll.

'Are you ready for a swift pint?' asked James.

His friend didn't need asking twice and, within five minutes, they were next door in the beer tent where Donovan and Kate were busy distributing drinks. They'd left the pub in the capable hands of Kate's sister and her husband who were always more than happy to stand in.

Donovan drew two pints of ale. ''tis a grand show, this. Those engines are spectacular, so they are.'

Kate flicked her tea towel at him. 'He's spending more time looking at those than working.' She shoved him. 'There's people over there need serving.'

James scanned the tent and saw Bert and Gladys sitting just outside so they went over to join them.

Gladys, as was her wont, wore bright colours. Today's outfit of a summer dress and yellow cardigan was in a startling canary hue. She was certainly a person you couldn't fail to miss in a crowd.

She sipped her shandy. 'Gawd, I don't think I've seen such a thing. All these engines and the lovely food and drink. It's a proper day out for me and make no mistake.'

'I'm glad you're enjoying it,' said James.

'A-are you here for the whole day?' asked Stephen.

'We're getting the four o'clock bus. It'll connect us for the bus up to London.'

Bert supped his beer and dragged his chair closer to James. 'I 'ad a word with the window-cleaner up at your club. Name's Del Sykes and he's been doing that round for twenty years.'

James couldn't help but be concerned. 'Is he all right with this? I don't want him to get into trouble or anything.'

'Nah, mate, he's fine. I said you'd give him a tenner to spend a couple more minutes on the window looking into Livingstone's office.'

'Ten pounds!'

'You can afford it.'

'Yes, but ten pounds for two minutes' work. He must be laughing at us.'

'That's as may be but he said for that money he'd do the best he could. Seems a decent bloke. Anyway, he's due to shimmy up his ladders on Monday.'

James positively glowed. 'I'm at the Wendover that evening having a spot of dinner with Swiss Cheeseman. Could I meet jim beforehand?'

'Nah mate, he's just looking. He's letting me know if he sees anything. There's a pub opposite, on the corner, the Lamp and Whistle. I'll see you in there. Seven o'clock suit?'

'Make it six.'

Bert tapped his nose. 'It's a date.' He turned to Gladys. 'Right, come on, I want you to 'ave a ride on the footplate.'

'But that's only for kids,' insisted Gladys as she was pulled from her chair.

'Kids, my foot. We're young at heart and my money's as good as the rest of 'em.'

She roared with laughter and waved goodbye as the pair of them headed off. James watched on fondly. As if reading his mind, Stephen voiced his wish aloud.

'They are perfectly m-matched and I think it would be lovely for them to spend their autumn years together.'

'We must let them make that decision in their own time. If you push Bert too far, he'll dig his heels in.'

They spent a few minutes in silence watching the scene. Around the edge of the field were a number of vendors selling hot dogs, sandwiches, candy floss and chips. At the far end of the field were four steam-powered fairground rides consisting of a merry-go-round, the Razzle-Dazzle, that tilted and rotated at quite some speed, a steam yacht that pitched back and forth and a big wheel where, on a clear day such as this, one could see beyond the Downs to the sea. The music from the fairground organs carried on the breeze and the smell of fried onions mingled with steam.

'Rose and Lilac t-told me that you had a chat with them. About their…worries, for want of a b-better word.'

'That's right. I'm jolly pleased that they're bringing everything out in the open. Have they told many people yet?'

He learned that they had confessed at the recent WI meeting. 'Anne said it w-was crowded because they were putting the f-final arrangements to the rally. She sat with them as they related what had happened. They a-added a final promise that they haven't done anything wrong since moving to Cavendish.'

'It's a brave thing to be able to own up to something like that. Let's hope this puts young Maximillian in his place. George is going to take a statement.'

The face Stephen pulled convinced James that the sisters now had second thoughts. 'Oh, don't worry, G-George took a statement from them but they're having s-second thoughts about standing up in c-court and giving evidence.'

'Won't a statement do?'

'You'll h-have to ask George about that. You spoke to some others, didn't you? Are they coming forward?'

James was confident that they would. Mrs Withers seemed unsure of what to do and clearly did not want to compromise the position of the high-ranking naval officer. But, she could also see that if she remained quiet, the threats would continue. Mr Sharpe, judging by how happy he seemed to be earlier, was firmly in the camp of giving a statement. 'George will do his best to get evidence where he can. Hopefully, he can pick up some fingerprints which will help to confirm things.' He heaved a sigh. 'This still doesn't get me any information on Theodore Livingstone. He's the one that I've been asked to take an interest in. So far I have nothing except an altercation between him and Paolo a couple of days ago. Paolo insists it was simply a mistake but I'm not so sure.'

'You c-can lead a horse to water but, r-remember, you can't make it drink.'

James finished his ale. 'You can, Stephen, if you put enough salt in its oats. I just need to find out how to go about that.' He rested a hand on his friend's shoulder. 'Thank you, by the way, for picking up Paolo's father. How did he seem?'

'Excited. Almost like a child. I-I believe this day may prove to him that he c-can come out of his shell and enjoy himself.'

The Charnley and Cavendish brass band struck up with 'Just the Way You Look Tonight'. There was something sentimentally appealing about the sound of a brass band and the pair of them listened for some time before resuming their chat. It was Stephen who spoke first.

'Y-you think that Paolo is mixed up with Theodore in some way?'

'His father is concerned about him. He's withdrawn, angry and reluctant to share what the problem is.' James repeated what Papa Rossi had said the previous day. 'Something's going on.'

'I hope and p-pray that this young man is not involved in drugs.' A familiar shout made Stephen look across. Luke and Mark were waving to him. They'd now been joined by Charlie Hawkins and his two children, Tommy and Susan. Charlie's hand signals indicated that he was taking them all onto the footplate of one of the larger engines. Stephen acknowledged him and rose from his seat. 'I'd best go and take some photos o-otherwise Anne will admonish me for not recording the day for posterity.'

Within two minutes, Philip Jackson, the local doctor, had taken the vicar's place. 'Wonderful day and a fantastic turn-out.' His wife, Helen, and their daughter, Natasha, were climbing on the steam merry-go-round just to the side of them.

James waved at them. 'I wonder if the Steam Guild would like to move this rally here permanently. What d'you think?'

Philip, whose dark smouldering looks melted the hearts of most of the female population in Cavendish, took out his pipe. 'If they're not agreeable, you could always arrange a separate event, perhaps over a weekend rather than a week. It's a wonderful thing to come to and I can tell you're in your element with all of these engines.'

His friend clearly knew him well and he considered how anything mechanical fascinated him. His racing days back in the Thirties had been a time of immense joy and a love of cars, engines and speed had never left him. It seemed natural to become a mechanic in the Royal Air Force during the war and, although the planes he worked on were used in conflict, he couldn't help but wallow in the excitement of seeing such splendid machines speed up into the clouds.

They chatted for a short while about the rally and watched as Helen took Natasha's hand to try her skills at winning a goldfish. Philip groaned. 'We already have two goldfish from fairs. She seems to be a dab hand at winning those.'

'Vet fees are pretty low though,' joked James as he cast a glance over to the entrance where another villager was taking over from Flora Armstrong. The young lady picked up her handbag and wandered toward the WI tent. She looked wary and as if she were searching the field. Was she looking for Ken? Perhaps. But why look so anxious.

Philip had followed his gaze. 'She's a timid girl, isn't she?'

'Mmm. Generally, when you get to nineteen or twenty, the shyness leaves you and you become more confident – making your way in the world and all that, seeing friends and going to dances.'

'I think she was beginning to get that way a few months ago. She certainly seemed a little more outgoing than she is now.' He drew on his pipe. James caught the sweet smell of Old Bruno.

'Ken told me she'd not been herself recently. I was surprised to learn that she'd gone on a couple of dates with Maximillian Livingstone. They seemed the most unlikely couple. Doesn't surprise me that it came to an end.'

Natasha came running toward them. 'Daddy, Daddy, I've won a goldfish.'

Philip turned to James. 'I told you!' He scooped her up in his arms and hugged her. 'We'll have to introduce him to the others.'

'It's a her. This is Goldie.'

He lowered his voice to James. 'They're all called Goldie.' He got Natasha comfortable in the crook of his arm and, before going, mumbled more to himself than anyone. 'That Maximillian ought to be ashamed of himself.'

All James heard in response was Natasha asking who Naxa Millie was. He wondered what Philip knew that he didn't. Perhaps Helen had divulged something. Or had Flora spoken to Philip in his professional capacity? Had Maximillian really swept her off of her feet and left her heartbroken? If that was the case, Philip may have given her something to calm her down.

He was about to go when Beth came across to join him. She'd bought herself an ice cream and was studying the best angle by which to attack it. 'Have you seen who's arrived?'

James perked up. 'No. Who?'

'Maximillian. It looks as if Theodore is waiting on the road in his Bentley.'

They watched Max as he strode through the entrance, ignoring Anne's welcome and Dorothy's offer of raffle tickets.

Anne yelled after him. 'It's a £2 admittance. No exceptions.'

Clearly angered by the interruption, Max stopped, put his hands in his pockets and flung several pound notes in her general direction. Anne rushed forward before the breeze took them. Several women surrounding her stared at Maximillian in disgust. He ignored their piercing looks and marched up to Paolo's van, flung an envelope at him and retreated to the passenger seat of the Bentley which promptly drove off.

'Well,' huffed Beth, 'how rude and boorish.'

James scrutinised Paolo who had been thrown out of kilter by the intrusion. He slowly regained his composure and focussed on his customers. The envelope had been thrust beneath the counter. His father was a short distance from the van but had seen what had happened. The old man's brow furrowed before he was encouraged by Professor Wilkins to view another engine.

James was suddenly aware that Beth had continued to rant. 'Why on earth does someone like that think they can just stroll in here without a by your leave and ignore the welcome of perfectly lovely villagers?'

He held her hand. 'Don't let the likes of them upset you. One day, they'll get their come-uppance.'

He hoped that day would be soon.

CHAPTER TWENTY

Del Sykes had been cleaning windows for most of his fifty-two years. His dad had done the same cleaning round in the centre of London and he'd begun helping him out at the age of seven. He knew the streets like the back of his hand and was on speaking terms with most of the people who lived and worked in the buildings in the busy thoroughfare that ran parallel with Oxford Street, the long road that swarmed with people scurrying in and out of the famous department stores.

The request from Bert Briggs had struck him as odd and he'd only gone along with it because he turned out to be a friend of a friend. Also, Bert had seemed like the salt of the earth and hadn't asked him to do anything more than spend a few more minutes on a particular window. He knew the office he was talking about because he'd seen the people in there and he only knew that because its regular user was Theodore Livingstone, Member of Parliament. Personally, he couldn't stand the bloke.

His wife thought he was a toffee-nosed snob just out to line his own pockets. Del hadn't disagreed. He wasn't a political man but Theodore Livingstone stood for everything he didn't: the rights of rich people to make themselves even richer. He wasn't interested in helping out the working classes and had proved to be very unpopular with ordinary families. This Bert Briggs seemed to be trying to find some dirt on Livingstone so he didn't mind participating one jot, providing he wasn't taking part in anything illegal.

Bert had reassured him. 'All I want you to do is spend a couple more minutes than usual on that window. See if there's a safe. If the geezer's in there, see if he's

196

got a notebook or ledger and let me know what he does with it. Does he keep it with him or lock it in a drawer? There's a tenner in it for yer. A tenner for an extra couple of minutes. I won't ask you to do anything else. I'll even make sure the window's dirty so you've got an excuse to spend time up there.'

He'd told his missus who'd brightened at the prospect of a ten-pound bonus. 'Think what we could do with that!' she'd said, already listing a ream of things that would have far exceeded that amount. 'Anyway, that Mr Briggs is right. All you're doing is looking through a window you've looked through for the last God knows how many years. No one can pull you up for doing your job.'

And that's how he found himself outside the Wendover on a Monday afternoon. It was his usual time and, as normal, he asked the doorman, Graves, for some fresh water.

'I've just taken a look and there's some muck on one of the side windows, first floor. It looks like it'll take some cleaning.'

Graves, wearing tails and a top hat, stepped onto the pavement and followed Del to the corner.

'There,' Del pointed.

'Where the devil has that come from?' Graves said with a clenched jaw, 'It looks filthy. I can't imagine what that could be.'

'Normally, it's bird doo-dah, ain't it, but that looks like paint or something. If it is paint, I'll probably need something to scrape it off. You got something?'

Graves said that he did. 'I'll be on the door. If you can't shift it, come in and we'll take a look at what's in the store cupboard.'

Del picked up his ladder and started at the front of the building, like he always did. He wasn't used to covert operations but he'd seen plenty of films where spies and undercover cops were part of the story and the secret was to act normal and stick to your routine. He was also aware that Theodore Livingstone arrived at a specific time, so cleaning the chosen window at this time would be pointless. With fresh warm water delivered, he shimmied up the ladder and began on the first-floor windows. Just along from him and across the road was the world-famous Liberty's store, a grand building with an exterior that reminded him of old Tudor structures. A number of well-to-do ladies came in and out of the building and a few chauffeur-driven cars waited nearby to load up with an assortment of shopping.

He polished slowly and methodically and came back down the ladder to move it along. He shifted his bucket and rags and went back to collect his ladder. Behind him, he heard Theodore's familiar Bentley Continental pull up.

'Cor, 'ow the other half lives,' he mumbled, thinking he'd need more than a tenner to afford that. He watched as Theodore Livingstone emerged from the car.

The young driver, with a similar appearance and complexion to Theodore, had got out and opened the passenger door. Del recognised him. Maximillian. Theodore stared at the bucket of water with a look of disgust and didn't acknowledge the brief 'Afternoon guv'nor' from Del.

'Good afternoon, Mr Livingstone,' said Graves.

Livingstone thrust his coat and hat at Graves and marched through the entrance with no response. Del brought his ladder over.

'He's a bit of a grump, ain't he?'

Graves' resigned expression suggested this was normal behaviour. He went to hang up Theodore's coat and hat. The Bentley pulled away.

Del made his way round to the side. The corner window on the first floor would give him the glimpse of the office Theodore used. Settling a flicker of nerves, he secured the ladder and made his way up with his bucket and rags. Theodore was just sitting down at the desk, which Del had a side view of. At least they wouldn't be looking straight at each other. Theodore considered him for a while then returned to shuffling the papers on his desk.

Comfortable on the rung he'd chosen, Del set about washing the windows, safe in the knowledge that he would have to spend some time on them as one pane had been splashed with paint. He wondered how Bert had managed to do this as it didn't seem to be anywhere else. But, it gave him more confidence to spend time on it. He washed the windows, all the while gazing at Theodore and his movements.

The MP was dressed in a pinstriped suit, the sort you used to see gangsters wearing in the 1930s. The white pinstripe was too wide for Del's liking and, having watched a number of American films recently, he could imagine the man having a Thompson machine gun hidden under the desk. He told himself to stop being so stupid and concentrate. His wife always said he had an active imagination. He was getting paid a tenner for this so he'd better do a good job.

He watched as Theodore made a couple of telephone calls but couldn't hear exactly what was being said. He spent quite a bit of time on one part of the window and scanned the room for a safe. There didn't seem to be one. Theodore slid open a couple of drawers but hadn't unlocked them. So far, there was nothing to report. He was just about to go down and ask for a blade and some white spirit when one of the waiters came in with a tray. Theodore bristled at the interruption.

With his heart thumping, Del rapped on the window. Both men stared at him. The waiter appeared a little alarmed and darted across to open it a fraction.

'Yes?'

'Sorry mate, I did 'ave a word with Mr Graves on the door. I need some white spirit to clean this paint off. In fact, it's pretty dry so a blade would help. Can you get them?'

'Yes, yes, of course.' He closed the window and disappeared.

Del gave Theodore a chirpy hello but received nothing in return. A minute later and the waiter was on the street below, waving a bottle and a blade at him. Del slid down the ladder, reached for another cloth and climbed back up. Whistling as he worked, he took his time removing the paint. Bert had done a good job. Not too much to raise curiosity but enough to keep him up there while he kept a close eye on Theodore. The telephone rang. When Theodore answered it, his expression changed. Del couldn't put his finger on it but, if he'd had to, he would have described it as menacing. Rubbing the window hard, he heard the tell-tale squeak of a clean pane. Theodore reached into his inside pocket and brought out a black book. He put the receiver on the blotter and came across to open the window.

The black book was open in his hand. 'Why are you taking so long? You're normally done in a minute.'

Del had no qualms in standing his ground. 'You obviously ain't seen the mess this window's in. This 'ere is paint and you can't wash paint off.' He glimpsed the book as he carried on. 'Paint's got oil in it, so water don't 'ave any effect and neither does soap. It needed to be scraped off and then I use white spirit and once I get that off, then I've gotta wash it again.' Theodore leaned toward him to peer through the window from that side.

What caused Del to be so brave, he didn't know, but the notebook was now next to him. He went to change rags and accidentally on purpose knocked the book from Livingstone's hand. As soon as he'd done it, he wished he hadn't.

'You blithering idiot,' Theodore raged. His face turned crimson and the veins swelled on his neck.

'Sorry guv'nor. I'll bring it back up.' Instead of sliding down the ladder, he took it one rung at a time. He was pleased to see Theodore had disappeared from view but could hear him on the telephone cursing the accident.

Del picked the book up and squatted down to get some more rags. While doing so, he flicked through the book. It was a list of names with figures and phone numbers. He didn't recognise any apart from contacts with the London Mobile Library and Barden's Dairy Deliveries.

'Hey,' Theodore bellowed from above. 'What the hell are you doing?'

Del snapped the book shut and turned to face him. 'Just getting clean rags.' He waved the book. 'Don't worry, got yer notebook 'ere.' He scrambled up the ladder and handed it over. 'Just missed the spare bucket of water. Lucky that.'

Theodore snatched the book from him and snarled, 'Get this window cleaned and bugger off.' He slammed the window to.

Del made to retaliate but thought better of it. He'd done what he was asked to do and more. As he finished clearing the paint, he wondered if Bert Briggs might add another fiver to the payment for going above and beyond the call of duty. That would be a nice start to the week.

CHAPTER TWENTY-ONE

The Lamp and Whistle was such a small pub you could easily have walked by and missed it. It took up a corner, squashed between a bank and a haberdashery. But what it lacked in size, it made up for in character. With one small bar, it catered for around twenty and only had room for a handful of wooden tables and chairs. The wall behind the bar was mainly glass which made the area look bigger than it actually was. Optics of various spirits were lined up and, to make it even more cosy, the landlord had strung up some tiny white lights across the ceiling. When James walked in, he felt as if he'd entered some sort of grotto.

As it was early evening, theatre-goers were either having dinner or were too early for a pre-show drink so grabbing a table was not too difficult. James ordered drinks and, by the time he'd returned, Bert had joined them.

'Oi, oi, Jimmy-boy. Beth, I didn't know you was coming up 'ere.'

'James' friend, Swiss, invited me along to dinner at the Wendover. I so enjoyed it the last time that I couldn't refuse the invitation. Anyway, I was interested in what you have to say.'

Bert tipped his head at James. 'You're getting as bad as 'im, wanting to solve bloody mysteries all the time; 'scuse my language.'

James sipped his drink. 'I rather think that Beth is gunning for Theodore Livingstone.'

She shuddered. 'The man is positively revolting.'

'Yer not wrong there. I ain't 'eard anyone say a good word about the geezer but then I only know the people in my circle. The bloke is mates with the Prime Minister and some of the royalty so he must switch on the charm a bit. And he got elected as an MP.'

'In Kensington.' James pointed out that it would have been a foregone conclusion. 'Kensington is a rich borough and men like Theodore Livingstone stick up for rich people.'

'You ain't in the workhouse. If he was your MP, would you vote for him?'

'No.' James didn't elaborate. His politics were his own but having met the man and seen how he treated people, it didn't matter what his policies were, if he had stood for the Cavendish constituency, James wouldn't have put a tick against his name at the polls. 'Anyway, enough of this. Do you have anything to tell us?'

His friend positively gleamed. 'You owe me a fiver by the way.'

'What for?'

'I gave 'im a tip. Well, he asked for one actually.'

'Well he'd better have something useful because if he hasn't, you're a fiver down.'

'Oh James,' said Beth, 'don't be such a grump. Bert wouldn't have paid him without good reason.'

Their friend brought his chair closer. 'Right. Del Sykes spent quite a bit of time looking through that window. I'd got a young lad to shimmy up in the middle of the night and coat some paint on the window so I knew he'd 'ave time to look. Well, he did exactly that. There wasn't a safe and the desk drawers weren't locked. The office was pretty sparse. There was a phone call but Del couldn't hear what was said.'

'Well I can't see that this is something that deserves extra payment. I could have done that myself if I'd gone up in disguise.'

He received a dig in the ribs from Beth.

Bert's eyes went heavenward. 'I ain't finished yet.' He took out his tin of tobacco and began rolling a cigarette. 'The phone call that came through, Del said there was a change in the bloke. You know, a bit shifty and he brought out a black book from his inside pocket.'

The news made James perk up.

'Well, he started getting annoyed about Del being there so he opens the side window and starts moaning. How long you gonna be, that sort of thing. Well, Del goes on about the paint and Livingstone leans out to take a look. Del saw the book and sort of knocked it out of his hand. Made it look like an accident.'

'Good Lord,' James said with sudden admiration for this window-cleaner.

Beth brought her hand to her chest. 'What did Theodore do?'

'Blasted him good and proper and Del said, no problem, I'll go and get it. Well he got down to the pavement and Theodore had gone from the window for a couple of seconds so Del flicks through the book.'

'And?' asked James.

'There were columns of names and figures.'

James went to ask if any of the names were familiar but Bert stopped him.

'I know what yer gonna ask. He didn't recognise anything much. Remember, he only had a few seconds. He was making out he was getting fresh rags. Anyway, he did recognise two names.'

James and Beth waited.

'The London Mobile Library and Barden's Dairy Deliveries.'

James sat back. 'I'm not entirely sure if that helps. It doesn't mean anything, does it?'

'It don't at the moment, no, but it may slot in somewhere. You said yourself, it's always like doing a jigsaw. It isn't until you get the right pieces that things make sense.'

Beth asked if there were figures by those names.

'Yeah, it was full of figures, dates, times. He said there were names under those businesses; like sub-headings.'

'I say, does he remember any other names, names he didn't recognise but perhaps can recall?'

'Nah mate. He didn't have that sort of time. But he does remember there were a lot of sub-headings.'

James brought out his wallet and handed Bert a five-pound note. 'He certainly did more than was asked. Do thank him for us and, if he remembers anything else, no matter how trivial, then let me know.'

Graves tipped his hat to welcome James and Beth at the Wendover. 'How lovely to see you again, Lord and Lady Harrington. Mr Cheeseman advised that you would be dining with him. Shall I escort you through?'

James and Beth left their coats with the cloakroom attendant and said they'd make their own way.

The Wendover had been a gentleman's club since 1890 but, in the last decade, the powers that be had decided that wives would be allowed to join their husbands for dinner. The decision meant that James and Beth had begun to visit a little more regularly, especially if they had booked to see a West End show.

The main lounge was typical of most clubs: a patterned carpet, leather wing-back armchairs, wood-panelled walls and a marble fireplace. To the far end was a small cocktail bar and, lining the walls, a collection of hardback books, mainly classics that gathered dust.

Copies of *The Times*, *Financial Times*, *Country Life* and *Sporting Life* graced the tables. A number of members lounged in chairs, smoking cigars or pipes. Very little chatter punctured the silence.

Beth whispered. 'Is it always this quiet?'

'I'm not here often enough to know. It is Monday, though. I can't imagine this is a busy day. There are a couple of rooms off to the side where you can play cards or chess but I've never known it be the sort of place to be rowdy. If you want that sort of thing, you tend to take yourself off to a jazz club or something.'

Beyond the lounge, he opened a glass door that led out to the courtyard. A few years ago, this was simply an open-air space for people to sit in when the weather was dry. When members expressed a wish to dine outside, funds were put aside to place a glass roof over the courtyard for year-round eating. Admittedly, in the winter, it remained quite chilly even with the heating on but, at this time of the year, the temperature was bearable.

Andrew 'Swiss' Cheeseman was already at their table and jumped up to greet them. 'James, Beth, how lovely to see you again. It's been too long.' He held out a chair for Beth.

A waiter appeared and took their order for drinks. James loosened his tie. 'We don't come up to London as often as we should. Beth is the one who organises me to do so.'

'If I have an excuse to visit Liberty's and Selfridges, I'll come up and we'll take in a show, too,' explained Beth. 'We tend to favour the restaurants around Shaftesbury Avenue because they're a little closer to the theatres.'

'That's true,' said Swiss. 'And are you seeing something tonight?'

'Not a show, no. We thought we'd head over to The Skyline.'

Beth had suggested it earlier in the evening and James had agreed that it was a good idea. Not only could they do a bit of sleuthing about Faith Simms but they did actually want to visit the club as it specialised in upbeat dance music. It opened at nine o'clock in the evening and didn't close its doors until the early hours of the morning.

'I've driven up,' said James, 'so we're not reliant on trains.' He picked up the menu card. The restaurant served light meals and James decided to have the Wendover Egg Mornay. This consisted of a circle of mashed potatoes, a couple of rashers of crispy fried bacon and soft-boiled eggs covered in a cheese sauce.

'I think I'll have the same,' said Beth.

Swiss signalled to the waiter and they placed an order for three of the Wendover specials. The waiter set down their drinks and delivered a plate of warm rolls and butter.

Their host tore open a roll and cut a sliver of butter. 'Now, I booked a table here in the far corner because most people tend to prefer being over there. It's a bit lighter but you said you didn't want to be overheard. I tried booking a side room but they were all taken up.'

Only two other diners were in the courtyard and were engrossed in their own business so James wasn't too worried. He hoped that nothing untoward would be said anyway and he was pleased to see that, to his knowledge, neither Theodore or Maximillian were in the main part of the building. He suggested they wait until their meals arrived, so they talked for a while about their families and what was happening in the world. Beth said that they'd enjoyed the film *Carlton-Browne of the F.O.* starring Terry-Thomas and Swiss agreed and mentioned his favourite scenes.

The meal arrived. The bacon was crisp, the mashed potatoes fluffy, the eggs perfectly cooked and the cheese sauce thick with grated cheddar.

James added a dash of salt and pepper. 'The reason we're here is to discuss Theodore Livingstone. You said you know him?'

'I'd rather say that I know *of* him,' said Swiss, adding that he had no wish to ingratiate himself with the Livingstones. 'He is a bigot, a racist and a walking ego with absolutely no consideration for anyone else.'

'I couldn't agree more,' said Beth. 'He and his son were extremely rude when we met them recently. He wouldn't even acknowledge me until he was introduced.'

'Ah ha,' said Swiss knowingly, 'once he heard the title, he probably couldn't do enough for you.'

She didn't have to say anything. Her expression alone revealed how unimpressed she'd been. James described their first meeting and how they had initially gone to see Dulcie Faye.

Swiss almost dropped his fork. 'Dulcie Faye? What a stunning girl she is. Does she look as good in real life?'

Beth didn't need much of an invitation to gush about Dulcie. 'She is an adorable girl, just like in her films, you know, the girl next door. I think she more or less plays herself on screen.'

He listened to her extolling the virtues of Miss Faye. 'Does she live in Cavendish, then?'

'Oh, you won't know, will you?' Beth said. 'She's being courted by Theodore.'

It was all Swiss could do to keep his mouth shut and swallow his food. He put his cutlery down and stared at James. 'She's stepping out with Theodore Livingstone! He's old enough to be her grandfather, isn't he? I've seen a couple of photographs in the newspaper but I thought that was just coincidence. Surely she could do better than attach herself to such a miserable specimen of a man.'

'I say,' said James, 'steady on. You told me you don't know him that well.'

'I know what I see and I know what I read in the papers. Reputable papers. I also know what I hear from people who move in the same circles.' He picked his knife and fork up again. 'You know we have a few MPs here who are members. When Theodore is here, I've not seen one person make the effort to pop over and offer to share a drink or a table with him. Actually, that's not true, it's normally the more prominent, egotistical MPs who share his company. Unless you're of some use to his cause, then you are treated as rubbish.'

'Do I take it that you approached him?'

Swiss took a break from dinner and sipped his wine. 'When he first joined as a member. I toddled over to welcome him to the club and stood him a drink. He had an interest in me first of all because I was reading a book about the Great War. That's a passion of his apparently. He said that at home he had several display cases of diaries, photographs and maps – that sort of thing. When he realised that I'd just found the book lying around, his estimation of me seemed to go down. Then he started questioning me. He asked what I did for a living and the man had the cheek to ask me what I could do for him.'

'In what respect?'

'He couldn't have been more direct. First, he wanted to know where I lived and, because, I wasn't in Kensington, he made it clear that he wasn't my member of Parliament. I couldn't give two hoots whether he was or not, but then he asked what I did for a living. I told him I was in finance, insurance, that sort of thing and he asked if I ever took any backhanders.'

James was about to put a forkful of bacon in his mouth but stopped. 'He wasn't joking?'

A shake of the head. 'After about ten minutes, Theodore Livingstone MP said cheers and swanned off to sit in an armchair. Didn't even thank me for the welcome. Any greeting I've made since has been ignored.'

The laugh from Beth came with an edge. 'How *did* that man become so rude and offensive.'

'And,' said Swiss, 'what on earth does the charming Dulcie Faye see in him?'

'Rather less than you may think,' said James who elaborated on further meetings with Dulcie. 'Our belief is that she is at his beck and call when he requires it. She has no say in the matter and appears thoroughly unhappy at times.'

'Well why on earth doesn't she stop seeing him?'

'We think,' Beth said lowering her voice, 'that Theodore has some sort of hold over her.'

Swiss rested his elbows on the table. 'What is it you need to know about Theodore? You've clearly put on your investigative heads and if I'm able to help you, and I'm not sure that I can, you'll need to spill the beans a bit.'

'Long story very short, we were asked to ingratiate ourselves with the Livingstones to see if we could spot any suspicious behaviour.' He gave a brief outline of

DCI Lane's and Superintendent Higgins' request. 'We are simply observing and feeding back.'

'But,' added Beth, 'they suspect he's a drugs baron and could be implicated in murder.'

Swiss mouthed a silent 'Oh'.

'The thing is, Swiss,' James continued, 'we've been doing a lot of observing and we keep digging dirt up on the son, Maximillian. We've got nothing on his father apart from rumours. Until today, that is.'

Swiss topped up the glasses. 'Oh?'

James told him about the window-cleaning ruse and the black book.

'I say,' Swiss said with a wide grin, 'your chap, Bert, is a good man to have your back, isn't he? And you say the book has names and figures? Could be sums of money owed, names of people who supply the drugs. But the two companies, the dairy company and the mobile library, are both well-known institutions. I can't imagine them getting involved in something as seedy as drugs.'

'But that's probably the reason why it works. Theodore has the ability to manipulate people to do his bidding. He has the McCalls in his pocket.'

James watched his friend flinch. 'They're as bad as they come. I presume this is where the violence comes from, the murder.'

James and Beth said they'd come to the same conclusion. James didn't want to get bogged down in the death of Faith Simms or her ties to a past crime so he decided not to dwell on that. That was George's job. After Bert's warning about not getting too close, and the decidedly unsavoury threat at the rally, he was more than happy to simply collate information. 'Thing is,

Swiss, what do you know? What does he use the room upstairs for?'

The waiter came and collected their plates. James and Beth put an order in for lemon tart and Swiss, true to form, requested the cheeseboard. Once the desserts had arrived and they were left on their own, Swiss scanned the room. The two gentlemen who had been at a nearby table were now gone and the courtyard was empty.

'After you telephoned me, I gathered that Theodore was subject to some sort of scrutiny so I sat and had a chat with Graves. Knowing Livingstone as I do, I thought he wouldn't take kindly to me asking questions and so the only person I could trust was our doorman. I mean, the man's been with us for decades and I know he's not Theodore's biggest fan.'

'Oh?'

Beth asked how he could be so sure.

'Theodore treats him worse than a slave on a plantation. To him, Graves is simply a servant and treats him as such. You'd think Graves was the invisible man. To our doorman's credit, he is always civil but I've seen the gritted teeth and the scornful looks as our illustrious MP throws his overcoat and hat at him. Never tips the man either.'

Thank heavens Swiss had thought to be so careful. If questioning the members had got back to Livingstone, he could well have been having a meeting with the McCalls. James warned Swiss that he was not to talk to anyone about their conversation and to simply carry on as if nothing had happened.

'Understood.'

'And whatever you do, if Inspector Fulton of Scotland Yard pitches up here, don't trust him. We believe he's in Theodore's pay.'

'Really. Right. This all sounds pretty serious.' He sliced a piece of Cheshire cheese. 'I waited behind to speak with Graves a couple of days ago. He was locking up and I pulled up outside, made out I'd left something in the lounge. There were only the two of us there so we had a convivial brandy and I asked about Theodore.'

James silently prayed that his friend had gleaned some information.

'Graves is, of course, the perfect gentleman's gentleman. You know he was a butler before he came to the Wendover, so he's terribly discreet. But, I managed to get him to open up a little with the promise that it was within these four walls.' He took a bite of cheese and continued. 'Theodore uses the office upstairs but he wanted to put a condition on it, that only he used it. But, those in charge of this establishment made it clear that it wasn't acceptable. There are two offices up there and they are for the use of all members. Eventually, after some blustering from the old man, he backed down. He generally uses it on a Monday and Tuesday. His son, Maximillian, comes in and spends an afternoon here on and off but he has no regular routine.'

'Did you ask Greaves if Theodore or his son leave private papers or documents upstairs?'

'I didn't but it's unlikely. The desks are not locked and simply store stationery, pens, envelopes, that sort of thing. There's no secure place to store anything because it's just an office for anyone to use. I went up there myself on Friday and had a scout around.'

'Does he use the same office?'

'Yes. I had a good search and found nothing. I even checked the waste-paper basket but there was nothing there. It's interesting that Bert's friend spoke about a notebook. I've seen him refer to it several times. He

214

always puts it into his inside pocket, left-hand side. Maximillian's a bit secretive too. Doesn't have a notebook, more like a folder of foolscap paper. He belongs to a wine club that I go to. He's just as boorish as his father and always carries that folder with loose bits of paper in. Doesn't go anywhere without it, even takes it to the lavatory.'

Beth asked if Graves had seen either the notebook or folder.

'He's never seen inside the notebook. Your window-cleaner man was lucky there. He did glimpse a couple of sheets of Max's foolscap papers when delivering drinks. It was something to do with that awful magazine of his, *Guess What?*'

Beth tutted. 'Probably research on what he's been able to dig up on his victims.'

'You're probably right, although I've heard the magazine is on its last legs. I know someone who works in the same building.'

'You know he's started publishing gossip affecting ordinary men and women, don't you?'

'I do, Beth, yes and I think that'll be his downfall. He's made a lot of enemies in the celebrity world and a chap here, one of our members, overheard that he'd been threatened.'

James asked for more information.

'I don't have any, just what I've told you. He simply overheard Max on the telephone to someone. Sounds like he may have met his match.'

This was interesting stuff and James felt that George would possibly have built quite a case against Maximillian for blackmail. But this still didn't help with Theodore. Gossip papers come and go and *Guess What?* was certainly one of the worst to be published in recent years and, if a conviction came, he'd be extremely pleased. Not only would it rid society of someone like Maximillian but it would let his victims go back to living life normally without the fear of blackmail and persecution. The big cheese was Theodore Livingstone, a bully believing he was above the law. And, if he was involved in dealing in drugs, James would love to be able to find evidence that would ensure he was locked up. He voiced those last thoughts to Beth and Swiss.

'And throw away the key,' said Beth. She excused herself to powder her nose.

'I take it that you're going to go after this notebook,' said Swiss.

'I'm tempted not to. If Theodore found out I was after that I wouldn't see my next birthday. He clearly keeps the thing on him at all times. I wonder what he does when he's sleeping. He must have a safe or something at home.'

'Perhaps the young starlet, Dulcie Faye, would know.'

'I'd rather not put her in that position. I don't know her well enough and we can't afford for this to get back to Theodore.'

When Beth returned, they settled the bill and Graves brought out their hats and coats. Swiss wished them well and said that he'd have one more for the road before heading back to his flat. It was nine-thirty and they decided to continue on to The Skyline for a couple of hours. Although he felt it unlikely, James hoped they would glean some information about Faith Simms while they were there.

The Skyline was in a trendy part of London's West End, just along from The Ritz hotel on Piccadilly. James had originally heard about the club from Beth who had read an article about it. It had become *the* place to visit for music and dancing and was considered to be the best venue in town for a night out. They discovered that it was a members-only affair but James used his title to good effect.

'I heard about it and wondered if we could perhaps spend an hour or two to decide whether it's for us?' he asked. He was pleased to find that both he and Beth could sign in as guests.

Inside, Beth stood mesmerised. 'Oh James, I feel as if I'm in Hawaii.'

They took in the main ballroom. Their surroundings were made to look as if they were sitting outside looking toward an ocean. A huge lighthouse dominated the corner of the room and very realistic-looking palm trees were strategically placed around the tables and the dance floor. Elegant girls dressed in red cocktail dresses paraded among the guests with trays of cigarettes and cigars.

On the stage was a wonderful band and their lead singer, a beautiful blonde in a full-length black satin dress, sang 'Stormy Weather'. The head waiter led them to a table by the dance floor and gave them a cocktail menu. James scanned the choices but his attention was diverted to the small print at the bottom. It showed a modern cartoon of Henry Stanley greeting Dr Livingstone. He nudged Beth to look at it and received a guarded look in return.

When the waiter returned James asked if the club had something to do with Theodore Livingstone.

'Oh no, sir. He's nothing to do with this. This is owned and run by Felicity Livingstone. She's his

217

daughter and very much the woman in charge. Can I get you anything?'

They opted for a dry Martini each and a small bowl of peanuts. The band took a break.

'Well, this is rather a sophisticated place, don't you think?'

'Oh sweetie, I think it's glorious. I honestly feel as if I'm on holiday; that if I step beyond the scenery there, I'll be on the beach. Look at the way they've painted the wall there, as if the sun's setting. And that lighthouse in the corner. We must bring Stephen and Anne here. They'd adore it.'

'Or Bert and Gladys,' he said with a grin. They chuckled at the image of the cockney pair in such an upmarket club.

'They wouldn't give two hoots,' Beth said. 'Gladys would be in her most colourful flowery dress and Bert would still have that old flat cap on his head.' She sipped her Martini. 'I didn't realise that Theodore had a daughter, did you?'

'No. No one has mentioned a daughter, not even George or Superintendent Higgins. Come to think of it, no one has made any mention of the mother either except, of course, that she's no longer around.'

'It would be nice to be able to speak to Felicity. I wonder if she's here.'

Scanning the room, they decided it would be very difficult to establish who Felicity would be. James thought that, if she was anything like her father and brother, she might dress quite formally but the people here were out for a good time. Formal wear was not the order of the day. The waiter returned to ask if they required more drinks. James put in a second order and tugged the man back.

'I say, is Felicity Livingstone in the building?'

'Yes sir, she's here every night, without fail. That's her over there, at the end of the bar, with the gold dress on.'

The bar was around thirty feet long with glass panels at the back reflecting the bottles and glasses in front. Leaning on the counter at the far end was a chic woman with a dark bob and a Twenties-style flapper dress. She oozed sex appeal and seemed as far removed from Theodore and Maximillian as she could be. They noticed their waiter pouring the drinks and whispering in her ear.

'Oh Lord,' he mumbled to Beth, 'I hope we've not landed ourselves in it.'

Beth automatically moved a little closer to him. Felicity swept across the dance floor toward them, the swing of her hips accentuated by the fringe on her dress. She held out a slender, manicured hand.

'Felicity Livingstone. And you must be Lord and Lady Harrington. I saw you come in and checked to see who you were. Potential members?'

James stood and pulled out a chair. 'Possibly. We read about this club in an article and thought we'd try it out.'

'We love to dance,' said Beth, adding that they might join and recommend it to friends.

Their hostess sat down and positively beamed. 'How fantastic. Was it the article in the *London News*? That seems to have brought about an increase in members.'

'Yes, yes it was,' Beth said, before admiring her necklace. 'I hope you don't mind me saying but it's stunning. It looks almost Victorian.'

Felicity fondled the intricate necklace featuring a small sapphire stone. 'It belonged to my mother. She wanted me to have it.' A pained expression crossed her face. 'She died years ago and this is really my only memento.'

'I'm so sorry to have brought up painful memories. It's a lovely thing to remember her by.'

Felicity thanked her.

'I say,' said James, 'are you related to Theodore Livingstone?'

The expression he received in return gave him the information he wanted. She'd drawn herself up and a look of pure dislike registered. 'By name only, Lord Harrington. I know it's not the thing to speak ill of your parents but my father is not a nice man. I cut ties with him a long, long time ago.'

'So, Maximillian is your brother?'

'Unfortunately, yes. He's in the same mould and I don't have anything to do with them.' She scrutinised them. 'Are you here on my father's bidding? To spy on me? Because if you are, I've dealt with the likes of you before. I have security here who can help you out of the building.'

James knew that he and Beth must have looked horrified at the notion and both were keen to play down any association. Beth, he was surprised to hear, continued to defend their position.

'I'm not a fan of ill-mannered, egotistical men, Miss Livingstone. Your father was incredibly rude to me recently, and also to my friend. I shan't be putting the welcome mat out for him any time soon.'

To James' surprise, Felicity put her head back and roared with laughter. 'I bet he met his match with you.' She ordered a Cinzano from the waiter. 'Do tell me. Was it one of those awful bloody social dos he goes to with that slip of a girl who looks about fifteen? I bet he totally ignored you. You know why? Because you're a woman, and a spirited, independent woman from what you've just said. Good for you. I hope you put him in his place.'

'It's rather difficult to be rude to someone who lives nearby,' said James.

'Nonsense, Kensington is full of snobs who don't give two figs about one another. Present company excepted. You seem a bit more down to earth.'

James corrected her. 'We're actually in Cavendish. Sussex.'

'Of course. I'd heard he'd got himself a place in the country. Best thing to do is simply treat him as he treats you. He hates that sort of thing, especially if it comes from a woman.' She frowned. 'He didn't recommend this place, did he?'

'No, no. As I say, we saw it featured in an article but there was someone who was a member. We didn't know her actually but she arrived in the village a few days ago.'

Felicity lit a cigarette. 'Oh? Who's that?'

James contemplated. He hoped that Felicity was genuine in her loathing of her father and brother. If his instinct was correct, she might be able to shed some light on things. If he was wrong, God knows how he would wriggle out of it. He took the chance. 'Faith Simms.'

He waited. Felicity flicked ash into a sculptured dish and ruminated. James rubbed a palm on his trousers. He saw Beth shift in her seat. Finally, Felicity picked up her glass.

'I think, perhaps, we should have this conversation somewhere quieter. Come through to my office.'

They found themselves in a spacious room. Velvet curtains, sumptuous cushions and soft pile carpets decorated the area and all the seats were comfortable sofas or armchairs. She spread her hands to indicate the seating options. A mahogany desk took up the far corner and James wondered if Felicity, like her father would no doubt do, may choose to sit behind it to give her control but the thought didn't seem to cross her mind. She sat alongside Beth.

'Lord Harrington, you're aware that Faith Simms died?'

James and Beth said they knew about it and simply added how tragic it was that such a young girl could take her life like that. Felicity pooh-poohed the idea.

'You disagree?' said James.

'That was no suicide, Lord and Lady Harrington. My father had something to do with that, you mark my words.'

Beth feigned surprise. 'But your father's a prominent man, Miss Livingstone.'

'Rubbish. He's a crook. He bought himself status. Being an MP opens doors, that's all he wanted. He doesn't have the ear of the Chief Constable or the Prime Minister for no reason. He's lining his pockets and whoever he hurts along the way, it doesn't matter. If you're a woman, or a man who is no use to him, he'll cast you aside. Even Maximillian kowtows to him.'

The outburst had astounded James. This was far better than he'd expected and the openness had taken him by surprise. He was speechless for a few seconds before Beth had the foresight to ask a most intelligent question.

'Did you know Faith Simms?'

James could have hugged her. Felicity put a call through to ask for more drinks and opened a silver box of cigarettes. She told them to help themselves if they wanted to.

222

'I didn't know Faith Simms until she happened upon me about three months ago. She'd joined as a member around two months prior to that.' She topped their drinks up. 'She joined, I understand, to get close to me. She thought I could help her.'

'How?' asked James.

'Lord Harrington, do you know anything about Jacqueline Simms, Faith's mother?'

James hesitated. Did he trust this woman? His instinct, again, said yes but a flicker of doubt was there at the back of his mind. Felicity read it.

'If I'm to be honest with you, Lord Harrington, you must be honest with me. I take it you're not sure whether you can trust me. You wonder if what you say will get back to my father. Let me make it clear. I have nothing to do with my father or brother. What happened to Faith was as a result of their interference and if I can get justice done for her, I will.'

'But,' said Beth, 'how can you be so sure that your father was responsible for what happened to Faith?'

'Because he puts spies everywhere. Even here. I found that out a few months ago. Every so often, something got fed back to him and I wondered how it was happening. Lady Harrington, he likes to be in control and he hates the thought that I am my own woman. One of our staff was in his pay. He informed my father about who came and went in the club and, of course, Faith Simms had asked specifically to see me. My father found out. Whether that information came from here, I don't know, but now that young girl is dead. She was no drug addict. She didn't kill herself. Poor thing was simply trying to find out the truth about her own father.'

James took a hefty swig of his Martini and set the glass down. 'Right, Miss Livingstone, we do know about Jacqueline Simms. Our source was Valentine Plumb, a doctor who worked at the same hospital.'

Before he could continue, Felicity spoke. 'He was our doctor for a short time. Faith mentioned Valentine and that he lived in Cavendish. Her mother had told her about how she became pregnant and the awful pressure she was under at the time of the trial. I believe they call it a deathbed confession, wanting to tell the truth about everything before shuffling off this mortal coil. Well, Lord Harrington, I honestly think the worst thing she did was to mention that trial. She didn't have to tell Faith anything. That girl had lived a perfectly good life without knowing who her real father was. Somehow, Faith's meddling got back to my father and he, as I've already said, has to be in control. The fact that Jacqueline spilled the beans meant she broke her agreement. And Faith Simms' father is now a prominent government official. Any scandal would have been bad for him.'

Beth caught her breath. 'Are you saying he had her killed?'

'I can't prove it. You never can. Father will always manage to be somewhere different and you can bet your house that he will have paid someone a decent price to do the job.'

'How awful.'

James decided that no matter what he said now, they had put their cards on the table. He might as well go the whole hog. 'Do you know if your father is involved in drugs?'

'Undoubtedly, yes.'

James started to ask another question but their hostess stopped him. 'What is your interest in this? You're asking specific questions. Your ruse of coming here because of an article is no longer believable.'

He cast a questioning look at Beth who simply shrugged in a way that said, *you've come this far, we may as well continue.*

'Miss Livingstone, your father's and brother's move to the village has caused considerable distress. Maximillian appears to have dug up some unsavoury information on a few of our residents and is attempting to blackmail them in return for being left out of that grotty magazine he edits.' He watched her shudder and mutter something quite obscene about her brother. 'I believe that your father may also be using people to shift drugs but we have no proof.'

'We?'

'One of my best friends is a senior police officer. In Lewes.'

She arched an eyebrow. 'Ah. And you think I can get you proof?'

'You seem an obvious person to ask.'

'Don't you think I would have brought him down years ago if I had the evidence you were seeking?'

Beth gave a despondent shrug. 'I guess we're never going to be able to secure an arrest.'

James asked about the notebook. 'Did you know he carried one?'

'I've heard rumours but I've never seen it because I never see him. If there is one, then it's likely to be your proof but how you'd get it, God only knows.'

'Does he have a safe at his home in Kensington?'

'Probably; but he wouldn't put it anywhere obvious. It'd be somewhere you wouldn't expect and he'd laugh at you because you wouldn't see it. It's little things like that that make him feel superior.'

Interesting. But it moved him no further forward. 'You're not able to help us?'

'I'll help you in any way I can but I'm not sure how. I don't want my father knowing that I am delving into his business because he will delve into mine. I vet my staff carefully now but I cannot guarantee that he hasn't planted someone here. Lord and Lady Harrington, I think you must be very careful. He may get word that you've visited me.'

James saw Beth look startled.

Felicity picked up the telephone and asked for someone to come to her office. When she replaced the receiver, she said: 'I have a suggestion.'

A few seconds later, a rather burly gentleman in a dinner jacket came in from the club and James' immediate thought was that he wouldn't want to get on the wrong side of him. He was a big, muscular man with a crew cut and a squashed nose. He remembered him standing on the door; he was obviously a bouncer of sorts.

'Lord and Lady Harrington, this is Alan Stubbs.'

Alan Stubbs held out a podgy hand. 'How do.'

'Alan, I'd like you to keep an eye on these two and make sure that my father does nothing to upset or intimidate them. Can you do that for me?'

The man looked as if all his Christmases had come at once. ''course I can. Where d'yer live?'

It turned out that Alan had a network of contacts in Felicity Livingstone's pay who, James discovered, were there specifically to ensure that Theodore and Maximillian did nothing to intrude on her domain.

226

Alan ushered them toward the door. 'I'll see to it personally, Miss Livingstone. I'll get my brother to stand in for me here.'

'Oh, and Alan.' Felicity grabbed two cards. 'Sign Lord and Lady Harrington up as members plus two guests. My compliments.'

Beth accepted them. 'Oh, how lovely.'

'Believe me, if you manage to do what I've been hoping someone would do since I was fifteen, I'll give you shares in the club.'

They laughed but, before going through to the main club, James asked about Felicity's mother. 'Forgive me if I'm being too intrusive but I sense that perhaps she is the one who turned you against your father.'

'My father is a bully, Lord Harrington. He mentally drove her into the ground, sucked every bit of confidence and life out of her until she was a gibbering wreck. She had a nervous breakdown and he put her into an institution which did nothing to help. Valentine, by that time, had decided to assign a different GP to the family. I don't think he was terribly enamoured with the way my father treated his wife. Father did everything he could to keep her in that institution. Fortunately, I was there for her and, much to my father's anger, I transferred her to my apartment. With months of care, love and affection from me, she began to get her life back together. I had no reason to suspect anything.'

'Suspect?'

'She took her own life.'

'I'm so sorry. You think your father was responsible.'

'I know what he's capable of. I was old enough to see what sort of man my father was and I didn't like him even when I was a child. Max was only three when she

227

died. He didn't know her like I did so father became his role model and he's been trying to emulate him ever since. He fails miserably, of course, and father treats him like the imbecile he is. Max is always trying to do things to please him.'

He reached for her hand. 'I'm so sorry.'

'Don't be. I'm a great believer in karma. It'll all come back to bite him one day.' She chivvied them out. 'And when it does, there'll be one hell of a party here. Now go and forget that loathsome individual and enjoy yourself. Alan: drinks on the house.'

It didn't take long for the foot-stomping music to take over, making a pleasant distraction from Theodore and Maximillian. They mingled on the dance floor and stayed far longer than they'd planned. It had been a while since they'd come across such a vibrant venue with lively music and a mixture of ages in the attendees. At one in the morning, they decided they really ought to be going.

On the drive home, Beth snoozed in the passenger seat. James avoided the country lanes and took the main A23 that ran from London straight down to the coast at Brighton. The route reminded him to think about entering for the Veteran Car Run, a historic drive between Hyde Park in London and Madeira Drive on the seafront, which had always been a tremendous spectacle. Only vehicles built prior to 1905 were allowed to enter and he had vowed, since the purchase of the old Mercedes, that he would put an entry in for this year. He made a mental note to do so.

As the lights of London faded in his rear-view mirror, he concentrated on the dark road ahead and reflected on his chat with Swiss and Felicity. There was only one thing that would convict Theodore Livingstone and he knew the answer was kept in Theodore's inside pocket. How on earth was anyone going to get hold of something like that? But at least they had Felicity on board. She would do anything to convict her father. He hoped that she would be of help but he didn't know how. Obviously, she didn't want to jeopardise the club in any way. He'd have to put his thinking cap on about that one.

A fox dashed out in front of him, he swerved and straightened the car.

Beth stirred. 'Are we home?'

'Just coming to our turn-off. I think a nice hot chocolate is in order when we get in.'

'Mmm,' she said sleepily.

The headlights lit up the Cavendish turn-off. As he signalled, the lights of a dark car followed him off the slip road but this time the sight sent a tingle of safety through him. Knowing Alan Stubbs was shadowing them made him feel a lot more settled.

CHAPTER TWENTY-TWO

The church hall, home to many events, including the Cavendish Players theatre group, was heaving with women preparing for the Whitsun dance.

The dance had evolved from just a handful of ladies during the Great War to around forty and, over the years, they had cobbled together an outfit to wear which had since been recognised as the Whitsun Dancers' costume. This consisted of a sky-blue cotton dress, with each lady sporting a different coloured cotton apron and scarf. They wore flat black dancing shoes with bells attached and every dancer had a half-circle garland made out of various materials that they held above them as they danced. Beth's dress was complemented by a turquoise apron and scarf and, at this moment, she was adding more turquoise off-cuts to her garland.

As more women had taken part, more dresses and accessories were needed and, in many cases, items had to be replaced. A few days before the event, the dancers gathered to make sure they were kitted out and spent an hour rehearsing the steps. Trestle tables dominated the centre of the hall and on them were different rolls of material and off-cuts. Anne and Helen were busy sewing hems on a couple of new aprons.

Rose and Lilac Crumb had set up the tea urn in the corner and were happy to simply serve tea and biscuits. At a quiet moment, James went across.

'Hello ladies. How are you?'

'Oh Lord Harrington, we can't thank you enough,' said Rose.

'It's true what they say,' Lilac said, 'a problem shared—'

'Is a problem halved. We have so much to thank you and the Reverend for.'

James dismissed the compliment. 'You have nothing to thank us for. The decision to tell your story was yours and yours alone and you should be very proud of yourselves for doing that. It's a very brave thing to stand up and admit a wrongdoing.'

For once, the sisters appeared bashful. Rose thrust a cup of tea at him.

'On the house, as a thank you.'

James accepted the tea and recalled Anne's conversation. She'd reported back on how the sisters' admission had gone down at the WI.

'They were so nervous,' she'd said, 'but Stephen and I sat either side of them and Stephen gave a bit of a lecture. He'd seen a couple of women look a little scathing and was keen to put them in their place. He said that thing about attacking your neighbour when you have a stone in your own eye.'

He'd roared with laughter. 'Anne, as the vicar's wife, I thought you would have known that story off by heart.' He'd corrected her: 'Why look at the speck in your brother's eye but fail to notice the beam in your own eye. Isn't that the quote?'

She'd shoo'd him away with a chuckle. 'I can't help it if I start daydreaming.'

'Ladies,' he said to the sisters, 'have you contacted George?'

'Yes,' said Rose, 'We're just not sure about going to court.'

'I'm sure if enough people come forward, that won't be necessary. Let me have a chat with him, see if he can put your mind at rest.'

231

'We don't want him coming to us,' said Lilac. 'We must go there.'

'Don't worry. I'll make sure he's discreet.'

The sisters visibly relaxed. Happy that at least two of his villagers would provide a statement to George, he put his mind to encouraging Mrs Withers and Mr Sharpe to do the same although Sharpe's behaviour had suggested he was more than happy to do so.

He sought Beth out. 'I'm popping over to the cricket club. George is there doing some batting in the nets and I need to update him on our visit to The Skyline. Shall I pick you up later?'

'Yes, I'll stay on here and have a chat. If it empties out, I'll go back to the vicarage with Anne.'

'Right you are.'

Twenty minutes later, James found himself in the grounds of the cricket club that they shared with their neighbouring villages, Charnley and Loxfield. It stood alongside the tennis club with a slightly larger pavilion than its neighbour. He spotted George in the nets. He hadn't bothered changing into cricket whites, simply taken his jacket and tie off and put on a pair of cricket pads. Charlie was running at some speed toward him to bowl. The red leather ball flew out of his hand and George only just managed to defend his wicket.

'That's quite a technique you have there,' James said to Charlie.

'I've been watching some of the cricket on the Pathé News. Trying to take a leaf out of Freddie Trueman's book.'

Freddie Trueman was considered to be one of the fastest bowlers in English cricket and Charlie had certainly made a good effort to copy his style.

George took off his gloves and came over to them. He handed the bat and gloves to James. 'Have you come to practice? If so, take these and see if you can face this man. He's going to be an asset when we take on Charnley in a few weeks.'

Charlie excused himself for a few minutes. 'I've got Tommy with me and I promised him a go in the nets. You don't mind, do you?'

James was more than happy. He'd discussed with Charlie the idea of Tommy coming to the club to play. Although he was only a boy, he'd shown a keen interest in sport and James wasn't about to let that interest wane. If nothing else, he would be a player for the future.

Waving Charlie off with the bat and gloves, he asked George how the investigation into the death of Faith Simms was going.

'Slowly.' He picked his jacket and tie up from the grass and they began a leisurely wander around the cricket pitch to the car park. The pitch had been perfectly mown and was surrounded by oak trees.

George repeated what Valentine Plumb had divulged to James when Faith was first found.

'And you know that Valentine was the Livingstones' GP years ago?' said James.

'Yes, I do.'

'Do you think it's relevant?'

'It was a long, long time ago. If the pair of them were feuding, I haven't seen any evidence of it. I made enquiries at the Wendover and no one's seen them together. Valentine insists that he simply disliked the man and asked for another GP to take over from him.'

'What do you know about the death of Mrs Livingstone, the mother?'

'Suicide,' said George. 'Suffered from depression and decided to hang herself. There was no evidence of foul play or anything.' He faced James. 'Do you think Plumb had something to do with this Faith Simms business?'

'Not at all. It's just that he is linked to the Livingstones, albeit in the past. He cut ties as the family GP because he felt uncomfortable with things.'

'It doesn't prove anything. I'll chat with Valentine about it though. The fact that he had ties with Livingstone makes it difficult to rule him out completely.'

'Kushal Patel, you remember him, don't you? Well, he sees Plumb now and again at various conferences and seminars and he's pretty adamant that he's not the type of man to go around killing young girls.'

His friend stared into the distance. 'I don't think so either.'

'When Valentine telephoned, the evening he found Faith Simms, he seemed anxious, scared. He searched her bag because he claims he didn't know who she was. I believe him, although I know I'm guilty of seeing the best in people.'

'If he is friends with Livingstone, he may be just as devious. Faith Simms could have come knocking on his door, fresh in the knowledge that her mother had been set up; she'd probably told Faith who her father was and how she'd been threatened. Faith comes over here, thinking Valentine will be a sympathetic ear and give her more information.'

'Instead, he's in Theodore's pocket and kills her.' He grimaced. 'No, I'm sorry, I don't see it. I think you're on the wrong track.'

George admitted he thought so too. 'It's frustration that's making me clutch at straws.'

'By the way,' said James, lighting a cigarette, 'do you have a conclusive cause of death? Was it as suspected, an overdose?'

'The girl had been given an overdose of heroin. Didn't stand a chance.'

'How do you know it wasn't self-inflicted?'

'No previous signs of drug abuse. There's bruising on her wrists. We think she was held while someone injected her. Looks like whoever it was may have knelt on one arm and put the injection in the other.'

James winced at the image.

'We've spoken to her friends and work colleagues. She was an ordinary girl who sang in a choir and made the occasional visit to London for dancing.'

'Ah yes, The Skyline. I saw the membership card. We went up there last night and had a rather interesting chinwag with the owner.'

'Oh?'

'Felicity Livingstone, daughter of Theodore.'

George swung round. 'I didn't know he had a daughter.'

'He may as well not have one. She hates everything he stands for and has nothing to do with him, or Maximillian. She's her own woman and has carved a career for herself without his help, much to his chagrin.'

He went on to tell him about her own suspicions and how she was sure her father was involved in drug smuggling. 'This notebook is the key to everything, George. Can't you get a search warrant or something?'

'Not without good reason. If I turned up asking questions without a shred of evidence, Theodore would be on to the Commissioner and he'd be completely untouchable.'

James groaned and asked how he was getting on with all this blackmail business.

His friend brightened. 'Well I can tell you that this is progressing nicely. Mrs Withers contacted me earlier and she's coming in to make a statement. I bumped into Mr Sharpe and he's already co-operated. I popped in and took some fingerprints and a statement at the same time.'

'Marvellous. I know the Crumbs have said their bit but did you know they are pretty adamant that they don't want to appear in court?'

'I'll call in on the church hall on the way back; have a word with them. It might not even come to that. They're small fry compared to some of the more famous people who have come forward.'

'Really! You have more people coming forward?'

A rare show of excitement answered his question. They'd reached the car park where George opened the car door. 'Only thing I can't fathom is where Maximillian is getting his information; I mean for the local people here. Everyone is so private there's not a chance in hell their secrets could have slipped out. The only one that applies to is the Snoop Sisters. I mean, the rumour was already there, wasn't it?'

'Perhaps these statements will find a common thread.'

'Perhaps. Right, what are your plans?'

'My first thing is to pop in to see GJ. Now you've taken fingerprints, I'll ask him to try and restore that painting of Sharpe's mother. Then I've to try and find a way to get hold of that notebook.'

'That's our job. Leave it. He'll soon know if you start sniffing around and that's a situation I don't want to have to think about.'

James got into the Austin Healey and returned to the vicarage to collect Beth; they enjoyed a glass of sherry there before making their way home.

Opening the door, James saw an envelope on the doormat. It was thick paper, the sort you purchased at a good quality stationer. The envelope had tissue paper lining. He checked the postmark and discovered that it had been delivered by hand.

'I wonder who sent this?' he mumbled more to himself than to Beth as he slipped out a handwritten card. 'Oh dear.'

'What is it, sweetie?'

'An invitation from Theodore Livingstone MP, for drinks up at his lodge.'

She took the card from him and then frowned. 'But he's only invited you.'

Slipping his shoes and jacket off, he could feel his heart racing. 'You know how he feels about the female of the species, Beth. Perhaps this is an all-male affair – a game of cards and a brandy cocktail or something.'

'It's the *or something* that bothers me. Why, all of a sudden, does he want to socialise with you?'

'He did suggest meeting at some point.'

'But that was at Harrington's, for dinner, all of us together. This is you being invited, alone, to his house which is in the middle of nowhere. Supposing he's heard that you've been asking questions.'

They went through to the lounge where James convinced her that someone like Theodore wouldn't be so overt. 'If he wants to threaten me, he'd rely on someone else. Like at the steam rally. I wouldn't think it's his thing to expose himself like that. He has a reputation to keep up with people like me so I'm pretty certain it will simply be a drink.'

Opening the French windows wide, Beth remarked that 'pretty certain' was not helpful. 'I don't want you to go alone. And when is it?'

James chewed his lip. 'Tonight. Seven o'clock.' He met Beth's anxious gaze. 'That's rather short notice, isn't it?'

Beth wrapped her arms around him. 'I don't like it. Call him and refuse. Tell him it's too short notice and that you have something on.'

He kissed the top of her head and held her close. 'If he has heard something about my asking questions, who could have told him? I've kept my cards pretty close to my chest. Only Bert, Stephen and Anne know how involved I've become. Swiss and Felicity, I'm sure, wouldn't have said anything.'

'But Mrs Withers, Mr Sharpe and the Snoop Sisters could have let something slip about Maximillian. Perhaps he's warning you off his son.'

'Well there's only one way to find out and that's to pop over and see him. But not without letting George know first.'

Beth's shoulders dropped in relief as he went back to the hall. He lifted the receiver and called back to her. 'I'll get Alan Stubbs to hover about in the shrubbery too.'

The telephone call with George was a constructive one; his friend insisted on certain criteria being fulfilled before James accepted the invitation. James was happy to go along with the suggestion and, after letting Alan Stubbs know about the projected visit, he placed a call to

Theodore Livingstone to inform him that he would be coming along.

'You haven't given me much notice, Mr Livingstone. I'm expected elsewhere so I'm afraid I can only stay for a while.'

'That's absolutely fine. I'll see you at seven.'

Later, James went upstairs to change. He spent ten minutes staring at the clothes in his wardrobe. Should he wear a suit or be more casual? He'd not seen Theodore in anything other than a suit. Even when he'd driven to the steam rally he had a shirt and tie on and nothing fitted terribly well either. The weather was balmy and a suit would be hot. The last thing he wanted to be was uncomfortable. He was anxious to be calm and collected and it was paramount that he felt he had the upper hand in any way possible.

Sliding the hangers along the rail, he settled on what Beth described as his Cary Grant look; a pale grey lounge suit with a glen check, gun-metal grey tie on a white shirt, grey socks and ox-blood shoes. It was stylish and he knew, immediately, that he would out-do Theodore Livingstone in style and perhaps make him feel a little uneasy. He picked up his sunglasses and trotted down the stairs where Beth gave him a conspiratorial once-over.

'Very elegant. Dressed to impress?'

'You don't think it's too much?'

'You've made the excuse that you have a function to attend later.'

He pecked her on the cheek, swung open the front door and turned to her. 'The Austin or the Jaguar?'

'Definitely the Austin.'

With a grin, he went on his way. He took the Austin on a rather long way around Cavendish to gather his thoughts. George had instructed him to simply be himself and stick to safe subjects. He wasn't to go wandering off looking for where a notebook could be hidden and he was to avoid getting involved in any subject that could lead him into difficulty. As a precaution, if he didn't feel safe, he was to go to the window and light a cigarette. This would be George's cue to come and knock on the door on the pretence that James' sister, Fiona, had been taken ill. Alan was instructed simply to stand with George and observe from a distance.

More than happy that he had everything covered, he drove past Dulcie Faye's cottage and parked outside Groom Lodge. There were no other cars there and he assumed the Bentley Continental was secure in the large garage to the side. Alan and George peeked out from behind an evergreen shrub. They silently acknowledged one another. He smoothed his suit down, checked his shoes and kept his sunglasses on.

He reached for the door pull.

CHAPTER TWENTY-THREE

James was pleased he'd kept his sunglasses on as the triumph he felt inside would have surely shown in his eyes when Theodore answered the door. The man had his suit trousers on but had discarded the jacket because of the heat. His tie was loosened, his face flushed and he perspired quite badly. For a split second, he saw a flash of irritation cross the MP's face.

James' lightweight suit, by contrast, was of a good cut and cool. At a suitable moment, he took his sunglasses off and put his hand out.

'Mr Livingstone.'

Theodore glanced past him at the Austin.

James allowed his smile to surface. 'Beauty, isn't she? Got her a couple of years ago hot off the production line.' He slipped his sunglasses into his top pocket. 'I've an old Mercedes, pre-1905. You may have seen it over at the steam rally in the classic car section.' Allowing himself to be guided through to a large lounge, he added: 'I'm thinking about entering her for the London to Brighton rally. Have you ever taken part?'

'As a passenger, yes. Make sure you keep yourself warm. It's bloody freezing if you're in an open vehicle.'

James undid the button on his jacket. 'I say, Mr Livingstone, this is a rather splendid place.'

'Just call me Theodore. What do I call you?'

This was a question James was familiar with. Someone who felt he could simply drift into first name terms on their first meeting. He had refused people before and, where Theodore was concerned, he had no intention of conversing with this man, or his son, on first name terms.

He put his hands in his pockets. 'Lord Harrington. And if it's all the same to you, I'd rather stick with Mr Livingstone until we know each other better.'

Blink and he'd have missed his host bristle. 'As you wish. Brandy?'

'Just a small one, thank you.' He wandered around the room and took a deep, silent breath. His mouth was dry but he was pleased that he'd scored points against this man and shown that he was not someone to be bullied. 'I was a little surprised to receive your invitation. You made it quite clear, at Miss Faye's, that you were not someone wishing to involve himself in village life.'

The look he received from Livingstone was nothing short of disdain, as if he'd invited a tramp into his house. James ordered himself to remain calm and composed. He accepted the drink. 'I mean, you've been here a few months now. Are you thinking of getting involved? I know that Miss Faye is keen to be part of the community.' James silently instructed himself to stop rambling. He turned to look at the collection of books.

'Not sure how long I'll stay here,' Livingstone finally said. 'You get a lot of nosy parkers in these types of places, don't you find?'

James was glad he had his back turned. Was that a comment aimed at him? 'I don't know about nosy,' he replied, staring at the books, 'I think it's simply that people like to take an interest. Not sure how people can be nosy about you when they hardly see you.'

'You'd be surprised at what gets fed back to me.'

The heart rate went back up. Stick to safe subjects. Don't get dragged into a topic that's difficult. He swung round and tilted his head at the books. 'I see you're interested in the Great War.'

The suspicious note he'd heard in Theodore's voice changed to one of enthusiasm. 'Oh yes. My father fought through the whole thing and came back with some stories and mementoes.'

Pleased to be on safe ground, James told him about the reunion they'd had at Harrington's over the previous Christmas. 'You ought to speak to some of our villagers, Mr Livingstone. Most of them have fathers or brothers who fought. We had a Pals regiment here, of course.'

Livingstone seemed genuinely interested.

The door swung open. Maximillian strode in with a face like thunder. 'They've given me notice on that bloody lease and I've had to ditch five of my stories. I'll…'

'MAX,' Theodore thundered. 'I've company. Get out and do something useful.'

Maximillian flinched and almost bowed. After the briefest of apologies, he was gone.

Well, well, well, James thought, there's someone who is not his own man. Notice on the lease, indeed. To his business? Five stories ditched. He hoped that these included the ones about the Cavendish residents who had decided to stick up for themselves. 'Do you need to sort something out with your son? I can always come back another time if you need to talk business.'

'Business! Pah.' He took hold of James' forearm and steered him to the next room. 'He's as good at running a business as he is running a marathon.' He spread an arm out. 'Here, look at this.'

James couldn't hide his surprise. The room had been transformed into a museum of artefacts and memorabilia from the Great War. There were three display cases, containing fragments of shrapnel, medals, diaries and letters. On the wall was a tatty, muddy Regimental flag and several photographs of various men in uniform.

He gazed at the cabinets and scrutinised the letters. 'You have quite a collection.'

'All family stuff. Things my father and his two brothers came back with. The photographs on the wall are all of family. That's my father, there. Joined the Yorkshire Regiment with three brothers and two cousins. One brother and one cousin fell at the Somme.'

'You should take yourself off to the museum on the south coast.' James described his visit there over Christmas. 'It's a wonderful collection and quite a few documents in the reference section.'

'I've been several times. They keep trying to get their hands on this lot but I won't part with it.'

'Would you not even loan it? I'm sure access to a prominent Member of Parliament's collection would go down well, not to mention the level of public interest there would be.'

The praise bolstered Theodore's ego. He ushered James back to the front room and offered him a cigar. James refused. They'd been here half an hour now and he was no nearer knowing why Theodore had sent for him.

He checked his watch. 'Mr Livingstone, I do have an engagement later. Is there a particular reason why you invited me here?'

'Mm? Oh, er… yes. I wanted to apologise for my behaviour when we met at Dulcie's. She was wrong not to let me know you were coming. You've got a status here in the village and I should have known. She put me at a disadvantage and I didn't appreciate it.'

It took everything James had to stop himself from launching into a scathing attack but he knew it would serve no purpose. He swirled the brandy in his glass, thinking of a delicate way to put things. Finally, he said: 'Mr Livingstone, it wasn't just me there. Lady Harrington and our friends were also present. Do you not think they deserve a personal apology?'

Theodore dismissed the comment. 'Pass my apologies on. I didn't have time to invite a whole load of people here. I'm a busy man. I'm not just organising village fêtes.'

The muscles in James' shoulders tensed. Struggling to remain calm, he said: 'Mr Livingstone. My role in the village is centuries old and I would be doing my ancestors a dis-service if I failed to carry on the village traditions. I make *my* living by running the estate and am equally busy. I make no profit from running village fêtes.'

'Yes, yes, of course. But being an MP can be a burden.'

'As can being a Lord. But you're not sitting in Parliament at the moment, are you? You're spending most of your time down here so, presumably, you're not too busy. Unless you have a business on the side.'

He received a dark look. 'What do you mean by that?'

'Simply that a number of MPs have businesses aside from working as an MP. I wondered if you were the same.'

'Has someone been saying something to you?'

James swallowed his drink. Blast. He was drifting into uncharted waters. 'Absolutely not. What could anyone possibly have said? I certainly didn't mean anything by the comment. I apologise if it's caused some offence.'

Although he'd declined it, Theodore came across and slipped a cigar into James' top pocket. 'You be careful when you listen to gossip. Don't do what some people do and stick your nose in where it's not wanted.'

A chill went through James. He took the cigar out of his pocket and returned it to Theodore. 'I take offence at your insinuation, Mr Livingstone. I have more important things to do with my time than listen to gossip. Thank you for the cigar but I find that brand leaves a bitter taste.'

He made his way out to the hall.

Theodore held the door open for him. 'Perhaps I should apologise. Again.' The sarcasm was not lost on James. 'I have an awful lot going on at the moment. I didn't mean to cause *you* offence.'

James put his sunglasses back on. He stood on the top step. 'The chances of our meeting socially are remote, Mr Livingstone, but, if we do, I suggest we remain civil. I have no animosity toward you except for the fact that you were completely disrespectful to my wife and to Mrs Merryweather. Where I come from, that is considered bad form. I only ask that if we do meet socially, you display better manners toward the womenfolk. Good day.'

Aware that he'd left Theodore without the last word and a face screwed up in annoyance, he jumped in the Austin and sped off.

CHAPTER TWENTY-FOUR

It ought to have taken less than five minutes to drive from Theodore's house back home but, again, James found himself going around the country lanes to arrive back some twenty minutes later. It had taken him all of that time to relax. Theodore Livingstone was a man who simply got his back up. The apology over his behaviour during that initial meeting was nothing but an afterthought and, by not inviting the four of them over, he'd just proved what an arrogant and conceited buffoon he was.

Aside from that were the hidden meanings behind some of the comments. The references to being nosy and interfering in business that had nothing to do with anyone else. That could only be a veiled threat. He'd felt so on edge during the whole episode, he couldn't help but think he'd been found out. Had that blasted Inspector Fulton followed him so closely that he knew everyone James had spoken to? Had that same Inspector threatened those people?

He pulled up by the garage. George parked alongside and jumped out.

'Blimey, James, you took the long way around, didn't you? I flashed my lights a couple of times and you totally ignored me.'

'Sorry, George. I took the long way home to bring my blood pressure down.'

Alan pulled up alongside as George demanded that he be told everything. 'Word for word.'

'Do you need me?' asked Alan.

James walked over to him. 'Having you around does calm my nerves considerably but, no, why don't you toddle off. Where will you be?'

'At the Half Moon.'

Donovan and Kate had rented out their back room. They were not aware of Alan Stubbs' background and thought he was a salesman. James said he would call if necessary.

In the hall, Beth dashed out to ask how it went. George suggested a brandy and Beth grabbed James' hand.

'Did something happen? He didn't threaten you, did he?'

James nudged them both into the lounge where George did the honours with the brandy. Once they had settled, he went through the visit while his friend made copious notes and, on more than one occasion, asked for clarification. At the end, James asked his friend for his thoughts.

George shut his notebook and reached for his glass. 'He was definitely sounding you out. There were a couple of veiled warnings there but that's all. Doesn't sound as if he trusts you very much but I'm pretty sure that he would have been more direct if he had something concrete to say.'

'I'm certain that the supposed apology for his behaviour was not his reason for asking me along. It seemed like an afterthought.'

George put his notebook away, swigged the rest of his brandy and got to his feet. 'He's wary of you James. You need to stay back. Don't ask any more questions.'

'I've no intention of so doing. We have plenty of things going on here for my attention. This will take a back seat.'

'Good,' Beth said. 'Let George take the information and you stay out of it.' She turned to George. 'Have you got any further with your investigation?'

They received a frustrated groan. 'We're getting a lot of information on Maximillian. Now people have started to come forward, we're building a good case against him. One of those people is a television celebrity who knows others who've had a visit from Max so I believe that his world will come tumbling down very soon.'

'I just don't understand how he found out about our villagers' indiscretions,' Beth said. 'I know his father doesn't think much of his son's business sense but he clearly researches his victims.'

'And whoever's passed this information on is just as bad as him in my book.'

'And,' James asked, 'you've heard nothing further about this drug smuggling that Theodore is allegedly involved in.'

'Not a dickey-bird. I made a few enquiries with those businesses that the window-cleaner chap mentioned but no one was saying anything. I'm either talking to the wrong people or they're too scared to say anything.'

'Are you talking to the senior management or the foot soldiers?'

'At the moment, I've made enquiries through the owners. I've to tread carefully, though, because I don't want our questioning being fed back to Theodore. I've researched those people who I feel I can trust. They've been genuinely appalled that their employees could be involved in drugs so they're keeping a lookout. I should go.'

They wished George luck as they showed him out. Returning to the lounge, James switched the television on. 'Come on, let's relax and watch something that doesn't require any thought.'

No sooner had they sat down when they heard the doorbell ring and a frantic tap-tap of the door knocker. He got up.

'Someone's in a hurry.'

At the front door, he couldn't help but look surprised. 'Ken!'

Ken Scott appeared distraught and the young man furtively glanced to his right. 'Flora, come on. They're in.'

Peering around the door, he saw Flora Armstrong wringing her hands, eyes red-rimmed. On seeing him, she shrank back.

He caught Ken's eye. 'What's the matter? What's happened?'

'Lord Harrington, we chatted, the other day, at the steam rally… it's just that we don't know who to talk to. You said…'

James swung the door open. 'Come in. Flora, come along. I don't know what's frightening you but I'm sure that if you share the burden, we may come up with a solution for you.' She remained rooted to the spot. Good grief, the girl was terrified. He softened. 'Flora, you have no need to be scared while you're here.'

Beth appeared beside him. She'd clearly overheard and did what she always did in these circumstances; put an arm around the girl and led her inside. 'Sweetheart, I'm sure that whatever's worrying you isn't as bad as you think.'

Flora burst into tears. Beth glanced sideways at him and pulled a concerned face. He closed the door and they all went through to the lounge. Ken stood uncomfortably at the entrance until James told him not to stand on ceremony. The lad took his shoes off and sheepishly entered the lounge, all the while looking in awe at the size of the room.

James poured a brandy for the two youngsters. Beth had already seated herself and Flora on the sofa. He invited Ken to sit down and picked out his favourite wing-backed chair for his own comfort. 'Now, Ken, Flora, what is it that brings you to our door?' He crossed his legs. 'Am I right in thinking this has something to do with Maximillian?'

A further cry of anguish came from Flora, who was now in floods of tears. Beth tended to her and shrugged at James. They weren't going to get much from her for a few minutes. He turned his attention to Ken.

'Ken, please do your best to tell us what you know.'

Ken took a sip of the brandy and coughed at its strength. Another slurp gave him the courage he needed. He cradled the glass in his hand and sat on the edge of his seat.

'Before me and Flora were seeing each other, she was seeing someone else.'

'You mentioned this in passing. Maximillian.'

'He was in the village looking at various properties for him and his dad to move to. It was about a year ago and he kept going into the post office to get the local newspapers.'

Flora sniffed. 'He was ever so nice when he came in.'

James shifted his attention to her. 'In what way, nice?' He had a pretty good idea but needed to hear it from her.

'Me and Mrs Bothy share the jobs. Someone's always got to man the telephone exchange and that's normally me but, if it's quiet, I help out at the counter. Max came in a few times to get information about the local estate agents and find out their telephone numbers.'

'I see,' said James, although if he was being honest, he didn't. A man like Maximillian didn't need to go into a post office to find these things out. He had people do that for him. 'And he befriended you?'

Another sniff and a blow of the nose. 'He was lovely, he really was. He said he'd never seen anyone so beautiful and asked me to dinner. Even came round to our house to make sure my father would agree. Promised to have me home by nine o'clock sharp.'

Beth huffed. 'That doesn't sound like the man we're familiar with. I guess he took advantage in some way.'

Flora closed her eyes in despair.

'Flora,' said James, 'a man like Maximillian latches on to women because he thinks they may be of use to him. I've a feeling that he did the same with you.'

Through the occasional sobs, he learned that Max had taken her out frequently over the course of a month. 'He took me to posh restaurants in the countryside and asked me all about myself and what I did.'

'And what was he really interested in?'

Ken's face was red. 'What d'you think, Lord Harrington? He was only after one thing.'

Flora tried to rise but Beth gently held her on the sofa. 'Flora. We've got this far. You came here for a reason and I suspect we haven't heard that reason just yet.'

The young woman stared at the floor. 'One weekend, he'd booked us into a hotel. He'd booked separate rooms. I told my parents I was staying with a friend. We went for a drink…'

Beth stared. 'And one thing led to another.'

A nod of the head.

James' heart went out to her. This slip of a girl, plain and naïve, was taken in by a bounder of the first degree.

The man had taken advantage and left her desolate. Flora blew her nose and composed herself.

'Ken's always been a good friend; we went to school together so he knew something was up. But I never told him any of this until a few days ago. He knew that Max had upset me but didn't realise the extent of things.' She gulped. 'I feel sick just thinking about it.'

Beth slid closer and cupped her hands. 'Were you pregnant?'

A hesitant laugh. 'No, you can't imagine how relieved I was. I went to Dr Jackson and he did some tests. I was off work for a week worrying about it. I said I had the flu. Just thinking about what my parents would say if I'd have fallen pregnant. And I'd lied to them.' She sniffed. 'They would have disowned me.'

James cradled his drink. So, Max had wined and dined this girl and put her in a compromising position. Once compromised, he had nothing more to do with her. It was pretty clear what was going on here. Her reaction to Max's name outside the Half Moon a few days ago wasn't that she didn't feel well or surprised by Ken's appearance. It was because she thought this affair might have come out in the open.

'Maximillian was blackmailing you, wasn't he?'

The tears fell again. Ken dashed across to sit at the other side of her and, between him and Beth, they managed to calm her down.

'But why?' said Beth. 'What could you possibly know that would interest Max Livingstone?'

A long silence ensued.

Finally, Ken knelt on the floor in front of her. 'Flora, tell them. Lord Harrington is a good friend of Inspector Lane. He can help sort this.'

James felt for his cigarettes. He didn't want to push her but he'd already fathomed it out. How else could Max have known about everyone?

He struck a match and lit the tip of his cigarette. A couple of minutes went by as she clung to Beth's hands; all the time her eyes darted here and there. He could see she was wrestling with her thoughts. Ken whispered in her ear. She sniffed, then met James' gaze.

'I don't drink normally, Lord Harrington, and when Max took me out, he always plied me with wine and I'd get a bit talkative, you know.' Her face took on an expression of horror. 'Oh, I don't mean anything by it but I got talking about my job. When I look back, well, that's all he really asked me about.'

'Your work at the telephone exchange.'

He saw that Beth had cottoned on. She turned Flora to face her. 'He wanted to know the gossip?'

Flora gave a curt nod and slouched in the chair. 'He made it sound like a joke, you know, kept asking questions like 'I've bet you've heard some juicy titbits in your time', that sort of thing. Well, I have but, like any good telephonist, I keep them to myself. But then after…, you know, after we'd spent the night together, he wanted more.'

The smoke from his cigarette swirled up to the ceiling. 'Did he ask you about specific people?'

'How did you know?'

Ken got back on the chair. 'What a b–, sorry, but how can someone stoop that low?'

'Unfortunately, both the Livingstone men are beneath contempt and it's upsetting that you were taken in, Flora. But taken in you were. My guess is that Maximillian had heard that a couple of our residents were related to people who were well known in their field, so any gossip would be ripe for his magazine.'

Beth inquired who Max had asked about.

'Mrs Withers who runs the sweet shop and newsagents, Rose and Lilac Crumb and Mr Sharpe.' On mentioning Sharpe's name, she burst into tears. 'He's such a dear man.'

'And the information you gave him ensured that he didn't spread rumours about you.'

Through the sniffs, James learned that since joining the exchange, Flora had listened in on a number of telephone calls but swore that she never told anyone about it. 'I just liked listening to what people were up to. I didn't mean anything by it.'

A part of James was livid. How dare this girl listen in on private calls? But then, he presumed, there were girls all over the country in these exchanges doing exactly the same thing. And, he was sure, some of them were happy to spread gossip, especially in the larger exchanges. The one at Cavendish was tiny with just Flora and her colleague employed to staff it. Max had picked on the one most easy to manipulate.

James stubbed his cigarette out. 'Flora, did you listen in to any calls to or from Valentine Plumb?'

She bit her lip and thought for a while. 'No. I don't remember any.'

A sense of relief went through James. Hopefully, the man had nothing to do with what had happened. 'What about Faith Simms?'

She thought for a while. 'I think there was a Miss Simms that put a call through to Mr Livingstone.'

'Max or Theodore?'

'Oh, Theodore.' She shot a look at him. 'She was the one found in Mr Plumb's garden.'

'I'm afraid so, yes.'

She flung herself at Ken. 'I'll go to prison. My parents'll find out. They'll disown me.'

Beth's pleading eyes sought him out. He frowned. What did she want him to do? He couldn't promise her that she wouldn't go to jail. He didn't know the protocol. She hadn't done this willingly; she was being blackmailed. She'd volunteered that information. But then, Max had plied her with drink. Perhaps that would be her defence. He hoped this didn't end in a prison sentence. The girl wouldn't last two minutes.

'Flora,' he said, 'I'm going to contact Detective Chief Inspector Lane and ask him to speak with you.' He repeatedly promised that his friend would be sympathetic and take everything into account, including the fact that she had been plied with drink. 'Ultimately, Flora, George wants to catch criminals. You are not a criminal, simply someone who was in the wrong place at the wrong time. I can't pretend that he won't press charges but George is someone who will see your side of things. You may simply end up with a telling-off.'

Beth lifted Flora's chin. 'Why don't we pop upstairs to the bathroom and get you freshened up?'

Flora turned to Ken. 'Will you sit with me when I have to speak to him?'

'Yeah, course I will.'

Beth led her out.

Ken shook his head. 'I can't believe someone would treat a woman like that. He's supposed to be well off, isn't he?'

James reflected on the lad's innocent view on life. If only life were that simple. 'Ken, you will realise that money doesn't necessarily make you a good person. From my experience, it is a person's upbringing that makes them who they are. We are mostly all taught the difference between right and wrong, what constitutes good and bad, how to treat and respect one another. Regrettably, there are some who fall by the wayside. People like Theodore and Max Livingstone are interested only in themselves and what they can gain. They are egotistical, greedy and downright rude. They ingratiate themselves with powerful people. They seek the same power and will do anything they can to exert that power.'

The young man stared at his hands. 'What can I do?'

As they got up, James asked how old Ken was.

'Seventeen.'

He slipped an arm over the young man's shoulders. 'As Flora's sweetheart, you'll need to be there for her whenever she needs you. Don't follow her around like a lost puppy.' He reached for his wallet and took out two pound notes. 'Take her to Elsie's for some tea and tell her you're there for her. Tell her you'll stick by her. Make her realise that whatever happens, you'll support her, even if it's simply as a friend.'

Ken accepted the money and thanked James.

'And now I believe I need to put that call into George. Let's get this sorted out once and for all.'

Lying in bed that evening, James sipped his hot milk. 'The mystery of how Max came to know about our residents has been cleared up. At least, now, one Livingstone will be off the streets for a bit.'

'Did I hear George say they have a search warrant?'

'For the *Guess What?* offices.'

'Why can't they extend it to their houses?'

'He was apparently told he was lucky to get the warrant he had. He did ask to search the houses but the

257

powers that be were reluctant, especially with the evidence they already have on Maximillian. Apparently, they think they have enough to convict. Searching properties owned by Theodore would soon get back to the Commissioner at Scotland Yard and he'd be asking questions.'

She snuggled into him. 'Shall we spend some time at the steam rally tomorrow and forget about this business? Bert said that he and Gladys were going.'

'I think that's a splendid idea. The weather's good. We'll treat ourselves to a meal out somewhere too.'

Turning the light out, he stared at the ceiling. With the statements and testimony of the residents and Flora's confirmation of what she had been asked to do, he was more than satisfied that Theodore wouldn't be able to get his son released, even with the contacts he had. He also wondered, with the Livingstone reputation being tainted and no doubt dragged through the mud by the press, if Theodore would start losing some of his high-profile friends.

The press would have a field day with Max and George was sure that, once his behaviour was out in the open, more people would come forward with stories of blackmail.

But how would this affect Theodore Livingstone?

CHAPTER TWENTY-FIVE

A few days had passed and there was no news from George. In a way, James was relieved. He'd never felt so anxious and he was pleased to be feeling more relaxed, especially as he'd not seen hide or hair of the Livingstones.

It was early Saturday afternoon, the last day of the steam rally, and they couldn't have asked for a better day. From the moment the gates opened they were blessed with wall to wall sunshine, clear blue skies, a gentle breeze and the promise of more of the same.

Crowds had flocked into the far field of Harrington's and the place was buzzing with activity. The steam fairground had queues of children waiting for their turn on the rides; every traction engine had its engines pounding; steam puffed out of the chimneys and whistles shrilled.

Mixing in with the smell of steam and oil were the various refreshments being sold: candy floss, hot dogs, hamburgers, along with Graham Porter's traditional hog roast. James and Beth caught up with him.

'Ah James,' the butcher said, 'you like crisp and salty crackling, don't you?'

'I certainly do.'

Graham carved off thin slices of the succulent pork and placed them in a soft roll. Beside him, his wife Sarah spooned over a good helping of apple sauce with a warning that it was piping hot. 'Be careful when you eat it. This apple will ooze out of the sides.' She reached across for a piece of crackling. 'And mind your teeth on that.'

Beth asked for the same order but without the crackling. 'I'm pretty sure my teeth aren't as tough as James'. How's it all going?'

'Wonderful,' she replied. 'Everyone's in good spirits and we've such perfect weather. Our two children are with Tommy and Susan riding on the footplates. They couldn't stop talking about it last night.'

'It is quite a spectacle, isn't it?' said James. 'And the colours are so vibrant.'

They paused for a moment to take in the scene. They were on a slight incline so could see the rally a little better and what a vista it was: the traction engines had been lovingly polished and wherever the sun shone, the paintwork glinted and gleamed.

Pink candy floss stood like cushions on wooden sticks, women wore colourful summer dresses, men were dressed in light linen trousers or shorts. Laughter drifted on the breeze and the call for customers at the hoopla stall carried along with it.

Luke Merryweather raced up to them. 'Uncle James, Auntie Beth, Mum and Dad are by the WI tent and said would you like to join them?'

Mark tripped up behind him then added: 'Mr Briggs and Miss Smith are there, too. She's got a really bright green dress on.'

James and Beth said cheerio to the Porters and chatted with the boys en route although they hardly needed open their mouths.

'We've been on Big Bessie,' said Mark.

Luke pointed in the distance. 'It's that one over there with the vase of yellow daffodils on it. It's the biggest traction engine ever.'

'And the man that owns it has shire-horses.'

'They're enormous. I've seen shire-horses before. They're gigantic.'

'He parks them at his farm.'

'He doesn't park them, silly, he keeps them in stables.'

'Well, anyway, he keeps them there and lets people ride them.'

'And that engine over there is called Tim and we asked why.'

'Yes, and the man said because it's one of the smallest. Its full name is Tiny Tim. The man that owns it said it was made out of bits of broken up engines. When he drives it around the fields, he says you can't always notice the difference except when you put it right next to a proper one.'

'He said it was his little gem hidden in plain sight.'

James ruffled the boys' hair in turn. 'And I'm sure he's right. Are you coming with us or just escorting us to the tent?'

'Just escorting you,' said Luke. 'Can you find your own way now?'

Beth smoothed his hair down. 'I think so, yes. Where are you two heading for?'

'Mr Bateson is going to show us the motorbikes and he's going to let us sit on some.'

'Be good,' Beth said, 'and don't forget that Uncle James is showing his car off in a little while.'

The boys raced off with the promise that they wouldn't forget. Beth slipped her hand into James'. 'What a shame that Harry and Oliver are not here to see this.'

Their twins were currently in the middle of their National Service and, now that their training was over, were beginning to enjoy themselves. They were stationed in Kent, had visited home quite often and were now waiting to be mobilised. Oliver, the budding teacher, was learning French and Harry was getting to grips with James' service profession of being a mechanic.

Before they reached the WI tent, James spotted Dulcie Faye chatting with Helen Jackson and her daughter, Natasha. They made a detour to go and speak with her. Although they hadn't actually seen George, they'd received word that he had taken down a full statement from Flora Armstrong. Ken supported Flora through the whole affair and had insisted that he remain with her. In the meantime, Mr Bateson had offered to help with any legal advice should it be required in the coming weeks.

Dulcie had squatted down and was chatting to Natasha about her pretty dress and the beautiful flowers in her hair. But Natasha was an incredibly quiet girl and always shy with new people. James watched as the small girl gazed at the glamorous film star while standing a little behind her mother. Helen coaxed her forward.

'Natasha, when someone says nice things about you, you should say thank you.'

She whispered a thank you and leaned closer to Helen, who had now seen them approach. 'Oh James, Beth, I keep seeing you here and there and never get a chance to say hello. What a lovely rally this is, so colourful and traditional.'

Beth agreed as she smiled at Helen's daughter. 'And I see you've met a real-life film star.'

Natasha gazed at Dulcie then whispered, 'I like her dress.'

'Thank you, Natasha,' Dulcie answered. 'That means so much to hear you say that. And I have a secret to tell you. Would you like to hear it?'

Natasha's big brown eyes stared in anticipation.

'I think you're the prettiest little girl here.'

She snuggled into Helen's skirt. Helen picked her up and groaned. 'You're getting too old to lift.' Natasha whispered in her ear. 'Yes,' her mother nodded, 'that's your father messing up a perfectly good shirt.'

James turned to see Phillip and Mr Bateson working on a motorbike engine. Luke and Mark were looking on and helping where they could. All four of them had oil and grease on their hands.

'We'd best go and see what he's up to, hadn't we, Natasha?' Helen rested a hand on Dulcie's arm. 'So lovely to meet you. Don't be a stranger, it'll be good to see you at some of our events.' She apologised to James and Beth for not stopping longer. 'We must meet and have tea at Elsie's one day.' She gave them both a subtle, perturbing nod toward Dulcie.

Her concern did not go unnoticed by either of them.

Dulcie teased her hair as she watched them disappear into the crowds. 'What a lovely lady. She's married to the doctor, is that right?'

'That's right,' said James, 'the one with the curly dark hair that has women queuing at the surgery with non-existent ailments.'

She laughed but it was almost forced. It wasn't until she faced them directly that Beth gasped.

'Dulcie,' she said, 'what happened to your face?'

Dulcie acted surprised, as if she'd forgotten about it. 'Oh this? I walked into the cupboard door in the kitchen. I forgot it was open and, bang, there it was. It looks worse than it is. It's beginning to fade now.'

As Beth sympathised with her James thought back to his time in that kitchen when he'd helped Tony Young with the tea. There were no kitchen cabinets at eye-level. They were all waist-height. An awful thought struck him but he erred on the side of caution with his enquiry.

'Is Theodore not coming today?'

She was upset, there was no doubt about it. As she composed herself, she said that he was busy. 'I think a few business things have come up. He was terribly annoyed last night but wouldn't say why. When I said that this was the last day of the rally, that he should come along because it would make a change to the dreary business lunches, well, h…' Her eyes fixed on James. 'He said he had too much on.'

James didn't know whether to pursue this or not but decided he would. 'Did Theodore strike you?'

The frankness silenced her for a moment but then she brought out a hanky. 'Yes, yes he did.'

Beth steered her to one side, away from the crowds. 'Dulcie, you don't have to put up with that. You're not married to the man, he has no hold over you, does he?'

'Yes and no,' said Dulcie blowing her nose. 'He has friends in high places and he managed to get me the two roles that you know me for.'

'In return for?' asked James.

'Simply that I be his escort at certain functions. If he asked me to attend, no matter what arrangements I have, I'm to be there.'

'But you've made a name for yourself now,' Beth said, 'you have no need to stay with such a bully.'

Her expression was helpless. 'You don't know Theodore. He got me the agent and he has friends high up in the industry. If I didn't toe the line, he said he only had to make a couple of phone calls and the film roles would dry up.'

James suggested she changed her agent. 'You've made a name for yourself, Dulcie. You could do what you want.' He lowered his voice. 'If you're worried about anything Maximillian may print in that magazine of his, there's no need anymore.'

A glimmer of a relief crossed her face. 'I know. The police raided his offices and took away a lot of things. Theodore was furious.'

'If that is not a worry for you, you have no need to stay with that man. The fact that he has to bully you proves that he needs control and that,' he said, pointing at the bruising on her cheek, 'proves that he's losing control. What exactly did you say to him to warrant this? Something must have happened?'

'I didn't say anything really. I think he lashed out. He started getting moody after your visit, Lord Harrington. He was fine before that because he came to the cottage and had tea with me. When you'd gone, he came hammering on my door and asked if I'd said anything to you about his business affairs. Well, of course, I said no. And that's the truth. He never speaks about his business to me and when we're at those dreary dinners, I tend to latch on to a friendly wife who puts up with these things like I have to. Never mind what I said. What did you say?'

Beth reminded him they were supposed to be meeting up with Stephen and Anne. James asked Dulcie to walk with them.

'Miss Faye, how committed are you in your relationship with Theodore Livingstone? Would you prefer that he was not in your life?'

They threaded a path across the green. 'More than anything. But he's a powerful man and if he wants to destroy you he will. I've seen him do that, Lord Harrington, and he told me once, months ago, that he could put me back where I came from, a shop girl in the Co-operative. Not that that was a bad thing. Sometimes I wish I had a more normal life. I'm not even sure that I like being a film star. It seemed quite glamorous to begin with, but it's not, not at all.'

Outside the WI tent James asked one more thing. 'Do you know anything about that notebook he carries with him?'

'Only that he's completely obsessed with it. I asked him what was so important about it. He's always feeling his inside pocket to make sure it's there. He even has a fastening on all of his suits so there's no danger of it falling out.'

'Does he have a safe at home?'

'I think he has one in Kensington, but not here. Why?'

'What does he do with it when he's here in Cavendish, lock it in a drawer?'

She shrugged. 'I've no idea. What's so interesting about it? And how do you know about it?'

'I'd rather not say and you're not to mention this to Theodore. The less you know the better. If you do mention it, I couldn't guarantee that he wouldn't become violent again. Are you sure you're all right living at the cottage?'

'Oh yes. Dealing with his temper is something I've had to adjust to.'

Beth frowned. 'Has he hit you before?'

'No. I thought he might do. Once, when we first met and… thinking about it… it's when he had convinced me to accompany him to a number of functions.' Her gaze was intense as she turned to James. 'I would like rid of him, Lord Harrington.'

'Sit tight. Act normal and don't give him any reason to suspect that you have spoken to me about this. I'm concerned that if you do, the pair of us will end up black and blue.'

Dulcie gulped and promised she would say nothing. Charlie Hawkins and his two children, Tommy and Susan, joined them.

'What a grand day out this is.' He waved his camera. 'I've changed films once already and the kids are having a whale of a time.' He turned to Dulcie and gawped. 'Blimey, what happened to you?'

James, sensing Dulcie's embarrassment, said: 'Fell over and bashed her head on the cupboard.'

'Are you on your own?' he asked.

'Yes.'

He crooked his arm. 'Why don't me and kids show you around?'

She slipped a hand through and, for the first time since they'd bumped into her, she looked genuinely happy. 'I'd love to.'

Before the Harringtons had time to discuss their chat with Dulcie, Gladys Smith accosted them.

'I'm 'aving a smashing day, I really am. I see why Bert keeps coming to Cavendish. And those Coffee Delights that Elsie has are the bees' knees.' She led them to a table outside the tent. 'We're over 'ere in the shade.'

Stephen pulled a couple more wooden chairs over. 'The m-most marvellous day. Luke and Mark have a-already made their minds up about w-what they want for Christmas.'

'Already?' said James.

Anne groaned. 'It'll change before the month's out. But at the moment it's anything to do with traction engines. Does Meccano make a traction engine set?'

'I'm pretty certain they do,' said James.

'They definitely do,' added Beth. 'I've seen one in the window of Hamleys in Regent Street.'

'We'll have to make some enquiries about cost,' said Anne.

Bert pulled a face. 'Oi, 'ave you forgotten who's sitting 'ere listening to this? Don't go into Hamleys, they'll rip you off. They always add a few quid on because you get it in their store. I'll ask the blokes up at Petticoat Lane. They'll get their 'ands on 'em. How many d'you want? Two? One each?'

Stephen stopped him. 'Let's m-make sure that's exactly what they want before you start stockpiling. Last year, th-they changed their minds s-several times before settling on books and a b-board game.'

Elsie brought out a tray of cups and saucers with tea already poured. 'If you want scones, you'll need to get them at the WI. I'm doing my normal thing. I provide tea, they provide scones.' She leant in. 'But I do have a few Coffee Delights left.'

As the group had snacked during most of the day, no one had an appetite for anything except tea. James studied Gladys in her bright green dress. She had a glow about her. She was always a chirpy individual, much like Bert really. Not well off, living from day to day and just about making ends meet but the glint in her eye caught his attention. It wasn't lost on Beth either who had commented on the same expression on Bert's face.

Bert slipped his cap off and fidgeted. 'Yeah, well, I took Gladys out for pie and mash yesterday and...'

James felt Beth grip his hand.

'I asked 'er if she'd like to tie the knot, you know, get married and all that.'

Before anyone else had a chance to react Beth had sprung from her seat and enveloped them in a hug. James simply sat, astounded, before rising from his chair to do the same. He hugged Gladys and clasped Bert's hand warmly.

'I'm so pleased for you both. You're made for each other. I couldn't be happier for you.'

'And we don't want our reception at Harrington's. I know you'd offer but we're 'aving a proper knees-up at the East End mission.'

'The vicar that helps out at the mission is gonna marry us,' said Gladys, 'and my son and daughter-in-law are gonna cater for it.'

'It's gonna be a proper party and you're all invited to the whole thing.'

'W-When is it all h-happening?'

The pair explained that they had a meeting with the vicar at the end of the week and they were thinking about October. The month, although dreary, meant a great deal to the pair of them as both sets of parents had also married around that time.

'As they're not 'ere to celebrate it with us, we thought it'd be nice to honour 'em.'

'Oh Bert,' Beth said, 'I can't believe it. I'm so happy.'

James excused himself for five minutes and came back with a bottle of sparkling wine and six glasses. 'Donovan didn't have champagne so I've got the next best thing. Put your tea to one side.'

The cork popped, the wine fizzed and some rousing congratulations came from the group.

As they settled down, Beth and Anne discussed outfits with Gladys and offered their dress-making skills, while Stephen went through some hymns they could suggest to their vicar.

James suddenly noticed the time. 'I'm popping across to the arena. The classic cars are being judged.'

'Who j-judging them?' asked Stephen.

'A chap from the RAC. The Steam Guild invited him down to do the honours so I can find out a little more about the veteran car run. I'll only be ten minutes.'

'I-I'll come with you.'

Bert slipped out of his seat. 'Me too. I don't wanna get stuck with wimmin talking weddings.'

'Go on wiv' yer,' chuckled Gladys, her cheeks rosy with pride.

On the way to the arena, Bert thanked James for his advice. 'I'd barely go' me proposal out and she'd said yes, then started nagging me about why it'd taken so long.'

'She thinks the world of you, Bert. Did you settle this business about where to live?'

'Come to C-Cavendish,' said Stephen, 'you spend m-most of your time here anyway and you're very well l-liked you know.'

'Nah, vicar, village life ain't for me. I'd go mad. It weren't really much of a decision. I spend as much time up in Bethnal Green as I do 'ere and I'm spending less time in Brighton. I'm going back to my home patch in the East End. Moving in with Gladys.'

'Splendid.' James suddenly felt that all was right with the world. Two dear people had come together in their autumn years and fallen in love. It sent a tingle of joy through him. He'd often worried about Bert spending his old age alone and that concern had now gone. He'd nabbed himself a soul mate and a ready-made family. Although grown up, Gladys' son, David and his wife were always helping at the mission and very much part of East End life.

At the arena, the vintage cars were lined up and were already being judged. The man from the RAC had a tick-sheet to adhere to and this meant studying the whole vehicle; the general condition, the paintwork, the state of repair inside, and finally the engine and tyres. James was up against some stiff competition and he was particularly enthralled by a 1924 Bentley open-top tourer with heavy leather straps that secured the bonnet. How he'd love to have a drive of that. And further along, a Bugatti, similar to the one he drove at Monte Carlo during his rally days. He'd loved the speed and the rush of adrenalin and, although he'd only ever been placed once, the thrill of taking part far exceeded any disappointment.

The man from the RAC had three rosettes which he duly fixed to the windscreens of those coming in the first three. Unfortunately, James' Mercedes was not included but he wasn't surprised. Some of the vehicles here were in mint condition and he still needed some work doing to his own car.

He felt Stephen's pat on the back. 'Never mind, b-better luck next year. I'm going to t-track down Luke and Mark.'

Bert, meanwhile, caught James' eye and jerked his head away from the crowds.

'That bloke that did the window-cleaning up at the Wendover. He got hold of me last night, said he'd remembered something about that notebook.'

'Oh?'

'Two things. First, he remembered another one of the names inside. Said it came to him because he'd seen the same name on a shop front in London. Rossi's.'

James almost took a step back as he absorbed the information. Then, a sudden realisation. The London Mobile Library, Barden's Dairy, Rossi's Ice Cream. 'Theodore's using mobile businesses to move his drugs. Despicable, yet utterly ingenious. What's the other thing?'

'That notebook 'as a black cover, leather. It doesn't say notebook on it though. There's a symbol on it. I asked him to draw it for me.' He handed James a piece of paper.

James unfolded the paper. It showed a lion, side on, holding the flag of St George, overlaid with a white rose. The banner at the bottom simply said Yorkshire. He gripped it tightly. 'Good grief.'

Bert stared at him.

'A gem hidden in plain sight.'

'Eh?'

'Something Luke and Mark said. Hidden in plain sight. If you wanted to a hide a notebook that is valuable, where would you put it?'

'In a safe, mate?'

'Yes, that's what I thought but he doesn't.'

'Whatcha getting at?'

'What I'm getting at, Bert, is that I know where he keeps the notebook.'

Bert felt his pockets for his tin of tobacco. 'Well, in that case, I've got an idea. It's been going 'round my head for a while, especially when you told me about that sister of Theodore's. Are you able to get in touch with her?'

'Felicity?'

'That's the one.'
'Yes. What do you have in mind.'

CHAPTER TWENTY-SIX

The rally began winding down at about four o'clock. Vendors packed up their trailers, the fairground people unscrewed huge bolts and folded their machinery down to the size of a caravan. Traction engines either powered themselves out of the field or were put on to lorries for the longer journeys. As spectators gathered their things and made their way through the exit gates, many made a point of speaking to the organisers to tell them how wonderful the rally had been.

By five o'clock the majority of people had gone and it was left to a group of volunteers to trawl the field and pick up litter and hand in any lost property to the Steam Guild. Donovan and Kate transferred unused beer and spirits into their Morris Minor van; Graham and Sarah made up small bags of hog roast for organisers to take away with them; most of the women were packing up their stalls from the WI and, once clear, the men took down the tents and bundled them into a waiting lorry.

It had been a glorious and enjoyable day, but a tiring one. James was pleased that his contribution to arranging this was simply to loan the fields out and suggest a few stallholders. Leaving everything in the capable hands of the Guild members, he focussed on his own arrangements, the first of which was to return home and put a direct call through to George.

George's news was good about the conviction of Maximillian Livingstone. A handful of trustworthy constables had searched the premises of the *Guess What?* offices and come up with enough incriminating evidence of blackmail to put the man in jail. 'But,' he said, 'we still have nothing on Theodore. That man will continue to get away with the crimes he commits, James.'

'And you have no reason to search Theodore's houses. It's just that I think –'

'Not on your nelly. I've already had the powers that be on the telephone giving me some verbal about going after Maximillian. Even though I had good reason, these friends of Theodore are a pain in the proverbial. You know that one of the people who rang me was the Deputy Chancellor?'

'He really does have friends in high places, doesn't he?'

'What were you going to say?'

'I know where that notebook is.'

He heard a long groan down the line. 'Are you absolutely certain?'

'Pretty much so. It's on him during the day but I am satisfied about where it'll be at night, when he's asleep.'

'Fat lot of use that is to me. No James, I can't risk it. I'll have a chat with Superintendent Higgins. We'll have to see if we can come up with a plan.'

James closed his eyes and built up the courage for his next sentence. 'Bert had an idea. He's already set it in motion. Can you come over?'

He received another groan before hearing the dialling tone.

At seven o'clock, James and Beth were sitting in their lounge with George and Dulcie, the latter, James noticed, becoming more horrified by the second. She sat alongside Beth and, with every new snippet of information coming from George and James, she became quieter and more disbelieving. But, as the information was being shared, she said that some of the things she'd heard and seen were now slotting into place.

'I was so involved in my acting that I haven't really thought about it before, but now I look back.' She elaborated on the fact that Theodore never allowed her to speak to certain people; the fact that he'd cut her short if she strayed into territory that he didn't want discussed; the odd, secretive talks that he'd had with people like Paolo Rossi.

'I remember him parking up by some of these places you've talked about,' she said. 'That mobile library, the dairy people. Theodore would get out of his car and chat to these people and none of them were happy. I thought, at first, they were constituents but then a lot of them weren't from Kensington. And when he started annoying that ice-cream man, well, I felt sorry for him. He seems such a nice man.'

'That's what he does,' said George. 'It sounds like he has a nice little network going. The drugs come in and he makes sure its distributed around the mobile units.'

'How the hell does he get people to do it?' said James. 'He must be paying an awful lot of money.'

'Not necessarily. There's plenty of money in the drugs business and he might pay a percentage. Peanuts, knowing him. But I think they're committed to his bidding because of threats. If the McCalls are part of this, that would convince people to do their bidding.'

An uncomfortable silence descended. James couldn't even comprehend the notion. 'You know, Valentine Plumb asked me if I'd ever come across evil. I didn't think I had. But now…'

Dulcie put a hand to her chest. 'I can't believe I've been taken in by such an awful individual and all to keep my career going. A career that I'm honestly not sure that

I want.' She straightened and looked George square in the eye. 'Whatever your plan is, I want to help.'

'I'm not involving you, Miss Faye,' said George. 'I don't want Theodore to have any suspicion that you're helping us.' He dipped his head at the faded bruising on her face. 'There's one reason why. And there is someone who has far more reason to want him in prison and that's his daughter.'

The young actress frowned. 'I didn't know he had a daughter.'

James related the details of his meeting with her at The Skyline and how Faith Simms had come to her for help.

'Oh heavens, this is too awful for words. Are you saying that Theodore killed Faith Simms?'

'I'm saying he had a hand in it.'

George insisted that it would be unlikely that Theodore would have carried out the act. 'He always makes sure he's at a function being photographed.'

James could see her mentally count back the days and then realisation dawned. 'That was the evening we went to that awful première. It was short notice, the day you and Lady Harrington visited.' She turned to Beth. 'Am I going to prison?'

A look of horror crossed Beth's face. 'Absolutely not. Whatever for? You had no idea about any of this, did she George?'

'None at all. You've nothing to worry about but I will need a full statement from you which will take some time. I need you to go through every detail you can about your life since you met Theodore Livingstone. I need dates of when you were summoned to accompany him and anyone he met.'

277

Without hesitation, she consented, then asked what their plan was.

James sought permission from George to divulge his idea. 'Dulcie, this notebook that Theodore carries, I'm confident I know where he keeps it when it's not on his person. We know that Theodore wants control over his daughter and her business. He abhors any woman who is able to stand on her own two feet and has, on occasion, tried to take her business over. Felicity has contacted her father and brother on the pretence of needing help. She's told her father that she's finding it difficult running the business, that it's all too much for her. He, of course, is delighted to learn that she's not coping and probably rubbing his hands in glee at taking the business off her hands. They're going there tonight.'

'But how do you know that Theodore won't take the notebook?'

'Because Felicity has told him to come as a guest on a themed night. Tonight, the theme is Bohemian and all guests must wear velvet frock coats.'

She let out a nervous burst of laughter. 'Sorry, it's just that I overheard part of that. I heard Theodore bluster about a wide-brimmed hat and how absurd it all was.'

'But he went along with it?'

'He was getting ready as I came over here. A delivery van came from a costume place with the coats. But surely he'll be livid when she tells him the club isn't in trouble.'

Beth was almost gleeful. 'I've a feeling that Felicity Livingstone is more than capable of looking after her end of things.'

'And what's happening now?'

'I don't know,' said James.

George shook his head. 'You must know something!'

James said he didn't. He knew his friend had severe doubts but James was adamant that he hadn't a clue. Bert had been confident about whatever idea had come to him but wouldn't tell James what it was. He just hoped the plan worked. The police had run out of ideas. Now, Bert had said, it was time to push fate along a bit.

Bert watched as Theodore and Maximillian got into the Bentley to begin their journey to London. He was surprised to see them in such elaborate clothing but then overheard them complaining about Felicity's absurd theme nights. The last word Bert heard came from Theodore.

'She's just like her mother. I told her she didn't have the brains to run a club and now she's come running to me. I'm taking that club over and she can work for me or find something else.'

Bert ducked back in the bushes as the car glided by.

Behind him was Alan Stubbs, doorman of The Skyline. They laid low in the bushes for some time, watching and studying the lodge. It was still light and difficult to see if anyone remained on the property but they stayed still for twenty minutes. Satisfied that no one was on the premises, they hurried through the shadows and to the back door.

Without a word, Alan clipped the wires to the alarm, took out a number of keys and examined the lock. After a few seconds, he selected a key, inserted it and manoeuvred it until he heard a click. The pair of them grinned and gently nudged the door open.

The evening light meant they didn't need torches. They stood on a door mat while Bert got his bearings on where they should be looking. James had described the

279

house as he'd seen it and, if his instructions were right, the room they needed was next door.

Before taking a step, they slipped their shoes off and kept their gloves on.

Bert led the way through to the room where Theodore kept the family's Great War memorabilia. It was a windowless room and he closed the door behind them before dragging a long draught excluder across to hide the light when he switched it on.

He'd provided Alan with a copy of the symbol they were looking for and, on checking the second display unit, they grinned triumphantly. Alan squatted down to check for any alarm systems but it appeared to be simply locked. He checked his set of keys and, with a determined nod, slotted one into the key-hole.

The first key didn't fit properly. The second was too loose. Bert could hear his partner in crime breathing heavily as he scrutinised the lock and keys again. Satisfied he'd picked the right one, he tried again. A slight click prompted a smile. Slowly, Alan lifted the glass lid. Bert slipped a hand in and brought out the black book. He flicked through it and gave a thumbs up: it contained a clear list of individuals, names, dates, figures and, in the back, pick up and drop off locations and the names of various boats and cargo ships docking in and around London. He put the item in his inside pocket while Alan fastened the display case.

The light was switched off. Draught excluder slid aside. At the back door, they slipped their shoes on. Alan locked the door and tried the handle. Satisfied with a job well done, they scampered back through the shadows to Alan's car, two hundred yards down the road.

Twenty minutes later, they were in James' front room, drinking well-earned whiskies and soda.

'Blimey,' said Bert, 'this bloke 'ere is a dream to work with.'

James shifted uncomfortably. He wasn't sure that he wanted his friend to expand on their exploits. He always thought the best of Bert but he knew the man skirted close to the law and, on this occasion, it was clear he had broken it as, at this very moment, James held the notebook in a handkerchief in his hand.

To say he was excited was an understatement. This is what they had been waiting for. Evidence. Evidence that would put away a murderer, a drug baron, a patronising bully who'd had his way for too long.

Beth brought him to his senses. 'George said he'll be back later. I honestly don't think you two should be here when he returns.'

Alan swigged his drink down and took the notebook back from James. He turned to Bert. 'Come on, mate, I'll drop you off in the city. Where d'you need to be?'

'Bethnal Green.' He turned to Beth. 'Dulcie's not going back 'ome, is she?'

Beth went through the plan that George had implemented. 'He's already driving her to her parents. She left Theodore a note to say that her mother was ill and that her father had come to collect her. She'll be staying there until this is all over.'

'Good. I'd hate to think she'd be on the end of that bloke's temper when 'e finds that book missing.'

James didn't even want to think about it. If Theodore were to have any idea that Dulcie was mixed up in this plan, he feared that not only would her career be cut short but her life too. He hoped Felicity was as strong as Beth seemed to think she was. She was playing a dangerous game teasing her father with false information about the club's finances. Alan was going straight to the club to deliver Theodore's notebook to Felicity.

An hour later and George was on the doorstep. A look of complete astonishment on his face. 'I've had a message patched through to me. Felicity Livingstone says she's got hold of her father's notebook.' He scrutinised James. 'I suppose you're not going to tell me how she obtained it?'

'I have absolute no idea.'

His friend's visible annoyance was not lost on James.

'George, you know as well as I do if word got out about who obtained it, they'd be dead within a week. All I can tell you is that the people who got hold of this have a grudge against the Livingstones and I'm not about to divulge anything because, quite honestly, I am in the dark about it myself.'

His friend muttered and bemoaned the fact that it all seemed very dodgy. 'But wasn't this Bert's idea?'

James hoped he could pull off a blatant lie. 'George, I'm offended that you think Bert would risk his life taking this notebook. It was he who kept telling me to stop listening to you and Superintendent Higgins.'

'And,' added Beth, 'when James asked for his help, he was very clear that he would not get involved in anything to do with Theodore.'

'That's right,' added James, 'he said he didn't want to end up with concrete boots, or something like that.'

To his surprise, George seemed satisfied by the explanation and mumbled: 'Perhaps I'm doing Bert a disservice. He wouldn't be that stupid. I hope the next bit of the plan'll work. We've pulled in some of our best people for this and it all relies on Felicity Livingstone playing a convincing part.'

'Will you get everything organised in time?'

'We're having a meeting tomorrow. Half a dozen people, all in the dark about what their mission is and most have been drafted in from the Hampshire constabulary.'

'A wise move,' said James. It would be unlikely that Livingstone would have any of them in his pay.

Beth breathed a huge sigh. 'We're supposed to be attending Stephen's Pentecost service tomorrow. Do you think he'll forgive us if we don't attend?'

George picked up his hat and said he wouldn't be going. 'I've to ensure this operation goes as well as possible and I've to sit down with Felicity and brief her. It'd be helpful if you were there. I know you'll want to be there so it's no use me ordering you to stay away. You may have some suggestions and you'll be a support to her, I'm sure. We're going through the logistics of it tomorrow and, on Monday, we'll get the equipment and surveillance organised and put in place ready for Tuesday morning. We've got one shot at this so it has to be right.'

Beth held James' forearm. 'I'll make sure he behaves.'

He thanked them for their help. 'To be able to chat to someone I can trust about this has been a great help. And, as usual, you've been able to glean more information for us.' And, with that, George went on his way.

James lifted the two crystal whisky glasses that he'd received on his commendation out of their silk-lined box. 'We never did give ourselves a pat on the back. Are you ready for another whisky and soda?'

Beth turned the wireless on. Frank Sinatra was singing 'Come Fly with Me'. She accepted the drink and rested her head back on the sofa. 'This reminds me of The Skyline and flying off to exotic climes.' She turned to him. 'Didn't you feel as if you were in Hawaii or the Caribbean when you were there?'

He sat down beside her. 'Yes, I did. Felicity's done a good job with the décor; created a unique atmosphere.'

'We'll have to make the effort to go when this is all over, especially as we're members now.'

'Absolutely.' They clinked glasses and James hoped that the club would still be operating after Tuesday's police operation. If Theodore had any say in the matter, he'd get someone to burn it down.

CHAPTER TWENTY-SEVEN

James and Beth, dressed in their Sunday best, arrived at the church later than planned. Stephen, who had already reached the second hymn, gave them a concerned look as they tiptoed down the aisle to take their seats. James smiled encouragingly at him, to indicate that all was well. He'd felt bad about missing the whole service and, while George and his team were having a break, he and Beth had nipped back to catch the last of the service.

Reassured, Stephen nodded and returned to doing what he did best, which was to lead his congregation as they sang with great gusto. Dressed in robes embroidered with orange flames, he conducted his parishioners with an invisible baton and, having learned the hymns off by heart, he could put all his efforts into raising the energy in the church.

At the end of the hymn, Anne, who was seated the other side of the aisle, gave them both a wave.

As was his custom, Stephen did not go on to the pulpit, preferring instead to wander up and down the aisles and engage with his congregation. Before any sermon, he made a point of chatting with everyone and shared a witticism here and there. How unlike the previous incumbent this man was. After a few minutes, he clapped his hands.

'Pentecost,' he said. 'The d-day we remember the descent of the Holy Spirit upon the apostles. A day of feast and celebration. We associate this day with symbols of flames, wind and doves.' He asked the congregation to look around. 'The ch-children have done a wonderful job of decorating our ch-church with these images.'

James scanned the church. Sure enough, on the walls were colourful paintings of fires and trees blowing in the wind. Hanging from some of the rafters were home-made doves, many of which he knew had been made by Luke and Mark.

Stephen continued but James found himself drifting into his thoughts. They were due to return to Lewes police station after the service where they would continue to go through the plans for Tuesday morning. Such was his loathing of Theodore and Maximillian Livingstone and his desire to see justice done, he used this time in the church to send up his own prayers.

Prayers for Jacqueline and Faith Simms who had been drawn into a web of deceit through no fault of their own. Prayers for Mrs Livingstone, a woman who had presumably loved her husband, only to be unloved and abused in return. His thoughts went out to those who, at this moment, were threatened in order to serve a purpose, be it drugs or money. He asked that Felicity be given the strength she needed to go through with the plan they'd proposed and he couldn't help but admire her forthright attitude over what had been suggested. There wasn't a moment's hesitation from her. She'd agreed before George had finished the question. He prayed that those involved in Tuesday's operation would be kept safe and that they would be able to gather the evidence they needed.

He felt Beth pull him up. The members of the congregation were on their feet. Bob Tanner began the rousing rendition of Pentecostal Fire is Falling. She leant into him.

'You've been in a dream since you sat here. Are you all right, sweetie?'

286

He picked up his song-sheet. 'Just sending up a few prayers of my own, darling.'

He put an arm around her waist. The hymn, again, sent goose bumps down his arms and he felt a rush of pride at being part of this wonderful community.

At the end, Beth whispered. 'I have no doubt that George will have every contingency covered.'

The service ended with a succinct prayer before Stephen reminded everyone that the church hall was now open. 'A f-few sandwiches and sausage rolls c-courtesy of the Women's Institute. Not exactly a f-feast but certainly a snack to continue our P-Pentecost celebrations.'

The villagers filed out and made their way next door. Stephen and Anne hurried over to James and Beth.

'A-are you well? We w-were quite worried when you didn't arrive on time.'

Anne added her own concerns. 'That Theodore Livingstone seems close to a heart attack. I saw him in the village earlier and asked if he would be coming to the service.' Her hand went to her chest. 'I've never seen anyone look like he did. I thought he was going to explode.'

'She d-didn't wait for an answer. Came l-looking for me. Do you know why he's so upset?'

James said that he did and left it at that. 'Stephen. Anne. I'm normally happy to share information with you but the Livingstone men are not to be given any leeway. The more ignorant everyone is, the better.'

Beth agreed. 'Once this is all over, we'll get together and spill the beans.'

They couldn't help but chuckle at Anne's excited expression. 'You mean the police have everything?'

'They do,' said James. 'We'll see you at the Whitsun dance tomorrow night, if not before. But, I'm booking a table at Harrington's Tuesday evening. Would you like to come?' He gave Anne a knowing look. 'George will be joining us.'

'Are you th-that confident?'

Earlier that morning, James would have said no; but sitting here, in the church, sending up prayers and thoughts for Felicity's well-being and strength, he had changed his mind. If anyone could bring Theodore Livingstone down, it would be Felicity and he had every confidence in her. He regarded them all before saying: 'Yes. Yes, I am that confident.'

'Are you coming through for some sandwiches?' asked Anne.

James declined. 'We have somewhere we need to be. We'll see you tomorrow at the Whitsun dance.'

As they turned to go, Stephen pulled him back. 'I-I shall send my own prayers, James. I think th-this particular case needs every bit of help it can get.'

James thanked him and caught up with Beth. It would be a long afternoon of checking and double-checking, looking for loopholes and taking the utmost care. But it would be worth it.

In a couple of days, he hoped to see Theodore Livingstone led away in handcuffs.

CHAPTER TWENTY-EIGHT

The next day, James again found himself relieved to be caught up in normal village life. The mysteries he'd helped solve in the past had been fascinating and enticed him to dig deeper. He loved putting the pieces of the jigsaw together and observing human nature. His interest in why people committed crimes pulled at him like a magnet. A puzzle to solve was something he loved.

But this time, there was no puzzle to solve. The criminal and his activities were obvious. Both Theodore and Maximillian had spent years surrounding themselves with the 'right' people who would resist hearing any suggestion of any wrongdoing by either of them. But the battle of how to break down that barrier had been a frightening and anxious one. Knowing how ruthless Theodore was, and knowing the contacts he had on both sides of the law, James knew he had trodden on thin ice. He'd simply been asked to observe and he'd gone way beyond what had been requested of him. God willing, this wouldn't come back and bite him.

Beth brought him out of his musings. She was dressed in her sky-blue and turquoise Whitsun dance costume and was fixing a turquoise tissue flower in her hair. With new additions to the group, over fifty women were on the cobbles outside the Half Moon and had managed to find different colours for each costume. Even those that had chosen reds and blues were in different shades of those colours. There was blood red, orange red, burnt red, navy blue, midnight blue, royal blue. All in all, extremely colourful.

Kate brought out a ship's bell and clanged it. The crowd hushed.

Mr Bateson, dressed in tails and a top hat, held a glass in his hand. 'In memory of the Cavendish Morris men who served our country during the Great War and in celebration of those women who danced in their place on Whit Monday. We salute you for carrying on the tradition and raise our glasses to you. To the Cavendish ladies.'

The villagers shouted out: 'The Cavendish ladies.'

The ladies shuffled into several lines, the bells on their ankles ringing. They held their garlands above them. Bob Tanner and Taverners counted themselves in and launched into a traditional tune called 'Off She Goes'.

And off the ladies went. The bells jangled as they skipped delicately along the cobbles. Unlike the leaping and bounding of the Morris men, the ladies were far more refined and trod a gentle step up and down the lines, weaving in and out and back and forth.

Three tunes were played, and three dances danced. It was a simple tradition that had stayed like this since the Great War. The only change was in the number of women taking part.

As the final notes rang out from the accordion and fiddle, the ladies took a bow and each accepted a complimentary glass of lemonade from Donovan and Kate.

Beth and Anne, flushed from their exertions, made their way to James and Stephen.

James pecked Beth on the cheek. 'As usual, the Cavendish ladies did the tradition proud.'

'I-I hope that the soldiers who left us d-during the Great War are l-looking down and smiling.'

'I'm sure they are,' said Beth.

Anne gulped her lemonade down. 'I'm glad we don't do this in the middle of the summer. I'd melt.'

Stephen checked they were on their own. 'Tomorrow's the d-day?'

James pulled a face to indicate that he wasn't looking forward to it. 'I'm anxious just thinking about it.'

'Is there anything we can do to help?' said Anne.

'I'm afraid there's nothing. Since we hatched this plan, my mind has been on nothing else.'

Out of politeness and obligation, James and Beth remained at the Whitsun dance for a couple more hours. They both put on a good show and to those who chatted and laughed with them, they would have seemed no different to normal. Every now and again, James slipped out of worry mode and forgot about the following day's operation; then, without warning, it crashed back into his mind and he could almost feel the blood draining from him.

What if Theodore knew James had played a part in his downfall? What if the plan went wrong? What if Felicity got cold feet and decided she couldn't go through with it?

Beth sensed his mood. 'Sweetie, it's half past nine. Why don't we make a move and have a nightcap?'

Happy to be on their way, he checked his rear-view mirror and flinched. 'We're being followed.'

Beth twisted round. 'It's Alan Stubbs.'

'What!' He let out a relieved laugh. 'Are you sure?'

'I saw him get into his car as we pulled away.'

His heart rate slowed as quickly as it had sped up. He couldn't remember the last time he'd felt so on edge. Once again, he found himself sending up a silent prayer that everything would go to plan.

CHAPTER TWENTY-NINE

A recently-closed florist on Brighton seafront served as the rendezvous for DCI Lane and his team. It was nine in the morning, the blinds were closed but, inside, the place had been a hive of activity since seven. Some, James learned later, had been in since the previous evening.

Among the six people who were there was DCI George Lane who was supervising the various jobs and positions for the men and women who'd arrived with him.

Their cars had been parked further along the front or up the side roads. Upstairs in the flat above were Beth and Felicity.

James watched as George's hand-picked team checked everything over. The large hatch between the service area and the back room had been replaced by a two-way mirror. Tables and chairs were rearranged, hidden wires led from the counter to the back room and a chat was taking place about one particular thing causing concern.

One constable scratched his head. 'This microphone's too big, it's difficult to know where to put it.'

'I think I may be able to help,' said James, seeking George's permission. 'Anyway, I feel useless standing here watching everyone work.'

Two men had set up a reel-to-reel tape recorder in the back room. George jutted his chin at them. 'You're good with electrics and mechanics, James. Go and help them. We need to get a microphone close enough to this table to record what's going on. It's got to be quiet and that microphone needs to be less obtrusive.'

'Right you are.' He dashed through to the back with a number of ideas already in his head. His years as a mechanic in the Royal Air Force had served him well in respect of engineering and electrics. The tape recorder was the size of a small suitcase. The first thing he requested was that they switch the thing on. They did so. He went back to the main room.

'I can't hear it out here. There is a background hum anyway from the traffic outside. I can't imagine that Theodore will notice it.' He asked for everyone's attention. 'Can you hear that?'

Everyone stopped and listened for several seconds without comment.

'I'll assume that's a no,' said James.

The constable held up the microphone. 'Couldn't we get something a bit smaller?'

The item in question was cumbersome and was the sort of thing singers used when recording albums. James asked why they'd chosen that one.

'The one that we normally use is broken. It was this, or nothing,' came a reply.

Between the two rooms, James squatted down behind the counter. 'Here's an idea.' One of the men from the back room joined him. 'This counter has a thin panel that joins the two main ones. How about taking that out and putting the microphone there? There's no lighting there. I can't imagine anyone will see it. This is an unused shop so it won't hurt to have a few panels and things out of place.'

'Yes, that'll work.' The man stood up and instructed his colleague.

Setting up alongside the recording team, behind the wall that separated the shop front and the back room, were two constables with notebooks and pens.

James peered out of the window. He recognised one of the constables who had served with George for over twenty years. He was dressed as a holiday-maker with a camera around his neck. To the casual onlooker, he was exactly that. Having spoken to him on the way in though, James knew that the camera he held was one of the most expensive on the market, able to zoom in at an astonishing level. He was, he'd learned, recording Theodore's arrival and departure.

He rubbed his hands together and asked George how much longer they needed to wait.

'We're all set. He'll be here at ten o'clock. Felicity is going to sit here, with Theodore opposite.'

That made sense: Side-on to the counter so the recorder should pick up everything said.

'Behind that wall, we've two people who'll be taking notes plus, of course, making recordings.'

'Are we certain Theodore will take the bait?'

'Felicity got in touch with Theodore last night. Told him that she'd got her hands on the notebook, that someone with a grudge against him had passed it to her anonymously. She's told him that he can have it back if he bails the club out for her. She's chosen this place because it's empty and it's away from their normal patch.'

James couldn't help but grimace. 'I hope she knows what she's doing, George. She's taking a big risk.' He put his shoulders back. 'Am I able to sit out the back and listen?'

'No.'

'I'll sit in the corner, by the two men taking notes. I could take notes too. Three pairs of hands are better than two. There's no reason why Theodore would race through there. And if things do kick off, I'll hide in the cupboard.'

The crackle of a radio interrupted them. 'Bentley Continental has left Cavendish.'

George shouted. 'Right, everyone. He'll be here in around twenty minutes. I want everyone where they should be and no shifting about. If you need the toilet, go now.' He nudged James. 'Come on, let's go upstairs.'

Upstairs, Beth and Felicity were drinking tea from a flask.

Felicity waved the black book at them. 'I keep asking Beth where this book came from but she's acting innocent.' She turned to James. 'I don't know how you managed to get this, Lord Harrington, but I will be forever grateful. My mother will be smiling down at us when the police lead my father out.'

George sat down opposite her. 'Miss Livingstone, you do realise that this is going to be difficult for you. You are on your own in trying to whittle a confession out of him. We've spent some time together over the last couple of days and you've not told me how you're going to go about it.'

'Oh, Detective Chief Inspector,' she said, sounding almost condescending, 'I know exactly what I'm going to do and what I'm going to say. I've wanted to see my father suffer for what he's done for a long, long time and I wanted it to be me that served the blow. I could never see how, though, and this is my opportunity.'

'Well, don't go taking risks. Remember, we're in the back room. Just get him to talk, that's all you need to do. Try to get him to say something that'll give us a conviction.'

With a check of his watch, George ordered Felicity downstairs. He reached for Beth's hand. 'Beth, you can't stay here.'

'I don't intend to. I'm walking to Rossi's parlour. It'll only take ten minutes. I want to speak with Papa Rossi and let him know that his son is not to blame for any of this. James, are you coming with me?'

'I'm taking notes alongside the two constables.' He ignored George's annoyance.

Accepting that she wouldn't be able to change his mind she wished him luck before slipping down the back stairs.

'Right,' said George, 'come on. Take your places.'

CHAPTER THIRTY

Downstairs, James was surprised to see a man in uniform. Around fifty years old, he had a ribbon of colours on his breast and pips on his epaulettes. He held his hat under his arm. He greeted George.

'This had better work, DCI Lane, or you're in for some explaining.'

'If it doesn't work, sir, you'll be seeing my resignation.'

James' mouth clamped shut. That was unexpected. Was George serious? The officer went through to the back room.

'Who's that?' asked James.

'Assistant Chief Commissioner, Scotland Yard.'

'Friend of Theodore Livingstone?'

'No, that's the Chief Commissioner. I know this man's all right. He's had his doubts about Theodore but couldn't convince his boss. He's good friends with Superintendent Higgins. He's spoken to the powers that be about this operation and it's all been approved. We've already arrested a few of Theodore's operatives thanks to the information in the notebook.'

Impressed by such efficiency, James settled down next to the two constables, stared through the two-way mirror and waited. Beyond the mirror, he could see Felicity, side on, looking exceptionally calm considering the circumstances. George placed himself next to the recording engineers. His jacket fell open and James glimpsed the handle of a revolver.

A tense few minutes went by until the radio crackled to life. 'Subject pulling up alongside.'

George instructed radio silence. He ordered the engineer to begin recording and alerted Felicity. 'He's arrived.'

James heard a car door slam and, a few moments later, Theodore blustered in, threw the door shut and took a seat opposite Felicity.

'You deceiving little bitch. You hand that notebook over or so help me I'll throttle you.'

Felicity smirked. 'That's no way to speak to your own flesh and blood, father. I asked you here to do a deal. You do something for me, I do something for you.'

He scanned the room. 'Why here?'

'It's empty and out of the way. You know, father, it's a bad idea to write things down. Doesn't matter how safe you try to keep things, documents often get waylaid and end up in the wrong hands.'

The veins on Theodore's neck rose. 'You stole from your own father.'

'I did no such thing. Anyway, it went missing the night you were with me.'

'One of your cronies then. Someone did it and you know who. You tell me or God help you, you'll regret it.'

'You're in no position to negotiate.' She teased her hair. 'I took a leaf out of your book. Made sure I was in the public eye while a crime took place. That's your MO, isn't it? You've been doing that for a few years, haven't you? Got that man Archibald Stanhope killed while dining with the Duke of Kent. And you had poor Jacqueline Simms under your thumb.'

James stopped writing and eased forward. He felt vulnerable behind this mirror, unused to not being seen through glass. Already Felicity had her father on the back foot.

'What d'you mean? What're talking about?'

'Oh, don't be so ignorant, father. You know exactly what I'm talking about. Jacqueline Simms. Don't you remember her and that little relationship she had with…what was his name, an MP…some useless individual that wasn't very good at his job. Still isn't, from what I read. Colin…'

He slammed the desk. 'Charles! It was Charles.'

'Oh yes, Charles. Charles Healy.'

'Hardy. Charles Hardy.'

'Imbecile.'

'A ruddy good Member of Parliament. In the Foreign Office now. That Simms woman was just a slut who got in the way.'

The two constables scribbled furiously. James was too fascinated to jot anything down.

'Like all women, father. That's what you think, isn't it? All women are there to serve you for one purpose only. Like mother. What that poor woman went through. At your beck and call twenty-four hours a day and for what? Just so that you can pander to your friends. The Prime Minister, the Duke of Oxford, Baronet Ogilvy.' A sarcastic chuckle. 'No *female* friends on the list though. And, of course, if mother failed to kowtow to your every whim, you saw to it that she paid.' She put her elbows on the table. 'How does it feel to hit a defenceless woman? Does it make you feel powerful?'

'Your mother lived the high life,' said Theodore. 'Her mind went.'

'And who made her mind go? It couldn't be anything to do with the fact that you drove her into submission. Every little thing, father. Every little thing. You criticised her, put her down, laughed at her, humiliated her. *You* committed her to that hospital. *You* signed the papers and you thought she'd stay there, didn't you? You didn't bank on little me helping her out. You didn't like it when she started to get better, did you? Started getting her confidence back, ignoring your demands and orders. You didn't like that, did you? She had to suffer, didn't she, because you had no control.'

'Damn it, girl, she had it coming.'

James' whole body tensed and he exchanged a silent shocked stare with George.

'She disrespected me every chance she had, humiliated me in front of my peers. I wasn't going to stand for that. She had to go.'

'What did that feel like, father, stringing her up.'

James couldn't believe what he was hearing. Theodore seemed to be enjoying the moment and, again, James was reminded of Valentine's question about whether he had come across evil.

A sneer spread across Theodore's face. 'I felt as if it couldn't have happened to a nicer lady.' The chair creaked as he sat back. 'What do you want? I can't bring your mother back. You want your club, I want the notebook. Let's do a deal.'

'I also want to know what happened to Faith Simms. Then I have a proposal.'

'Faith Simms asked too many questions and was making it difficult for Charles. He was married, got a family, couldn't have that sort of publicity.'

'And you played God and had her killed.'

'But, my darling, my hands are clean. I was at a function with Dulcie.'

James wondered if his own expression was as satisfied as the one he saw on George's face. Felicity was performing extraordinarily well. The next question Felicity asked pulled his attention back.

301

'This little notebook of yours. You're running drugs, aren't you?'

'And how did you work that out?'

'It's obvious. The way you've written the book up. Names, dates, drop off, pick up, consignment, weights, the people you use. Dairies, mobile libraries, ice-cream vans, painters and decorators; all mobile businesses, making it easy to distribute the stuff. It doesn't take a genius to work that out. But then, father, you think the female of the species is dim. I have been your undoing and there's nothing you can do about it.'

'You want money? I'll give you money. You hand that notebook to me now and I'll write you a cheque. How much?'

She laughed. 'Do you think I'm an idiot? The moment I walk out of that door, you'll cancel that cheque and probably find a way to have me institutionalised. No, I want cash and I want a written agreement.'

'Don't get greedy.'

'Why not? You're greedy. Max is greedy. Why aren't I allowed to be greedy? I want one hundred thousand pounds in cash.' She brought the notebook out of her handbag and flicked through the pages. Theodore's eyes sparkled. 'Now, father, when's your next collection? Ah, here we are, a ship coming in. The Felixstowe. Is that the name of the boat?'

Theodore went to snatch the book but Felicity took it out of reach and, with her other hand, pointed a small pistol at him. 'I only have to fire this and Alan Stubbs will come running.'

James swallowed. Did George know she had a gun?

Theodore held his palms up and sat down 'I sent you to a good school, girl. If you're so intelligent you should

302

know that the port is Felixstowe, the name of the boat is Blue Oyster. If you read the columns the right way around you'd see that. That's why I don't think women are any use to me.'

She checked again. 'Ah yes, Felixstowe, the Blue Oyster. That's a fishing vessel by the sounds of it? You hide it in fish?'

James couldn't believe how calm she was being. Deliberately acting the fool. Her expression turned to one of acute confusion.

'Why fish? Isn't that awfully smelly.'

Theodore gave a sarcastic shake of the head. The man was being reeled in like the fish he hid the drugs in.

'The men I use don't care about the smell of fish. They get a good cut.'

'They gut the fish and hide it inside?'

He roared with laughter. 'You really are as stupid as your mother. The drugs are all sealed, ready to pass on. They just hide them at the bottom of the ice stores and get them out once everything's unloaded.'

'It's very ingenious, I must admit, father. To use mobile businesses to distribute your wares.'

'That's why I'm where I am. I cover my tracks too.' He put his elbows on the table. 'Now, how d'you want to do this? I take it we'll have another rendezvous to swap merchandise.'

'Why won't you let me help you?'

Theodore's brows knitted together.

'I'm a successful businesswoman, father. My club is not in trouble and I'm making money, legitimately. But it looks like you make an awful lot more dealing in drugs. What sort of drugs?'

'Heroin.'

'Give me a cut of the business. I can look after the money side of things – make sure the deals are done properly.'

For a moment Theodore seemed interested but then he answered her with a sneer. 'Why should I trust you? Your sibling is useless; a hopeless businessman. He's the one I would have liked alongside me but he's proving to be as useful as a chocolate teapot. Always trying to please me. You know it was him that killed Faith Simms, don't you?'

James swallowed hard.

Theodore harrumphed. 'Thought he was pleasing me but even screwed that up. I mean, why the hell put her in Plumb's garden? Why not just dump her in the Thames? Bloody idiot's a thorn in my side. And, anyway, you're your mother's daughter. Too headstrong.'

'I could go to the police with this.'

A sarcastic chuckle was the response. 'You don't have the Commissioner of Scotland Yard in your pocket. Why would he believe *you*? You be careful, girl, if we don't arrive at a deal that satisfies me, you might end up like your mother.'

'You're prepared to kill me?'

'I wouldn't be that heartless but perhaps you need to see a doctor.'

Felicity replaced the notebook in her handbag. 'Your loss. You really can't put up with any woman being in your camp, can you?' She shrugged. 'Oh well. I don't really want to work alongside a murderer and a drugs baron. That, for me, would be stooping low. You may think you're superior to me, father, but I'm having the last laugh.'

He sneered. 'Oh yes, and how would that be?'

She remained quiet as DCI Lane appeared in the doorway between the two rooms holding his warrant card. Theodore's eyes widened in shock and a guttural gasp came from him. With a screech of his chair legs he stood and bolted for the door, only to be confronted by two burly constables.

He snarled at Felicity. 'You bitch! You'll pay for this.'

George accepted the notebook from her and began reading Theodore Livingstone his rights. 'I'm taking great pleasure in ensuring that you and your son and off the streets for a long time.' The two constables marched a still protesting Theodore to an awaiting police car. George turned to Felicity. 'And as for you, young lady, I don't think I've ever witnessed such an accomplished performance but, I don't recall giving permission for a weapon to be used.'

Felicity handed him the gun. 'It's not real but I thought I'd need something to keep him in his place.'

James popped his head around the door. He couldn't help but give Felicity a big hug. 'My word, you really had him eating out of the palm of your hand.'

'My father thinks he knows best, Lord Harrington. The problem is, he never took the time to get to know me so he had no idea of my capabilities. I didn't sleep last night. I worked everything out in my head about what to say and how to say it. I rehearsed it and rehearsed it until I was blue in the face.'

'Well, Miss,' said George, 'I think you need to get some rest and perhaps I can come by later for a chat.'

'We can do it now. The adrenalin alone will keep me going for a few more hours. Alan Stubbs is waiting in the car over there. We'll follow you when you're ready.'

James was aware of a man at the door. Oh Lord, Inspector Fulton.

George, to his surprise, welcomed him warmly.

James frowned as Fulton marched over to him. 'I think I owe you an apology, Lord Harrington.'

'What's going on?' said James, a little reluctant to engage with the chap.

George chortled. 'He was working undercover, James.'

James stared at Fulton for several seconds, then let out a hesitant chuckle. 'Why didn't you tell me?'

Fulton laughed. 'For a start, I wouldn't have been undercover. No, your Lordship, I needed to stay in character and I needed you to think I was one of them. Two reasons. They had to believe I was on their side and it was vital that you didn't get too close.'

The admission prompted James to shake his hand. 'You play the part convincingly, Inspector. But what happens now?'

'Now, I'm retiring. That was my last job and one that I volunteered for. I've had my sights on Theodore for a long time but could never get close. Aside from what's happened here I've managed to get plenty of witness statements over the last few days.'

'What about Theodore? I mean, even from prison, he could reach you.'

'I'm off to New Zealand. I've a son there; off next month.'

James grinned. 'Not only did I have Alan Stubbs looking out for me but you too. I'm grateful, Inspector Fulton. I had a few sleepless nights because of you. Was that you following me half the time in that car?'

The sheepish expression told him that it was. 'And I was the man who threatened you at the rally. No hard feelings, your Lordship, and we've a big catch to be proud of.' He turned to George. 'I'm reporting back to Scotland Yard. There'll be a few red faces in London once this gets out.'

An hour later, the shop had returned to its empty state. Beth was waiting inside Rossi's and James could see the relief on her face when he entered the parlour.

Papa Rossi pulled them to one side. 'My son, he was stupid. Taken in by that man.'

'Mr Rossi, I think it's important you understand that he was threatened. It's been explained to me that Livingstone told Paolo that he had evidence, which he didn't have I hasten to add, to send you back to Italy and, of course, Paolo didn't want that. If he'd not done as he was told, he might very well be dead. That's the sort of man Livingstone is.'

'But Paolo, he will go to prison?'

'Oh, Mr Rossi,' said Beth. 'I'm sure the courts will take everything into consideration. If he tells George everything that happened, they may be lenient with any punishment.'

The old man wasn't so sure but said he would do everything he could to stand by his boy. With sincere wishes, the Rossis waved them goodbye.

James grabbed Beth's hand. 'There's a little café around the corner. I can't wait until we get home to tell you what happened. You won't believe what a show Felicity put on. She deserves an Oscar.'

307

CHAPTER THIRTY-ONE

Adam had taken the orders. George, Stephen and Anne had opted for the *boeuf bourguignon*, Beth requested the salmon and James, eager to see how Didier would elevate the dish, requested the gammon.

He had experienced a number of emotions following that morning's operation: anxiety to relief mixed with horror and elation. He'd arrived home with a stinking headache but a restful afternoon and some aspirin had done the trick. Feeling much better, he'd insisted on opening a bottle of champagne to celebrate.

As they knew so little about the case, he, George and Beth had updated Stephen and Anne on how Theodore and Maximillian had finally faced arrest; from the very first chat at the police awards ceremony to the role brave Del Sykes played and the mysterious theft of Theodore's notebook. During this particular topic, George had again pushed James to elaborate on who had obtained the document but James said nothing.

'I know it was a plan that Bert concocted but he wouldn't tell me about it and is unlikely to do so. Anyway, the fact is, it enabled you to get your man.'

Dinner was served and, as always, James was in awe of what was produced in the kitchen. The tender beef fell apart, the gravy was thick and the addition of green broad beans and new potatoes had turned a winter dish into one suitable for spring. Beth's Scottish salmon was, as expected, succulent, flaky and lightly smoked.

His own meal, one normally associated with cafés, had, as Didier had predicted, been elevated. The thick, deep-fried chips were disc-shaped; the gammon, a thick slice of home-cured bacon from Graham's smallholding had been cut into three spheres and the poached egg, too,

308

was spherical. Didier had steamed and slightly smoked the gammon to hold in the moisture and, like the beef, it fell apart. James was reluctant to cut into the food as his chef had made it into such a work of art.

After a few minutes, Stephen took a sip of champagne. 'Do y-you think Felicity will be safe? I mean, he can get at her from i-inside a prison cell, can't he?'

George settled them down. 'We have someone with Felicity wherever she goes. Scotland Yard has suggested she change identity and move to another city, but she loves London, so it'll take an attempt on her life to convince her to do that.'

'We should pray that it doesn't come to that,' said Anne. 'She's very brave to have confronted her father like that. And what about Dulcie Faye?'

James loaded his fork with gammon. 'Back in her cottage in Cavendish. She's going to keep the cottage and is seriously thinking about giving up her career.'

'Why?' asked Anne with an incredulous look. 'She has the world at her feet now.'

Stephen said that he sympathised with her. 'I-I only met her a handful of times b-but she struck me as someone who'd want to settle down. She d-didn't seem to like being the centre of attention and she mentioned to me that the occupation is not what she thought it would be.'

'I think you're right,' said Beth with a glint in her eye. Anne spotted it immediately and pushed her for her secret. She sparkled, with a knowing look at James, who rolled his eyes. Beth leaned in and lowered her voice. 'I think that she and Charlie Hawkins are smitten with each other. She told me this afternoon that she's going to commit herself to the short run in the West End with Tony Young and then give up her career.'

'Blimey,' said George, 'I didn't see that coming.'

Anne clasped her hands together. 'Oh, how wonderful! They would make a perfect couple.'

Stephen had to admit that he felt the same. 'Charlie is s-such a kind man and the l-loss of his wife was so terribly sad for that family. I-I've always hoped, since moving here, that he would find a l-lady to share his life.'

Beth turned to James. 'Sweetie, you don't think we'll be in any danger from Theodore? He doesn't know we had anything to do with getting that notebook.'

'We didn't,' said James. 'I'm absolutely confident that we have no worries. Once I'd had that drink with him at the lodge, we did nothing. And I'm sure Inspector Fulton kept the notion of our involvement to mere gossip.'

George admitted that Fulton had carried out his role with the utmost professionalism. 'Fooled everyone, including me. It wasn't until I told the Superintendent about how he'd threatened you that he let me in on the whole thing. But I was sworn to secrecy. He wasn't in Theodore's inner circle but he pandered to the Livingstones. Theodore loved having someone inside the force under his thumb. He used him for inside information but, along the way, Fulton was able to gather a few names and quite a bit of intelligence. But, that notebook was the thing. I can't believe some of the high-profile names that'll be going to court alongside Theodore.'

'Not the Prime Minister,' Anne said.

He smiled. 'As far as I know, no.'

'And M-Maximillian,' asked Stephen. 'What's h-happening with him?

'Trial date is set but I understand he's pleading guilty. There's too much evidence to fight it.'

'Well I, for one, am thankful they're off the streets,' said Beth. 'I hope we never come across people like that again.'

'And what about Valentine Plumb?' said Anne. 'Is he coping?'

'Still upset about Faith Simms,' said James, 'but his book now has some meat to add to the bones. He's been discussing Theodore and Maximillian with Kushal and they believe there is a way to integrate an account of their activities into Plumb's current project. It would certainly make for an interesting read.'

'And h-how is Paolo?' said Stephen, adding that he seemed a little brighter.

George explained that those people affiliated to the mobile business had all come forward, with the exception of two people. 'You always get a couple of rotten eggs and they'll be standing trial. But, where Paolo and the others are concerned I've got some very in-depth statements that'll put Theodore Livingstone in jail for some time. They'll have to go to trial, the same as the rest but the fact that they were in fear of their lives and the knowledge that, prior to meeting Livingstone, they'd been law-abiding citizens, well, that'll go in their favour. I'll do my best to show Paolo in a good light.'

Paul, the *maître d'* hovered by the door and requested George's presence. He whispered a message and they all looked on as a deep frown appeared on George's face. He returned to the table.

'What is it, George?'

'It appears that Theodore Livingstone is dead.'

A gasp went round the table. James put his drink down and couldn't begin to find the words.

'He was being transferred from Lewes police station and, somewhere along the country roads in Westerham, the car was held up and Livingstone was shot. They were waiting for him.'

After a stunned silence, James muttered: 'Good Lord.'

Stephen made the sign of the cross and sent up a prayer.

Anne gritted her teeth as she joined him but couldn't help but mumble: 'He doesn't deserve a prayer, Stephen.'

He rested a hand on hers. 'Anne, e-everyone deserves a p-prayer. Him more than anyone.'

Beth asked if they'd arrested the killer.

'My guess is the McCalls. He could have landed them right in the doo-dah if he'd given evidence. Theodore was the sort of man who would take everyone down with him.'

'That makes perfect sense,' said James, adding that he couldn't summon up the energy to feel one ounce of pity for the man.

'Me neither,' said Beth. 'At least people like Felicity can go about their business without fear of retribution. I do hope things will turn out all right for Paolo.'

'Me too,' said James. He picked the champagne out of its bucket and topped everyone's glasses up. 'Don't let me stop you from ordering dessert. I'm pleased to say that I've lost some of that weight I've put on so I'm still cutting down a little. But, I think a well done to us all. To George for pulling off a peach of an operation; to Stephen and Anne for keeping us sane and to Beth, for supporting me through what turned out to be a rather unpleasant enquiry.'

Beth clinked her glass against his. 'If you get involved in any other mysteries, try and avoid people like that.'

'I will make it my aim to do so,' he said, as he kissed the top of her head.

THE END

See over for Grandma Harrington's German Pancake recipe.

For more information on the Lord James Harrington series of books, please visit:
www.lordjamesharrington.com

Follow me on Twitter @cosycrazy

GRANDMA HARRINGTON'S GERMAN PANCAKES

This a lovely group snack. It's the type of dish you simply place in the middle of the table and invite guests to tear strips from.

This particular recipe will serve around six. Double up on the quantity for bigger gatherings.

6 eggs lightly beaten
A pinch of salt
Four drops of vanilla essence
50g/2oz butter
125g/4oz plain flour
250ml/9 fl oz milk

Pre-heat the oven to 180°C or Gas Mark 4.
Melt the butter in a medium-sized baking dish
Meanwhile, mix the flour, milk, eggs, salt and vanilla. (I also put a pinch of baking powder in but that is personal choice.)
Make sure the butter has melted, then pour the mixture into the baking dish.
Bake for around 30 minutes, possibly more depending on your oven. The fluffy pancake should be golden brown when you take it out of the oven.

Serve with whatever you prefer as accompaniment: lemon, sugar, cinnamon, jam, maple syrup etc.

36894085R00175

Printed in Great Britain
by Amazon